Pia Guttenson

Swap husband against a man in a kilt

Translated from the original German by:
Fritz Rauer

This work, including all illustrations, is copyrighted. Any use not allowed by the Copyright Act is illegal without the author's permission and may be prosecuted.

Story and characters of this work are freely invented. Any resemblances to actual names of living or deceased persons are unintentional and are not meant to defame or accuse anyone.

Copyright © 2015 Pia Guttenson

Cover Design: Basil Wolfrhine

English Translation: Fritz Rauer

All rights reserved.

Pia Guttenson
Silvanerweg 17
D-74376 Gemmrigheim
Germany

Herstellung und Verlag:
BoD – Books on Demand, Norderstedt
ISBN 978-3-7412-0805-8

Sometimes you think strength lies in keeping hold.
But it's letting go that shows true strength.

For
Basil,
Simone & Corinna
You're my personal „Dream-Team",
without which this book would never have seen the light
of day!

Not the perfect start

Lou was a nervous wreck. The flight from Germany hadn't been so bad, though it had taken ages for her completely distraught dog, Doc, to be restored to her, and all her luggage to be securely stowed on the luggage carrier. The real nightmare had started with the car rental. She hardly understood a word, as her English really had gotten a tad rusty. Further, the nice little compact car she had booked had turned out to be a monstrous Jeep. Naturally, with a stick shift. On the wrong side for her. While pulling out of the parking space, she had already killed the motor three times, had barely remembered to drive on the left, and had started out by ramming the curb. After what felt like a hundred roundabouts later, she was bathed in sweat and near tears.

Hours had passed since then. Now, she stood in the middle of the Scottish Highlands, whose stunning landscape she had been so eagerly looking forward to. Unfortunately, at that moment, the landscape seemed anything but charming. Not to mention that not a single romantic character had crossed her path. That another cloudburst was threatening wasn't helping, either. There was no sign of the landlord of her cottage. She had rented the holiday cottage through an advertisement, as it had promised both comfort and seclusion. The nearby village of Kildermorie had turned out to be a disappointingly tiny hamlet, however.
Sighing, Lou tugged and wrenched at her heavy suitcase with all her might, but it stubbornly refused to move a millimeter out of the muddy gravel bed, in which its tiny wheels had mired. To top it all, Doc was making a big hassle on the front passenger seat, because he wanted to finally get out and get some air.

"Goddammittohell" she swore, as the spike heels of her expensive Jimmy Choos sank into the sodden mire. How did she deserve this? Who invented such tiny wheels? It had to be a man. All the men in the world seemed to want to make her suffer, after all!

Why in the world was everything in her life going down the drain? All right – Scotland, Jimmy Choo high heels, and a Jil Sander costume, went about as well together as the Pope and Marilyn Monroe. Granted, she should have put on her hiking boots, hidden somewhere down in the depths of her suitcases. Only, in which of the five?

In the meantime, it had begun to rain once again. Doc's pitiful howling was the only sound that cut through the driving rain.

"You ham actor!" Lou hissed angrily at Doc, while pulling her heel out of the ground. Great, the shoes were as good as ruined!

Annoyed, she swung her foot and gave the suitcase a good kick. With a splash, the treacherous item fell over and a shower of mud hit Lou. Horrified, she gasped, and could no longer hold back her tears. It seemed as if a dam broke inside her. Here, in the middle of nowhere, her brittle self-confidence folded like a house of cards.

Deep sobs wracked her, while tears, mixed with rain, ran down her cheeks like a small waterfall. Couldn't something go smoothly, for once in her life? Why had she ever had the apalling idea of fleeing to the solitude of the Scottish Highlands? Because of the film adaption of a novel, with a hero every second woman was in love with, and a series with awesome imagery that wouldn't let her go?

Without meaning to, she thought of the breakfast on the occasion of her fortieth birthday. Hard to believe that was only a few hours earlier. Forty years old, and obviously totally loony! Had a midlife crisis hit her, after all?

Why else was she standing here in the pouring rain, soaked to the skin, and splashed with mud? When, at that very moment, she should have been dancing and having fun at her, most likely exorbitantly expensive, birthday party. Heavens, Alexander would go crazy when he found out she was missing!

Germany
The previous morning …

   The designer kitchen was a bustle of activity. Rosalita, the Spanish cook, and the only one who could really use the expensive cooking pots, was whirling through the kitchen like a tornado. In her freshly starched white apron, the fiftyish cook looked like someone from a corny soap. Smugly, Louise's menfolk let her wait on them. Lou hated the way they took Rosalita's service as a matter of course. What had she done wrong in bringing up her sons? Absolutely everything?

   Alexander had left the house an hour ago, without a kiss, much less any birthday felicitations. The only thing marking her birthday, was a large bouquet of flowers. That had been obtained by Mrs. Bott, her husband's personal assistant, who was also the good soul of the house. Like every year. There was also an awful cellophane structure with an oversized red bow, containing a jewelry box from Cartier. New jewelry again. Jewelry she only wore when she had to. She had been married to Alexander for so many years, and he still hadn't realized that she didn't care for such trinkets. The penetrating smell of the lilies was already giving her a headache.

   I hate lilies. Do I look like I want to go to a funeral?, Lou moaned silently. Deeply disappointed, and terribly frustrated, she stared into her cup of tea. Tried to calm down. Everyone seemed to be treating her as if she wasn't even there. Was it too much to ask for some recognition or appreciation?

"Ma, did you remember to pick up my favorite shirts from the cleaners? Oh, and how about the appointment for my haircut, is that fixed?", her older son asked with raised eyebrows. His gaze appeared slightly irritated, as usual.

"Well…", she started, somewhat befuddled, but was immediately interrupted.

"Dammit, Ma. You really forgot, didn't you?"

With a jerk Louise got to her feet, glaring at her son.

"Maybe I did. You're 21 years old. Maybe you could do such things for yourself in future!", she snapped furiously.

"Oh, come on! Are you in a huff, because I didn't wish you a Happy Birthday right away, or are you really in a midlife crisis? All right. Congratulations, Mama. That it? Now, could you please do what you're there for? Please!"

Doing what she was there for? Had it come to this?

God, how I'm looking forward to the chaos that will break out around here, when I'm in Scotland! I should have cameras installed, so I could see your stupid faces!

Grinding her teeth, Lou ignored her visibly annoyed son, who shouted an insolent "As if you had so terribly much to do, Ma!" after her.

With resolute strides, she fled to her bedroom. She simply didn't have the energy for yet another debate. Deep inside, Lou knew that, if she didn't manage to leave today, she would inevitably end up depressed and in a clinic. Doc watched everything she did with knowing canine eyes. Deeply saddened, she sank to her bed. She had already deposited her suitcases at the airport the day before, with some help from Tobi. Her alarm clock showed her she still had an hour until her birthday brunch with her friends. New tears came to her eyes.

Carefully, she took Alex' portrait from her bedside table, lovingly stroking the contours of his face behind the glass. How she would have loved to do the same to the living original. Touched him. But she hadn't come as close to Alex as this portrait in years. She had tried everything to save their mutual feelings. Of course, she realized that the time for butterflies in the stomach had passed. But, was the craving for physical closeness so wrong? She had even gone to one of Constance's horrible dessous parties, spent an exorbitant sum for a wisp of fabric.

It hadn't been a success. Certainly, she and Alex had had sex that evening. To be exact: boring, 'get on – get in – get off – finished' sex. A whole ten minutes long. Two months later, she had embarrassed herself again, meeting Alex with nothing on but dessous, high heels, and Rosalita's lace apron.

Unfortunately, this had been the one evening he had had Mrs. Bott along, because of a meeting. She had wanted to die of shame.

At some point, she had stopped begging for intimacies. Instead, she had buried herself in romance novels. She regularly wrote reviews of so-called 'bodice rippers' for a book blog.

She loved this side job, devouring loads of books, as well as e-books. The ones she loved best, however, were those dealing with the goal she dreamed of, Scotland. Lou had never been to Scotland. That would change this very evening, however. Sighing, she took a well-thumbed book from her nightstand. One of the 'Highland Saga' books, by Diana Gabaldon. Her favorite among the Scotland novels. Like so many women and men who had succumbed to Scotland's charm, she loved this author's books.

She had hardly been able to wait for the filming of the series by an American TV channel, had already seen all there was to see. In the end, the series, combined with an advertisement for a vacation cottage, had done it. Booking a flight, and reserving a rental car, had been easily done. Keeping everything a secret, however, had been much harder to do.

She knew, of course, that characters from a novel, like Jamie, or Mr. Darcy, were not to be found in real life. Also, she couldn't imagine living in a previous century, romantic as it might be. What she was absolutely certain of, though, was that she was going to end in an insane asylum, if she didn't change something in her life now. Newspapers and magazines were full of women with burn out-syndromes and depressions. She, however, seemed to be in a mid-life crisis.

An hour later, makeup had concealed the redness around the eyes, from crying. From the shop window she passed, her reflection looked back at her with a practiced smile. As on her previous birthdays, she had reserved the big table in the back room of Coco's. All her women friends, as well as her gay brother Tobias, who more or less counted as a woman, had come.

"Happy Birthday, sweetheart!"

Constance pressed her in a close hug. As so often, Lou felt like an ugly duckling next to her friend. Constance was head of a successful consulting firm, and had been one of her closest friends since Lou had married Alex. It didn't surprise Lou that Constance, in her late forties, had already been married three times. She had a calculating air. No man seemed to be able to measure up to the stylish woman. So, granted, there were quite a few parts there, that weren't natural. But the same could be said of Eve's breasts, and Desiree's lips.

Since Alex had come into her life, Lou had been consorting with the rich and the beautiful, or, as her best friend Debbie like to say, with the Botox and lifting monsters.

Rolling her eyes, Debbie handed Lou a champagne flute. "I'm so looking forward to seeing the faces of these would-be 'ladies', when you scoot off to Scotland. You still want to go through with, don't you, sweetheart?"

"Of course. If I don't do it now, Deb, I'll never be able to look myself in the eye again."

"Whatever happens, Lou, you know you can always come to Chris and me."

"You mean, ever since I defended you against Jo with a shovel, in the sandbox."

Lou gave Debbie a conspiratorial wink.

"Among other things", her best friend answered with a broad grin. "But seriously, Lou. I know you hope Alex will show himself to be a romantic, and bring you back. I just don't want you to be disappointed, when he remains the asshole I take him for!"

"I just hope you choose your words with a little more restraint at kindergarten", Lou joked drily. "All right. I know what you're trying to tell me in your own blunt way, sweetie. I won't cave in. I promise!"

"Good. Then stop looking like it rained on your parade! Tobi, Chris and I are backing you all the way! With Chris, you have a great lawyer standing ready, and you can easily do without these other *ladies* here!"

Despite all the good cheer around her, Lou couldn't get into a party mood. Which was not least the fault of one of her many arguments with Alex, that was still haunting her.

"I don't understand how you could do this to me, Louise! Nude people. You painted totally nude people, having sex.

What the hell are my business partners going to think of me? Isn't it enough that my wife publicly reviews bodice rippers?", Alex had shouted at her last night, while tearing at his hair in a helpless gesture. He was acting like a tiger, pacing up and down in his cage.

"… but that's art, Alexander. I don't understand… Besides, I paint under an assumed name…", she had tried to explain, wringing her hands. Not to mention that Sofie and Kai, the nude models, hadn't had sex, but had just lain there in a close embrace.

"Art with no money in it! You understand me perfectly, Louise! Your so-called reviews of those terrible sob stories, and this tactless painting, are just a waste of time, and cost a fortune! Besides, they make us… make me look like a fool, in front of the whole business community!"

"That's just not true, Alex… Besides, it's my time. And don't act as if we can't afford a few brushes and canvas…", Lou had objected, but had only managed to turn Alex's complexion into an unhealthy red.

"Did turning your hair to blonde affect your brains, too? Don't you get everything you want, Louise? Don't I fulfill your every wish? I let you and the children do anything you want. Other women would be happy to have a maid, a cook, and a personal trainer", he ranted on.

Doc interrupted his tirade, by taking a protective stance in front of her and growling.

"Kindly take your hideous brute away, when I'm talking to you!"

"Dog isn't a brute. He's a dog", she retorted indignantly, but prudently sent the big mongrel to his spot, where he curled up, still growling softly, and watched them suspiciously.

"Money isn't everything, Alex. At least, not for me", she

reproached him. Trying to keep calm, she dug her nails into the couch upholstery until they hurt. Lou was so terribly disappointed.

"What are you trying to say, Louise? I think we should simply act as if nothing had happened. You're just having a little… let's call it midlife crisis, darling", he said soothingly in a dangerously low voice, seemingly sympathetic. He was on the verge of leaving.

Lou knew very well, it would really be better to hold her tongue. She could feel that she was on very thin ice indeed. After all, she had been married to Alexander for over twenty years. But hadn't she done that long enough? Hadn't she held her, supposedly, loose tongue for long enough?

"I'm not having a midlife crisis, Alex", she answered, as calmly as possible. Stubbornly, she ignored the angry crease between his brows as he turned back to her.

"I majored in marketing and art. I was the best of my class. Do you realize that? Have you ever thought about what I gave up? Our children are old enough, but you still won't let me work. Instead, I have a husband who prefers his work to his wife. A husband who doesn't even kiss me, let alone sleeps with me. Do you even feel anything for me anymore, Alexander? What am I to you?"

Her husband's whole body was stiff. With an agitated hand, he loosened his tie and opened the top two buttons of his shirt to get some air. "What's this all about, Louise? Look around you. All this luxury is thanks to my hard work. Don't you think it's unfair to reproach me with that, of all things? You are the mother of my children, and, by the way: sex takes two. Don't act as if you want sex more than I do!"

"Have you ever considered that, maybe, I don't always want to have to indicate when I feel like sex? That maybe I want to be courted, or swept off my feet?"

"You forget yourself, Louise. I think you read too many of those terrible bodice rippers. Besides," he pointed a stiff finger at Doc, "you prefer him to me anyway!"

It was true that Doc slept in her bed. However, he hadn't done so until Alexander had insisted on a separate bedroom. Supposedly, so he wouldn't disturb her, coming home in the middle of the night, after a long, hard day at the office, as happened so often. "That is so typical of you, Louise! As always, I'm the asshole, and you're the angel!", he threw at her, and disappeared with a loud bang of the door.

She could still remember every word of their argument, which had wounded her more deeply than she was willing to admit. You could never argue with Alexander. He needed to control everything, and everyone.

"What's the matter with you, Lou?", Tobias brought her back to the here and now. He studied her carefully. Immediately, the incredible noise level, generated by seven loudly chatting women, died down. All eyes were glued to her lips, spellbound. Lou swallowed.

" I have to tell you something", she began, drawing a deep breath.

"I knew it! My God, I'm so sorry for you, darling. How long has it been going on?", Constance feigned sympathy.

"What do you mean, Constance?", Lou answered, irritated.

"Well, with a man like Alexander, it's no wonder", Michelle put her oar in.

"And just what are you trying to say, Michelle? Louise is very beautiful herself, after all!", Tobias defended his sister angrily.

Lou felt compelled to intervene. "Stop it, please! Alexander doesn't have someone else…"

"My goodness, I'm impressed, Louise. I didn't think you

had it in you!", Constance cut in.

Lou had to control herself not to break her friend's neck. "Just to make it clear, for all of you: neither Alexander nor myself is having an affair!", she growled.

"You aren't pregnant, are you?", Catherine started carefully.

"Heavens, no! Will you finally let me finish, please", she exclaimed, with an irritated roll of her eyes.

Tobias' look seemed to say: "I'm all agog!"

"I'm going to take some time off from my family, and, yes, from Alexander. Two months."

Everyone stared at her, shocked. Only Constance's affected laugh broke the silence. "Why do you do that to him, Louise? Alexander grants your every wish. God, the man looks like the twin of George Clooney."

"Goodness, girl. You don't have to do a thing at home", Gabby reproached her, receiving assenting nods.

"Money isn't everything", Lou whispered in a choked voice.

Tobias pressed her hand sympathetically.

"But he doesn't even play around, Louise. Right? Besides, you have children. You have duties. I think it's totally wrong, what you intend. Why don't you go to a psychiatrist? I can recommend mine."

„I certainly won't do that, Catherine. I'm perfectly all right!", Lou spat indignantly.

The whispered "midlife crisis" was easily audible to all.

"I heard that!", Lou growled angrily. Ignoring her trembling legs, she got up and whirled in place.

"Just look at me! This isn't me. I train for three full hours every damn day, with an expensive personal trainer. I nibble salad like a stupid rabbit, and deny myself the slightest unnecessary calorie. I've forgotten how chocolate even tastes!

My hair is bleached blonde, even though I was always perfectly content with my own light brown hair. But blond is soooo hip! My fingernails are manicured, with false nails applied. Damn! The only thing left, is for me to have plastic surgery", Lou moaned.

"But you look fabulous, darling! It's all been worthwhile!", Constance objected.

Lou shook her head. "But I haven't been happy for a long time now, Constance. What's left of me in all this? You don't even know the real me. You've never really gotten to know me," she accused her friends.

"Nonsense, Louise. You're totally exaggerating. Of course we know you!", Catherine disagreed confidently.

Lou smiled sadly.

Tobias whispered: "Bet you don't!"

"In which clothes do I feel most comfortable?", she asked of no one in particular.

"Your red Armani costume, with your Jimmy Choos", Constance answered promptly.

"No. No. Lou prefers faded jeans, sneakers and that checked flannel shirt, that's just about worn through at the elbows. At least, when she's not painting in a smock and torn overalls", Debbie contradicted calmly.

Lou nodded gratefully.

Her friends stared at her, stunned.

"I don't even like George Clooney, even though Alex looks so much like him…", she admitted, with another sad smile.

"Nope. My sister likes rugged men like Gerard Butler, or that hero from her favorite novel, Jamie Whatsit", Tobias confirmed with a grin, while he gave her a thumbs-up.

"That's why I could never understand her choice in men. You should have taken Achim. Back then", Tobias said, with a wink.

On her friends' faces she could see surprise, disbelief and horror.

"You can't be serious, Louise! And what about your party this evening…?", Constance answered, totally confused.

"Will have to go on without me!", she answered with a sigh.

"But the children?"

"Heavens, Catherine. Richard is 21, and Philip 17. That's old enough to finally stand on their own pampered feet. My flight to Scotland leaves this afternoon", Lou declared firmly into the shocked silence.

"Why Scotland, of all places? It rains all the time there. Besides, the people there are all so odd", Constance began, uncomprehending.

Lou didn't feel like laughing anymore. She just felt empty. What had ever connected her to these women? "I don't really like heat, Constance. To be precise, I never had any use for the Maledives, or the Côte d'Azure. Besides, I get seasick. Unfortunately, no one ever bothered to ask me. I like to be close to nature, chilly and solitary. Besides, I always wanted to visit Scotland sometime. I'm looking forward to bringing the magic of those landscapes to my paintings. I want to devour books before a crackling fire, eating a whole sinful bar of chocolate", she tried to explain her decision to Constance.

And who knows, maybe I'll meet a Scot like those in the books, she thought, without saying it aloud. It wouldn't have mattered, though. Constance already looked as if Lou had just smashed her whole world view.

Scotland

A checkered handkerchief in her field of vision, followed

by an umbrella floating above her head, tore Lou from her memories. Goodness. She must look like a scarecrow.

"You all right, Miss?", a voice in broad Scots dialect met her ear. Totally discomfited by the piercing blue eyes meeting hers at the same height, not a single word came from her lips.

"Just great. She's mute, too", came an unfriendly growl. Shaking his head, that piercing gaze rested on her shoes, whose heels had already sunk deeply into the sodden earth.

"Well, I….", she stuttered. Any further explanation was cut off, as the stranger simply picked her up like a small child, and carried her toward the house, grumbling softly. She was put down roughly on the small veranda. The large man inserted the key in the lock, and opened the door, acting as if the whole situation was commonplace and totally normal.

"Alasdair Munro. Who are you? And what the hell are you doing on my property?", he uttered, with an irritated undertone, and a rolling 'R' that went right through her.

"Lou… um… Louise Schulzinger, pleased to meet you", she stuttered, totally confused, while automatically putting out her hand to shake.

The Scotsman ignored it with an inscrutable look. "Louise Schulzinger, not Louis?", he growled. "Dearg Amadain!" Without another word, he turned and stumped back to her car. The fellow acted as if the driving rain, which by now had turned to a deluge, didn't even exist. Seemingly unconcerned by Doc's barking and dangerous growling, and before she could call a warning, he opened the trunk of her Jeep. The Scotsman took her luggage out, retrieved the suitcase she had left standing, and carried them, two at a time, to the house, cursing loudly at the last ones, which were pretty heavy, due to her many books.

His unintelligible mumbling wasn't helping Lou to calm down, either. She had never felt so out of place in her whole life. Real life simply wasn't like a novel.

Thanks to the dark gaze the Scotsman rested on her, she didn't dare say a word. His look wasn't hard to interpret, though. Blonde bimbo, thin figure of a model, high heels and miniskirt, which, together, meant: Totally dim and conceited.

Why, oh why, hadn't she changed her dress, and the shoes? Apprehensively, she stood on shaky legs, and watched as all her luggage landed in the gloomy vestibule, where she had dodged, soaked to the skin. She was unable to do anything at all. The taciturn man frightened her a little. He looked like a dangerous brute. No, he didn't resemble a hero from a novel in the slightest. Desperately, she tried to inconspicuously smooth her miniskirt a bit further over her thighs, while gazing at the muscular upper arms of the man, which were apparent through the snug jeans shirt.

The face of the Scotsman was anything but handsome. It seemed angular and hard, an impression that was reinforced by his heavy stubble. The color of his cropped hair reminded her of stained oak. A large scar disfigured one cheek. Together with the piercing gaze, from almost incredibly blue eyes, it lent the fellow a dangerous aura. Involuntarily, she broke out into goose bumps, retreating until the roughly plastered wall stopped her. She almost felt like prey.

Along with her last suitcase, the man opened the front passenger door without any hesitation, letting Doc free. Horrified, she held her breath, watching her four-legged monster. Doc was a mongrel mix of Irish Wolfhound and Doberman. Against all expectation, however, the dog didn't attack the stranger. To the contrary, the huge beast wagged his tail like an idiot, even let the stranger rub his ears, as if they had been best friends for ages. Incredible!

"You traitor!", Lou exclaimed indignantly.

Damn.

The expected male tenant had just turned into a tarted up female tenant. As if he didn't have enough problems already. Couldn't anything in his screwed up life go right for once? Bad luck couldn't stick to his boots all his life, could it?

Alasdair could smell trouble coming. Instead of going into the house and getting dry, as anyone with common sense would do, this tourist stood immobile in the door and watched him open-mouthed.

He shook his head glumly.

"She'll take her death, the stupid female", he cursed quietly in Gaelic, while he opened the car door for the ugliest dog he had ever seen.

He let the animal sniff at his hand, and the dog's low growl turned to a joyful whine. He talked to the animal quietly.

Marge had been nice enough to prepare the house for the arrival of his new tenant. She had probably even filled the refrigerator, if he knew his mother.

The good woman would never realize these weren't friends they were hosting, but tenants. In any case, he certainly wasn't about to enter the house. It held too many bad, and only a few good, memories for him. Once again, Alasdair asked himself why he hadn't sold the ramshackle building. Because it had been owned by his clan for hundreds of years? Or was there a small part of him that still held on to the few happy moments of his marriage to Felicitas?

"Fool", he berated himself. Groaning, he lugged the heaviest, if luckily also last, piece of luggage up the washed-out gravel walk, which the rain had turned to a morass. *Cac. Another thing I have to do right away: Spread new gravel!*

Arriving at the house, he dropped the suitcase roughly next to the others he had lugged up under the suspicious eyes of the German woman.

"Thank you", the foreign woman whispered, with chattering teeth and eyes that seemed filled with fear. He noticed her trembling lips were almost blue with cold. *A Dhia. Damn.* His gaze touched her fingers, whose nails looked strangely deformed. She immediately tried to conceal them behind her back, as if she had noticed his look.

For sure, those hands have never built a fire in the hearth. Damn. With a man, there would have been no problem here. A crackbrained idea, renting to tourists of all people. Now an A'gearmailteach makes me enter this damned house, after all these years, he growled silently.

He sent a furtive look at the woman from the corner of his eye. She was only a little shorter than his 185 cm, which was somewhat tall for a woman, he thought. She was thin, though. Much too thin, in his opinion. That made her look like a nervous fawn. Her friendly face was streaked by black smears of mascara. He had to force himself to look away from those wounded brown eyes, which affected him so deeply. Doe eyes. A sigh escaped him. Oh yes.

He couldn't escape raising a fire on the hearth, as the old-fashioned house had no central heating. With, it seemed, a mixture of fear and suspicion, the woman watched him take off his muddy work boots. He silently cursed the hole in his left sock. More resolutely than he really felt, he entered the gloomy vestibule. The woman seemed to wrinkle her nose. Embarassed, he asked himself whether his work pants smelled of cow or sheep dung.

As if I care, what some tarted up blonde from Germany thinks of me, he thought. He was a farmer. No more and no less. He hadn't entered these rooms for more than eight years.

Felicitas had left him exactly two days after the birth of

their daughter, Grace. She hadn't had room in her life for the child of a sheep and cattle farmer, who operated an unprofitable café in his sparse spare time. Felicitas' life was lived on the great stages of the wide world. Not a piddling jerkwater town, lost in the endless expanse of the Scottish Higlands, living with an ugly fellow.

Even when, after three months, it had turned out that Grace was deaf, she hadn't come back to him and their daughter. He had only heard from her two more times. Once, when he had received the divorce papers, and again on the day of their divorce, on which she had appeared personally, with a popinjay in a suit and tie at her side. She hadn't once inquired about Grace. There had been no mail on any of her birthdays. Never in his life would he have believed a mother could be so heartless.

From that day on, Grace had become the centre of his life. What else could he have done? Grace was his flesh, his blood. He had renounced women, apart from occasional sex affairs. That wouldn't change for any German blonde, either!

Louise, not Louis, pfffft… A missing 'E' was going to bring him a lot of trouble. He pushed past the woman in his holed socks, into his former living room, where he lighted the oven with a practiced hand. He didn't touch the light switch. He needed no light.

Alasdair didn't want to see the place where he had once sat, entwined with Felicitas, before the fireplace. No feelings – no entanglements, and so, no heartache! Carefully, he tried to avoid each creaking floorboard and the associated memories. He took two stairs at a time on the way to the bathroom, to avoid at all costs the creaking one where Felicitas had once bloodied her knee. With a sure hand, he felt for the little cabinet and pulled out a towel. Grinding his teeth, he ignored the familiar delicate smell rising from the toweling.

Hastily, he returned downstairs. Without a word, he pushed the towel into the woman's hands. Just before reaching the door, he thought better of it, and turned around to the foreigner, who was at least now standing in the dining room, though she still seemed totally unsettled. But that wasn't his problem, was it?

"Always open the cover, before you light the fire. There's wood behind the house, Miss…"

"Schulzinger. Louise Schulzinger", the German woke from her numbness. "What about the central heating, Mister.. ahm, Munro?", she asked.

„There is none", he answered shortly. Embarrassed, he tore himself away from the large, teary doe eyes. Before Mistress Schulzinger could make new demands, Alasdair slammed the door behind himself, and rushed off. No compromises. No ghosts from the past, and so, no new injuries! Annoyed, he cursed quietly, running his hands through his wet hair. Had he lost his mind? A tourist. A tarted up model.

God above, a woman!

Why had he rented his property to her? Granted, he was in deep. Devil take it. Yes. He had no idea how he would pay the next vet's bill – and that would come, as sure as taxes. But renting his property to an A' ghearmailteach? Damn missing 'E'!

A Dhia. *I hope the woman doesn't burn down the whole house*, he prayed silently. After all, he wasn't exactly overinsured, was he?

The rude fellow had just left her standing there. Without batting an eye, he had just left. No central heating? What did that mean? It seemed, *warm* meant something different in Scotland than in Germany.

The slamming of the door had wakened her from her

lethargy. Shakily, she tottered on. Sank into a wing chair. For minutes, Lou just stared at the water that ran from her hair, across her back and the long legs, before pooling on the floor in front of her.

 Damn, she would ruin the wooden flooring.

Doc seated himself before her, watching her from his loyal brown eyes. One ear pricked, the other folded down, he whined insistently. Sighing, she wrapped the scratchy towel around her head, while lovingly running her hand through his wiry wet pelt.

"It's all right, big fellow. Mistress has pulled herself together," she murmured to him. The cold had stiffened her limbs. She got up awkwardly, to find some more towels.

Finally, she as well as Doc were dry, and all signs of water had been eliminated. In a tiny kitchen, she managed to brew some tea in an old-fashioned tea kettle, despite an unfamiliar gas range and burned fingers. Lou mentally put some matches at the top of her shopping list. She simply couldn't use a cigarette lighter, without burning herself.

It didn't help that her nails were much too short, because she had had her false nails removed. In the confusion and the half-light, she hadn't been able to find an electric kettle.

Now she sat, with an old patchwork quilt she had wrapped tightly around her, in the worn wing chair, right before the open fireplace. Tired, she stared into the crackling flames. She felt totally worn out. Empty inside. Hadn't even found the time, to take a look around the cottage. She was usually the nervous type of woman, who locked everything up. She always made sure she was alone, even looking under the bed and into the large wardrobes. As if a burglar couldn't kill her doing that, just as easily. Strangely, though, she didn't feel any such fear in this little cottage. In spite of the grumpy Scot, she felt at home. Even welcome. Besides, there was always Doc, who hopefully wouldn't see just any Scotsman as a friend.

A look out the window showed her darkness, as well as the silhouettes of large trees, whose tops bent in the driving wind and rain. But even that sight didn't bother her. She suddenly thought of the smartphone in the pocket of her blazer. She pulled it out to take a look at the time.

It showed the time to be shortly after nine p.m. But was that German or British time? She also had thirty-two missed calls, and twelve messages. Lou gulped, incredulous. Resolutely, she pressed Delete, without reading a single message, or listening to any of the voice mails. Then she feebly let the smartphone fall to the couch table. From her hand luggage, she pulled out a package of dry dog food as well as a bottle of whisky, which she had bought at the airport. She knew a little about Scotch Single Malts, and had bought a fifteen year old Cardhu.

After pouring a generous portion of dog food into a soup plate for Doc, she poured herself a couple of fingers of whisky into her empty tea cup. Not in proper style, but good enough, lacking a whisky glass. Again, she nestled into the colourful blanket, settling comfortably on the sofa. Doc followed her with questioning eyes. When she patted the sofa next to her invitingly, he jumped up and rolled up at her feet.

"Lucky guy", she murmured gloomily. Her whole life was a disaster. Maybe it really was a mistake to follow one's secret dreams? Exhausted, she closed her eyes.

Simultaneously in Germany
Everything was perfect. The strings filled the large hall with pleasant music. Opulent candlelight, as well as large bouquets of lilies in all colours, provided a festive air. By now, the guests were all present. Only the birthday guest of hon-

our was missing. Where in the world was Louise? It wasn't like his wife to be late. When they had first dated, she had always scolded him for his tardiness. She had actually gone so far as to advance all their dates by a half hour, after which they had both always arrived at the same time.

"You look very handsome again today, if I may say so, my dear Alexander", Constance, who had approached him unseen, said archly. Smiling, she toasted him with a glass of champagne.

"I can't possibly compete with your beauty, my dear Constance. You don't happen to know where my darling wife is?", he answered gallantly, and had to pound Constance on the back, whose champagne had just gone down the wrong way, turning her face an unflattering shade of red.

"Whoops. Are you well, Constance?", he asked considerately, and took her glass, while she gasped for air.

"She didn't tell you?", Constance wheezed, incredulous.

Alexander felt his facial muscles freeze. "Didn't tell me what?", he responded, while he took her firmly by the arm. "What didn't Louise tell me?" Roughly, he pushed his wife's friend out into the empty anteroom. A cleared throat behind him made him flinch, feeling oddly guilty. Alarmed, he turned around, and saw his hated brother-in-law.

"Tobias. You're here?" he greeted him frostily, though surprised.

"Surprised, Alexander?", his brother-in-law answered his greeting, with a grin that had alarm bells going off in his head.

"Don't worry, you'll be rid of me right away, dear Alexander. I guess Constance was trying to tell you that Lou should have arrived in Scotland by now", Tobias explained

cheerfully.

Alexander had to clench his fists to avoid wiping the smug

grin from his brother-in-law's face. He had been married to Louise twenty-two years. He had married her against the wishes of his own parents, though she, eighteen at the time, had been beneath him socially. He had never liked her brother. This had to be another of Tobias' stupid jokes. Louise couldn't really have left him? He was a Schulzinger, dammit! No one just up and left him!

„Stop your insolent jokes, Tobias. You, of all people, should know I can't stand that kind of thing."

Tobias shrugged scornfully.

"I believe Lou told you often enough what she wants, and what she doesn't want. I was just supposed to tell you. Also, that Richie and Flip can stay with me anytime, if it gets too much for you!"

„Richard and Philip are going nowhere. Least of all to a … a… "

"Gay? Homosexual? One isn't made gay, one is born gay, Alexander. So you don't need to fear I'll assault my nephews."

Alexander broke out into a cold sweat. With trembling fingers, he pulled his iPhone from his jacket. Hectically, he punched Louise's number.

She didn't really do this to me? Not after I gave a huge feast for her and laid the world at her feet… his thoughts screamed desperately. Louise didn't react, no matter how often he dialed her number. Only her mailbox started up. With hate filled eyes, he stared at Tobias, let the iPhone fall carelessly to the floor and threw himself at his brother-in-law. Hands twisted in his collar, he shouted at him: "What did you do? Where, exactly, is my wife? Where's Louise, you gay asshole?"

He had lost control. Was in a total rage. But before he could throw further obscenities, or violence, at his brother-in-law, he received a skillful uppercut. Stunned, he sank to the floor. Around him, the guests streamed into the anteroom, looking for the source of the commotion.

"I hardly think that's the way to get Lou back, Alexander. I also doubt she'll answer her smartphone, if you're the one calling!"

Without another word, Tobias rearranged his shirt, turned around, and left the birthday party, strolling insouciantly. Alexander painfully straightened up, ignoring Constance's helping hand.

"Excuse me", he snapped and started for the second floor, holding his bloody nose. He had his office rooms there. Behind him, he could hear Mrs. Bott following on his heels, spouting "We'll fix all this, Mr. Schulzinger. You'll see, Mr. Schulzinger!".

Alexander fled into the bathroom. Trembling from head to toe, he slammed the door with a loud bang. Furiously, he ripped off his jacket and the ruined shirt.

Then he sank to the toilet, groaning, and put his head in his hands. How could Louise do this to him? He toiled night and day at his company for his family. He had never even looked at another woman, though the fair sex swarmed around him. And how did Louise thank him for his loyalty, for all the deprivations he had endured for the sake of his loved ones? By simply disappearing?

"My God. I've been embarassed before all my colleagues, friends…", an agonized moan escaped him. Granted, she had told him a dozen times she didn't want a big party. Yes, he knew she had ardently wished for a holiday in Scotland. But, a small party was beneath her. Why couldn't she understand that? And why would she pick Scotland, of all places, when she could fly to Mauritius in a private jet?

A knocking on the door woke him from his vale of tears.

"Mr. Schulzinger? Mr. Schulzinger, are you all right?", he

heard from the other side of the door. He could always count on the good Mrs. Bott. "Do you need anything, Mr. Schulzinger?"

Yes, dammit! My wife!, he wanted to shout, flicking tears from his eyes.

"A fresh shirt, Mrs. Bott. Could you bring me a fresh shirt, please", he said instead. He congratulated himself, silently, that his voice sounded quite calm again.

"Coming up!", Mrs. Bott cried, relieved. The clacking of her heels on the marble floor was audible all the way to where he sat. Not ten minutes later, he was sitting at his desk, freshly washed and combed, and with a pristine white shirt.

Uncomprehending, he stared at the envelope sitting next to the unopened Cartier jewel box, still in its cellophane with the huge red bow. Louise hadn't even opened his present. Jewelry for over a thousand Euros, and she hadn't even looked at it. Instead, she had placed it all provokingly on his desk, along with an envelope with his name on it.

The only place she could be sure of him visiting. His office. Shaken to the core, he reached for the envelope with trembling fingers and extracted the note. He was interrupted by Mrs. Bott, however.

"Excuse me, Mr. Schulzinger, but the guests are asking after the birthday guest of honour, and your lady mother is also getting somewhat anxious."

"Thank you, Mrs. Bott. Please excuse us. Just tell them my wife is indisposed, and I'm looking after her. Oh, and please tell my mother I'll look her up later. Ask the guests to please start on their dinner", he declared, in a voice that brooked no arguments. Mrs. Bott nodded understandingly, and left with swift strides.

Alexander took a deep breath, stroked the letter.

Oh God, his mother was all he needed now. She would be even more down on Louise, when she heard about this mess. Tiredly, he ran his hand through his hair. Breathed deeply. Finally he opened the letter, his heart beating erratically.

Dear Alexander,

by the time you read this letter, I'll already have left. I can't continue like this! I don't know how often I've tried to explain to you recently, what I feel. For you, I've become commonplace, part of the scenery. You've made me an artificial trophy. A blonde Barbie you can show around.

That's not me! Married twenty-two years, and you still don't understand me in the least! I don't want your money! I want the man back, who made me laugh. The man I talked to through the nights, with whom I burned the candle at both ends. I want love and sex. Not a pencil pusher, who hides behind his work, and ignores me. I'll be in Scotland for two months. Don't try to call or find me. When I know how I want things to go on with us, I'll get in touch with you of my own accord.

Lou

P.S. I'm not crazy, and I'm not having a midlife crisis!

Rage filled Alexander. He crumpled up Louise's letter as hard as he could. As usual, he was the culprit, of course! The scoundrel! He, who worked from dawn to dusk, like a maniac. Slaved for the good of his family.

He jumped up like a scalded cat, and threw the paper ball in the trash. She couldn't do this. Not to him! Hectically, he searched for the calling card of the detective bureau he sometimes used for his firm, searching for delinquent debtors.

The spare iPhone pressed to his ear, he hastened up to the penthouse. He stormed through the entrance door, and directly to his wife's bedroom.

"Is that the detective bureau Osanowic? Alexander Schulzinger, speaking. I need your help. I want to hire you to find my wife!", he barked loudly into the phone.

Half an hour later, he was poorer by several thousand Euros. The detective firm had already started the search for Louise. His eyes wandered through the spacious room. He noticed that her mutt's basket was missing, as well as toiletries, jeans and all the paraphernalia Louise needed to paint. Exhausted, he sank to the bed, burying his head in the pillow and breathing deeply of her scent. How had it come to this between them?

Yes. Yes, it was true. She had tried to talk to him again and again. And yes, he was very busy with his company. But she was comfortably off. She had servants, a fitness trainer, wellness and beauty treatments, women friends, and clothes from the most fashionable designers. Louise's jewelry alone was worth a fortune. Wasn't that what all women wanted?

By God, it wasn't as if they were a dysfunctional family. So why should he have acceded to her request for marriage counseling? Was Louise really going to just throw away twenty-two years of marriage? What the hell should he tell his sons? God, how was he going to explain it to his mother? He could already hear her "What did I always tell you about that woman?". Could Louise have a lover? It couldn't be her personal trainer, that was a woman. A real looker, he had to admit. Unless…. Troubled, he thought of Tobias, but then discarded the thought as totally absurd.

Deeply hurt, he gazed at the chaos he had caused.

A cottage in the middle of nowhere

Scotland

Warm, bright light on her face induced Lou to slowly wake from a dreamless sleep. Drowsily, she rubbed her eyes, only to immediately defend herself from Doc's wet tongue that tried several times to lick her face.
"Yuck! Down, Doc! No, stop that, bad boy!" she scolded indignantly, while the dog looked at her with loyal eyes, wagging his tail. "Anyone would think you hadn't seen me in ages", she murmured fondly, for who could long remain angry, seeing such a hangdog look. Next moment, she found herself sprawled under her monster dog, who had joyfully jumped on her stomach.
"Ow! Darn… get off. Down Doc. I can't breathe, you crazy beast!" she exclaimed, laughing. She sat up with some effort.
The sun shone on her through the large windows. Delighted, she watched two squirrels playing right in front of the window pane, untroubled by her gaze. Spellbound, she watched the idyllic scene, her hands stroking Doc's wiry hair. Only small puddles were left of yesterday's rain, the rest had already been dried by the sun.
If she bent her head forward a bit, she could get a glimpse of blue sky, with white cotton-wool clouds. A tiny feeling of joy spread through her. She had actually done it. Had done what she had been meaning to do, for years. Her whole life, she had always put other's concerns first. She had almost lost herself doing so, without anyone so much as noticing.
　　　Barefoot, she padded to the window, pulled back the last bit of curtain with a jerk. Blinded by the light and beauty she saw, she stood rooted to the spot.
"Enchanting", she sighed rapturously. She had actually reached the native country of her romantic hero.

"Thank you, Ms. Gabaldon", Lou murmured happily.
Yesterday's storm had passed. The tall pines and firs in her garden swayed to the imaginary beat of a mild breeze. Dust particles danced in the sun's rays, birds chirped. It was just as she had hoped for, but she had expected a morass of a garden, after last night's pouring rain. Relieved, she saw that the lawn, with its many colourful blossoms, hadn't been damaged by the deluge. Though it was already deep into autumn, the splendid garden seemed almost like springtime. She even imagined she could smell the aroma of that carpet of blossoms.
"Well then, let's see where we've landed, Miss Robinson", she told herself, and winked at Doc, who followed her gladly. The floor under her naked feet was cold, creaking with each of her steps. Seen by day, the furniture in the small living room had a rustic charm. The couch was covered in worn corduroy, just like the old-fashioned wing chair. Faded flowered pillows, whose pattern was repeated in the patchwork quilt, lent the room some colour. Everything was clean, and smelled slightly of fabric softener. The furniture consisted of just a few old wooden pieces, that looked as if they had mostly been passed down, from generation to generation. They looked old, in any case, possibly even antiquities, judging by their lathe-turned wooden elements. Colourful, seemingly handwoven carpets covered the wooden parquet, which looked its age. The living room merged seamlessly into the dining area, where a massive table, with a corner bench and two chairs, invited a meal. Wistfully, Lou stroked the wood, which felt soft and warm under her hand. Scratches and several dents told of regular use. She probably wouldn't spend a lot of time here, as her cooking skills were almost nonexistent. A fresh bouquet of roses occupied the center of the table, exuding a lovely fragrance.

"Ah, this is where the flower scent comes from", she thought aloud, with the beguiling scent in her nostrils. *The middle of autumn, and there are still roses*, she rejoiced. The kitchen was right next to the dining area. It was so small, there wasn't room to swing a cat, as the saying went. If she stood in the middle, she could comfortably reach all the drawers and cupboards at the same time. The only large item in this room was the overlarge, American-style refrigerator, including an ice cube maker. Unfortunately, as it proved, it was also the only modern appliance this kitchen boasted. Neither microwave, nor electric kettle were available, much less a dishwasher.

"Darn!", Lou grumbled, while yanking open door after door, hoping to find a microwave somewhere. No luck. At the thought of two months of dependence on her terrible cooking skills, her stomach began rumbling with hunger. There was a note on the refrigerator, with a telephone number, annotated with "A. Munro" and two exclamation points. There was also another note, with the address of the local grocery store, as well as a small road-map, showing the only two roads the town boasted. A slightly crumpled flyer picturing a minibus, and the day-tripping excursions it offered, completed the note collection.

A look into the refrigerator showed Lou eggs, bacon, local sausages, toast, and various jars with jam and pickled vegetables.

Shorty afterward, she tucked in with gusto to burned toast and bacon and eggs, also somewhat burned. She washed it down with huge amounts of tea. Refreshed, her gaze came to rest on her mutilated, burned fingertips, whose nails still needed to regrow.

"Never again artificial nails. Never again bleached hair", she murmured determinedly. Motivated, she began to unpack.

Comfortable pants and baggy sweatshirts didn't even fill a quarter of the cedar-smelling oak cabinet, that took up the whole of the only straight wall in the bedroom, up in the attic. Her favorite pillow, signed by her children, landed in the middle of a soft heap of bedding, of starched pristine white linen. This lay on the largest bed she had ever seen. Wide-eyed, she asked herself how this monster bed had ever passed through the small staircase, or the narrow door, on which she had banged her head.

"Only in pieces", she mused aloud, repeatedly shaking her head in disbelief, as she circled around the bed that took up almost the whole floor space in the room. It was of dark wood, ornamented with carved Scottish thistles. Hand carved, probably unaffordable nowadays. Hesitantly, she tested the springiness of the matress with her hand. Suddenly, a grin appeared on her face. Warily watched by Doc, she suddenly couldn't resist the childish temptation, and jumped right into the middle of the soft pile. Lou immediately sank, along with Doc, who hadn't been able to resist following his mistress. Piles of blankets and innumerable scatter pillows buried them both, as the soft matress made them both roll to the middle of the bed.

"Heavens… I'll sag to the floor. How am I ever supposed to sleep in this?", Lou moaned. With an effort, she fought her was out of the bed and back on her feet.

Exhilarated, she went back downstairs. She brought all her toiletries to the tiny bathroom with the slanting walls, which, surprisingly, offered an extra large bathtub. The, at first unimposing, room proved to be a very oasis of wellness. Sand-coloured floor tiles gave the feeling of walking on a beach. The walls were covered with terracotta, or ocean-blue tile chips that formed waves and alternated with real sea shells. Looking closer, Lou discovered jets in the tub. A Jacuzzi.

The only thing that caused her concern was the hot water boiler she discovered behind a rattan panel.

Oh oh. Looks pretty ancient!

She'd probably run out of hot water before the jets were even halfway covered. It was worth a try, though. After some searching, she found the ON switch for the boiler and pressed it. Cheerfully, she grimaced at her reflection in the mirror. Finally, she read the instructions on the packet of hair dye carefully, which she had purchased from her hair stylist in Germany. Light brown. Her natural hair colour. It was time to find back to herself. New life – new hair. At least, that was how she had imagined it.

Once she had put on her old painter's shirt, she looked at her long blonde hair, for the last time.

"Bye bye, Barbie doll", Lou murmured, determinedly ripped open the package, mixed the dyes, and put on the plastic gloves. Carefully, she spread the stinking pink mash on her head. She washed off the gloves, and put them aside for later. Then she opened the faucets of the bathtub. Luckily, the hot water reached to the jets after all.

A miracle!

Ecstatically, she seated herself in the bubbling tub. The bath was a godsend. She felt as if a huge burden had lifted from her, for the first time in ages.

Deeply relaxed, she mused on her life. How had their marriage gone so terribly wrong? Granted, at just eighteen, she had been somewhat young when she married Alexander, who was more than ten years older. Richard had been born exactly one year later. Four years later, Philip. At the exact same time, Alexander had taken over the family company. Now that she thought about it, it had started even then.

The highly talented art student, with advertising major, hadn't turned into a celebrated artist, but into a pregnant housewife. Somehow, somewhere along the way, Alexander had managed to turn her into a trophy wife. Though never to the satisfaction of her parents-in-law. He had lavished designer clothes on her, bought her the most expensive jewelry. Suddenly, she had a personal trainer – female, mind you – a cook, a maid and, in the end, even her own chauffeur, since her driving was supposedly suicidal. The down-to-earth Lou Mayer had turned into Louise Schulzinger. Little by little, she had lost all her old friends. All except Debbie, her very best friend. Small wonder, with all that luxury, which her friends hadn't been able to match. Lou couldn't blame them. Her life, at the time, had had more than a touch of *Cinderella turns princess*.

Her father had died when she was just twelve years old, her mother shortly after Philip had been born. Tobias was all the family she had left. He was like a red rag to a bull for Alexander, his homosexuality not fitting into the world view of a high society businessman. The man she had adored, had locked her in a golden cage. He had lavished everything money could buy on her. Only with love, had he been stingy.

Alexander let her wither on the vine. The more she had burned for his love, the less she had received. No hugs. No kisses. Nothing much in the bedroom, for years now.

The separate bedrooms had killed the remainder of her love. In a last bout of desperation, she had nervously visited a sex shop, clad in a trenchcoat and with sunglasses, like a secret agent in a cheap film. She had bought a virility tonic, as well as some absolutely trashy lingerie. At home, she had poured half the bottle in Alexanders' evening beer. Unfortunately, the result had been a disaster. Nothing had come of it, but a stomach disorder, and a loudly snoring husband, as well as a nasty rash, from the latex inlays of the lingerie. After this disaster, she had finally given up.

She had never been a prude, of course. Naturally, there were many ways to have a full sex life these days without a man. It was a fact, though, that no piece of latex or rubber could replace a man of flesh and blood. At least, not in her opinion.

The water was getting cold. Besides, it was about time to rinse off the dye. Unfortunately, there was no hot water anymore. Lou was forced to sluice off with cold water.

"Typical!", she shivered, annoyed. The dye would have to remain where it was for the moment, as it would probably not come off properly with cold water. Clad in her bathrobe, she flitted to the kitchen, where she put on the kettle. At least, this time, she hadn't burnt her fingers while lighting the cooktop. While waiting for the water to boil, she opened the door to the garden for Doc. Nervously, Lou prayed her hair would really be brown and not, for instance, pink, after leaving the dye on so long. The fresh air, and the earthy smells that reached her nose, managed to abate her panic a bit. Heavenly. In spite of the fiasco with the water, which she really should have foreseen, she felt free.

A renewed euphoria took hold of her. The last time she had felt this way had been, when she had brought Doc from the animal shelter. Lou smiled to herself, watching her huge beast, as the vicious, so-called 'attack dog' tried to catch a butterfly. She immediately felt warmed by the sight. She had deliberately chosen the ugliest animal she could find. At the time, Doc had already spent half a year, of his one and a half years of age, in the animal shelter. Not because he was vicious, or unpleasant. Rather, because he looked more like a plucked hyena than a dog. Lou had meant to pass him by, but her shoelace had come undone. So, she had been forced to kneel on the ground, right in front of his wire cage, to bind it. Doc's wet, doggy nose had nuzzled her, curious. A single look in his eyes had been enough, and she was lost. Beauty was in the eye of the beholder, after all! Alexander had thrown a fit. God, how he had shouted at her. He had implied that she was endangering herself, and her children, with a vicious attack dog. A grin came to her lips. The attack dog had turned out to be a champion smoocher. Instinctively, Doc had never really accepted Alexander. Now, she was certain Doc had been meant for her.

The shrill whistle of the tea kettle interrupted her regard of her happy dog. The handle of the hot kettle, wrapped in dish towels, in one hand, an empty bucket for mixing water in the other, she hurried up the stairs to the bathroom. Unfortunately, she tripped over one of those stairs, banging her knee painfully on the edge of the next one. The kettle rattled over the tiles, while the bucket flew through the air in a graceful curve.

"Goddammittohell!"

Tears of pain shot to her eyes. Suspiciously, Doc put his head around the corner at the bottom of the stairs, probably to see what all the noise was about. Lou waved him away with her hand. Her knee was bleeding from a scrape. Annoyed, she scooped up the bucket, then limped carefully into the bathroom.

"Would have been too much to ask, for something to work out without complications, Lou. At least, the kettle just slid", she hissed. After pulling a wooden splinter out of the wound, she pressed a handkerchief against it. It stopped bleeding after a few moments. The knee was already swelling a bit, and turning blue. No wonder, with her graceful stork's legs.

Bravely, she ignored the painfully throbbing wound. Using the bucket, she mixed cold water from the tap with the hot water from the kettle. Armed with gloves, shampoo and lots of rinse, she then attended to her hair. Watched part of her life flow down the sink in pink swirls, to go gurgling down the drain.

"Good riddance, Blondie!", she murmured. Then she viewed the result in the mirror. "Not very satisfactory", she told her reflection disappointedly. The hair color was okay. The rest of her hair style left a lot to be desired, though.

A bit like a mangy dog! Drat!

Now capable of anything, she limped down the stairs to the kitchen. She searched through the drawers, until she finally found a pair of scissors, with which she hurried back to the bathroom. It couldn't be that hard, after all. "It always works in the movies", she encouraged herself. Concentrating, she pulled her wet hair into a tight braid, fixing it in place with a hair tie. Taking a deep breath, she started in with the scissors. Unfortunately, the old device was quite dull, so she had to work very hard. She needed several tries, and a lot of endurance, before she finally held the severed braid in her hand. Unfortunately, after she took off the hair tie, her hair didn't look any better.

"Oh my God…oh no!", she exclaimed. Tears of rage ran down her reddened cheeks. This couldn't be happening! Now, she looked like a plucked chicken!

While blowing her wet strands dry, she desperately tried to remember whether there was a barber on Kildermories sole commercial street.

"God, I look like a scarecrow", she groaned aloud. Resolutely, she put on a pair of jeans shorts, sneakers, and a shirt. "Don't get upset, Lou", she told herself. "Don't panic. You have a laptop, and there's the Internet. You're sure to find a hair stylist somewhere nearby!"

A few minutes later, Lou sat at the dining table, looking for an internet connection. No result. No connection, neither with internet stick, nor without. Nothing doing. "This can't be! What kind of dump did I rent, anyway? Where's the promised internet connection?", Lou cursed angrily, while giving Doc an apologetic shrug of her shoulders, since he was looking at her as if she was now totally crazy.

"Don't look at me like that, dog. That miserable Scot, Munro, promised me modern comforts. Laughable!"

Naturally, her smartphone also showed no connection, though showing a dizzying number of missed calls, and even more messages. But, if incoming messages and calls were shown, there had to be a connection somewhere? Didn't it? With smartphone in hand, she searched every square centimeter of the cottage for a connection. She crawled on the floor, held the phone to the ceiling. Walked around the house. No connection. Incredible! Once again, she deleted everything, without reading, or listening to, any messages. By now, she was walking very carefully, bending her knee as little as possible. It throbbed with pain. Damn, that hurt!

In the kitchen, she at least found the first aid kit right away, which she had noticed by accident, while searching for the scissors. The non-sticking plaster she unearthed was the last straw to unleash her fury. Cursing loudly, and stamping with her healthy foot, she threw the whole first aid kit to the floor. The brittle plastic casing split neatly up the middle. A flood of old bandages, safety pins and various other items spread at her feet. With forceful strides, ignoring the pain in her knee, she grabbed her shopping bag, along with her purse, hissed "Come on!" to Doc, and set out. Behind her, the door closed with a bang, followed by clattering.

Why in the world am I so clumsy, all of a sudden?

Her ironic laugh made Doc put his tail between his legs. Ears hanging, he trotted obediently at her side. God have mercy on that Scotsman, if he should happen to cross her path just now. She felt like strangling him with her bare hands.

"Pah. Modern comforts!" Her eyes came to rest on the sagging door of the shed, which nestled against the wall of the cottage. Curious, she went closer, and took a look through the crack left by the warped wooden door. She thought she could discern the outline of a bicycle in the gloom. With an effort, she pulled open the door, to take a closer look at the heap of rubbish. Her discovery really was a bicycle. The light in the shed left something to be desired, like so much else here. She couldn't get a good look like that. She pulled it out into the open, uncaring of dust, dirt and several spiders. It turned out to be an elderly, and somewhat rusty, man's bike. The tires hadn't enough air, but, with the conveniently provided bicycle pump, she could fix that problem immediately. The porous tires should be able to support a lightweight like herself. She wiped off the spiderwebs with her hand. Courageously, she took a rather large specimen of a daddy longlegs by one leg, and carried it off a short distance, where she let it run free. After a further quarter hour's fight with the bicycle pump, she had an acceptable vehicle. Did the bike belong to her landlord, Alasdair Munro? The size might fit. A good thing for her, too. Munro was just about the first man she had met who was significantly taller than herself. Alex was just barely as tall as she. He always hated it when she wore high heels.

She hung the shopping bag on the handlebars. For the luggage rack, she had found an old wicker basket in the shed, which she clamped there. Awkwardly, she swung into the saddle. Doc bounded ahead, looking forward to some exercise. She followed him, a bit wobbly at first, almost as if she were riding on uneven stones. But with each further meter, she became more confident, though her knee pained her badly. At least it wasn't bleeding anymore. To compensate, it was more than colourful.

The enchanting landscape so captivated her gaze, however, that she soon thought of nothing else, but perfect places to paint, or she imagined Jamie and Claire rolling around on the grass, necking. Her rage at Alasdair Munro had evaporated, at least for the moment. Maybe there would be a pub in the village, where she could get a hot meal for lunch. Who knew, she might even meet a nice, handsome Scot in a kilt there? Wasn't it said that every hamlet in Scotland, be it ever so small, had its own pub? Not so?

The burned breakfast was like lead in her stomach. Besides, this way she could find out right away whether there was a barber in town.

Not fifteen minutes later, the first houses of the hamlet came in sight. At her command, Doc slowed down and stayed close at her side.

Good boy!

It seemed she hadn't done anything wrong in training her four-legged friend, at least! Come to think of it, he was also the only male who didn't patronize her, or contradict her all the time.

The day before, she hadn't seen much of the town. She had been much too nervous and scared. Not to mention having to fight her monster of a jeep. She looked around all the more curiously now. A pub, some houses, a shabby café with a bakery, and a rather small market, that was Kildermorie.

"Dammit, no barber. There's no barber in this darned backwater", Lou cursed in despair. She ran her fingers through her mane of hair, which still felt strange. Her gaze wandered erratically, still searching. Thus, she didn't even notice the oncoming figure. Lou crashed into the pedestrian.

She tottered, and would have fallen, if a hand had not held her upper arm firmly, until she had both feet on the ground. Startled, she looked into the ocean blue eyes of Alasdair Munro.

Oh no. Not him again!

Lou could see the Scot openly appraising her from head to toe. There was, again, an annoyed set to his full lips. Could this fellow ever look friendly? Seeing her hair, his eyebrows lifted inquiringly, but he remained mute.

"I'm very sorry, umm, Mr. Munro. I wasn't paying attention", she heard herself say. The Scotsman didn't meet her gaze, instead rubbing Doc's ears, who pressed against the big man's legs, wagging his tail.

"If you have to borrow my bike, Mistress Scherzinger…"

"Schulzinger, Mr. Munro, my name is Schulzinger. And, regarding your bike, I took the liberty of restoring it to working order. Of course, I'll be sure to take good care of it", she interrupted him. Annoyed, she felt her cheeks heat and, surely, also turn red.

Alasdair Munro rose to his full height. He returned her gaze, while repeatedly glancing at her wounded knee.

"Aye, lass. You're a danger to traffic, even in a hamlet like this. Ever heard of driving on the left side? In Scotland, we drive on the left, not in the middle of the street, or on the curb, as you just did", he accused her.

Unable to respond, Lou gasped for air. With trembling knees, she got off the bike, and let it fall against the Scotsman's legs.

"And you…you obviously not only have a problem with simple courtesy, but also a damned problem with stairs", Lou hissed angrily. She turned on her heel, head proudly held high.

"The seventh step from the top?", she heard him ask, but

didn't answer, instead walking unswervingly to the little café on the other side of the street.

Feeling Alasdair Munro's gaze on her back, Lou entered through the door of the shabby building, which she would otherwise certainly not have entered, and probably not even noticed. Surprisingly, she found herself in the salesroom of a small bakery, which smelled wonderful. Various baked goods were lovingly arranged behind an old glass countertop. The sight alone was enough to make Lou's mouth water. Doughnuts, apple tarts and savory filled turnovers – called bridies – were to be seen, as well as bannock bread. Curious, she glanced around the corner into the adjoining café.

It was rather small, but, though it seemed somewhat old-fashioned, just like the bakery, it was quite charming. She immediately fell under its spell. Two round and three four-cornered tables, with pretty tartan tablecloths, waited for guests. Everything was neat and scrupulously clean. One wall held bookshelves, bowed under the many books filling them. An old jukebox stood right next to them. She could only see a single guest, besides herself. A young girl, of perhaps eight years, sat at a table in the farthest corner. She took no notice of Lou, drawing or writing something with full concentration. Lou stood a moment, looking at the girl's brown curls. A friendly voice woke her from her contemplation.

"Can I be of some help?"

Lou turned at the voice. She saw a rather plump woman, who was wiping her hands on a large apron, a motherly type with round cheeks, two heads shorter than herself.

"Yes, umm, thanks. I'd like to buy something, and then eat it here in the café", she answered. She answered the woman's winning smile with a friendly one of her own.

"Gladly. Come along and choose something", the woman

said. Lou followed her back to the bakery.

"Is this your dog?", the woman asked, while fearlessly stroking Doc's huge head, who sat immobile, wagging his tail.

"Yes. Umm…I hope it's okay to bring him in here?"

"Don't worry, as long as he doesn't attack any customers, it's no problem. We're in the country here", the woman explained, with a conspiratorial wink. "You must be the German lady who rented Al's cottage. It's not the most modern of houses, but I think it has the most wonderful view", the woman chatted cheerfully, took a china plate, and looked at Lou expectantly.

She didn't really want to discuss the pros and cons, or the missing modern comforts, of the cottage with a stranger or local. "Um, yes" was all she said. It was really difficult to choose between all the offered goodies, especially since her belly was beginning to rumble embarrassingly. At last, Lou decided on a bridie filled with haggis, with an apple tart as dessert and, of course, a pot of coffee.

"Thanks. Yes, um, the cottage is very nice", she mumbled again, intimidated by the lady's questioning gaze.

"My name is Marge Munro, by the way. I'm your landlord's mother", the woman explained, and sent her over to the café. "I'll bring everything to your table in a moment, lass", Marge chirped.

His mother, of all people! Why do these things always happen to me?, shot through Lou's head. What luck that she hadn't listed all the shortcomings of her lodgings! Now, she would have liked to run for it. Since that wasn't possible anymore without making an absolute fool of herself, she made for the tables in the café, with Doc following behind. She decided on a table next to the window. For one thing, she didn't want Doc to disturb or frighten the young girl at the back table. For another, this way she would have warning if that sourpuss Munro should appear. After all, the fellow knew where she had landed. Unfortunately, right in his mother's café!

The girl still took no notice of her at all. Lou gazed along the street. A bit further down, and across from her, she could see the pub's signboard, naming it The Green Hunter. Lou decided she would eat her evening meal there.

The aroma of fresh coffee tantalized her nose, as Marge Munro set down the tray with the goodies she had ordered.

Suddenly, however, a strangely garbled yelling reached her ears, or rather, a sequence of strange, inarticulate sounds.

Marge seemed unmoved, quite unlike she herself. The fright almost made her drop her cup. Nonplussed, Lou watched the woman rush toward the girl, gesticulating with her hands, while the girl, crying angrily, threw both paper and pencil to the floor. The young girl also gesticulated wildly in answer, waving her hands in the air.

With an apologetic shrug, Marge turned to Lou:

"I'm sorry, lass. This isn't like her. But the wee one, my granddaughter, has some difficult homework. She just can't draw that stupid animal", she tried to explain, while Lou just looked at both of them uncomprehendingly. Marge Munro interpreted her look correctly.

"Oh, I keep forgetting. Grace is deaf. That's why her speech sounds so strange."

"Maybe…", Lou started, then suddenly didn't know how to go on. Grace. That was a strange coincidence. Lou's second name was also Grace. A strange feeling spread through her. Touched her heart. Grace.

"You wouldn't know how to draw an elephant, by any chance, would you, lass? I certainly don't, God save me.", Marge continued hopefully.

Lou got up without hesitation, and headed over to their table: Doc followed on her heels, as always. The big dog then laid his huge head on the crying girl's lap, as if that were the most natural thing in the world. Surprised, she stopped crying immediately. Hesitantly, she stroked Doc's head with gentle fingers.

Encouragingly, the dog licked the girl's hand.

"You've got a wonderful fellow there, lass. Only her father can quiet her down that quickly, usually. Right, Gracy?" Marge asked, tousling her hair lovingly.

Lou smiled back at Grace, squatting before her, so their eyes were at the same height.

"May I?", Lou asked, with exaggerated lip movements. Marge patted her shoulder approvingly. The girl pushed a sheet of paper and a gnawed wooden pencil at her. Lou smiled. She still did that, too, gnawing wooden pencils at their end when she was concentrating, or thinking.

Turning to Marge, she explained what she was doing. "I'm sorry, I don't know sign language. But it will be enough if Grace just watches. There's a very simple trick, for children to draw animals of any kind. The animals consist of circles, ovals, squares or triangles, which just have to be connected appropriately. Then you just erase the reference lines."

With a practiced hand, she began with a large circle. With an encouraging look, she had Grace follow her lead. Very soon, they had created a grand elephant together. Marge brought her coffee and food over to the girl's table, allowing Lou to eat on the side, whenever it was Grace's turn to draw. After finishing the elephant, they tried several other animals, because they were both having so much fun with it. Lou couldn't remember when she had last been so happy, as just at that moment with Grace.

"You have a way with children, lass."

"Thank you, Mrs. Munro. Just call me Lou, please", she answered, somewhat embarrassed. Marge Munro laughed cheerfully.

" 'Lass' is a pet name for girl. But Lou is also a nice name. Is it short for Louisa?"

Lou smiled back, shaking her head.

"Unfortunately, no. It stands for Louise."

Marge waved dismissively. "Aye, I understand. But that's not such a bad name, either. Just call me Marge, please. But, if you don't mind, Lou… about your hair…", she clicked her tongue disapprovingly. "Is that the new fashion? It doesn't really suit you, I'm afraid, my dear", she said.

Tears came to Lou's eyes. She shrugged helplessly. "I had hoped to find a barber here…", she managed despondently.

Marge waved that aside. "Afraid not, Lou. But still, no reason to cry. Don't worry, I'm sure we'll find a solution!"

She really liked Marge. She reminded Lou painfully of what she missed.

Oh Mama. I really need you now!

The girl, on the other hand, was simply sweet. How could a sourpuss like Alasdair Munro have such an agreeable mother? And how in the world could he have such a delightful daughter? And where was the mother?

Why did this have to happen to him, of all people? A woman, instead of a man. Daingead cae! A woman, who had brought all her worldly goods, including bricks, judging by her suitcases. That miserable female! He should have known! After all, he had been driving tourists from all over the world, mostly women, to see the sights of his native country. Women came in droves, looking for the famous heroes from the novels, and since the highland saga 'Outlander' had been filmed, even more came. Which was good, in a way, since in brought more income. On the other hand, those tourists had ridiculous mental images of the typical Scot. They ranged from muscular, and always wearing a kilt, to heroes saving female tourists, naked from the waist up. Several whisky brands had been taking advantage of those images, for their advertising, for some time.

Alasdair himself couldn't bear to hear the name 'Jamie' any longer. Not for the first time, he asked himself why his tenant hadn't just joined one of those series-backdrop round trips, instead of getting on his nerves. She was obviously no better, looking for the ostensible embodiment of Scotsmen. At least, judging by her looks at him. A living Barbie doll. Most of Louise Schulzinger reminded of exactly that, in any case. Annoyed, he gripped the old bike. Damn, his shin would probably show wonderful shades of blue next day.

Actually, he hadn't really cared about the rusty old bike. If Alasdair was honest with himself, the sight of her had caught him cold, even shocked him. The platinum blonde hair of the day before was gone, replaced by a light brown mop of hair, with a terrible hairdo. A weird mix of a poor man's Tina Turner, and a highland cow. Louise Schulzinger didn't look a bit like his ex-wife, but at first glance he had thought he saw Felicitas riding his old bike. Yes, dammit. It had given what was left of his heart a nasty little jab, seeing the foreign woman that way. Now, to cap it all, she had vanished into his own café.

Marge would kill him, when she heard how he had treated the German woman. What in the world was it about this woman, to make him lose his composure so? She wasn't his type at all! Morosely, Alasdair wheeled the bike across the street, and leaned it on the wall of the café. He had been on his feet since the early morning hours. First, several hours in the bakery, then on one of the far pastures, checking on the sheep. He had repaired fences, and several gates.

He had just come to have lunch, and to ask Grace how things had gone at school. Lately, the girl had had some problems with a teacher. He sometimes asked himself, anxiously, whether he had brought her up right.

 It wasn't easy, being both father and mother. He definitely lacked a feminine side, he knew it himself. He simply wasn't a man of many words, or for female stuff. How many times had his ex-wife complained of his lack of romanticism? Alasdair had always been more of a rough-hewn man. Since Grace had been going to school, she had been even more withdrawn than before. He knew she didn't tell him everything that was wrong. She was constantly coming home with new bruises. He felt totally helpless. The school for the deaf in Inverness was expensive. But it was, barring an operation, the only chance for Grace. He had refused to let Grace be operated on, even though he knew that such an operation was routine nowadays, and would even be paid for by the National Health.

Grace would have a real chance of being able to hear. But she could also die. An operation wasn't a walk in the park. The risk had simply seemed too high. He would probably soon be forced to sell his café, including the bakery. Right after he sold the only other thing he really valued. His Harley Davidson 74 Knucklehead, his baby. To which he was attached, not only because it was a rare and valuable collector's item, but because the kilt belt of his ancestor on his father's side, an heirloom of the family, had been worked around the tank, as well as a brooch fitted on the filler cap.

The sentimental value of the machine was beyond price. Unfortunately, he had responsibilities. Both for his girl and for his parents, who were getting on in years. If Grace were to have a future, he had no other choice.

If only he knew what he was doing wrong. Why wouldn't his girl tell him what was weighing on her? He didn't want to bother Marge with it. She was already doing far too much. Her advice was priceless, but didn't always help him. And his father was of no help with such concerns.

Brooding, he entered the shop. Marge was serving Stuart at the moment, and nodded to him. As soon as Stuart left, she would bring him his lunch, as always at this hour. Purposefully, he went over to the café, then halted in the door, dumbfounded. He couldn't believe his eyes, so strange was the scene. Louise Schulzinger with his daughter Grace, their heads together, concentrating on something on the table.

"Just look at that, Al", Marge whispered to him conspiratorially, having come to his side.

He couldn't take his eyes off them. The foreigner was taking the pencil from Grace's hand, to show her something. Not enough that Grace was letting herself be touched, she seemed to be happy about it. Suddenly, the girl clapped her hands excitedly.

"What the...?", he uttered, dumbfounded.

"Lou was nice enough to help me out. You know I can't draw, aye. Gracy was supposed to draw an elephant. A difficult homework assignment."

"Lou?"

"Louise, the German. A wonderful lady. I was beginning to think Gracy would never calm down, she was so frantic. Then she came. Now the both of them have been drawing for quite some time. You're late today. How long have you been standing in front of the shop, laddie?"

"Too long, it seems. Don't you think the A' gearmailteach has other things to do than babysit your granddaughter, Marge?", he muttered gruffly, starting toward the table. Actually, he felt panic rise in him, seeing them together like that. Blind panic. This miserable woman was waking feelings in him that he didn't want. Feelings he damned well couldn't afford. He was getting angry.

And yet, there was no rational reason to feel that way. Alasdair felt as if he were champing with rage like a mad bull. Controlling himself with difficulty, he planted himself by the table. The stranger winced nervously. Her charming smile froze to an artificial grimace. Grace, though, beamed at him happily, unconcerned.

"Look, Pa, what Lou showed me. Mrs. Dunnen is sure to give me at least a B+ for that. Lou even said she'd go to school with me sometime. Isn't that grand of her, Pa?", his daughter explained in sign language with flying fingers, until Alasdair felt compelled to hold her hands still.

Uncomprehending, Grace's eyes looked at him like big, gleaming blue marbles. It hurt him terribly, to have to hurt his girl. On the other hand, he couldn't let a stranger, a tourist who would only be in Scotland for a short time, turn their lives upside down.

Daingead! Neither Grace's heart, nor his own, could be given to a woman like this, who was probably only knowledgeable about fashion and jewelry. No feelings – no heartache.

"Thank you for your help, Mistress Schulzinger", he managed, still barely under control. Paying no attention to Grace's signs, he repacked her pencils in their case.

"You're..."the German answered, cleared her throat ".. you're welcome, Mr. Munro", she stuttered. She got up so suddenly, that her chair fell over with a loud bang.

"The bicycle is outside", he answered quietly.

Louise Schulzinger's face hardened. Her eyes flashed. Taking no further notice of him, she tousled Grace's hair fondly.

"Thank you", she mumbled, taking the wrapped bread,

that Marge proffered her with an apologetic shrug, from her hands. Even the dog trotted at his mistress' heels with a resigned look.

The Devil take take that woman, Al thought angrily.

A moment later, Marge placed the dish with his lunch in front of him with a loud crash, making her feelings quite clear.

"What is it, Mother?", Alasdair growled.

"Not all women in the world are like your ex-wife, Al. What did the poor woman do to you, that made you act so rudely?"

"I didn't…"

"You certainly did! I didn't raise you like that! Your father would be horrified at your bad manners, aye!", his mother cut him off.

Lou all but fled from the chilly atmosphere in the café. All coziness had disappeared the moment Alasdair Munro had entered the café. With trembling hands, she grabbed the decrepit bike, which leaned against the wall, awaiting her. What a terrifying man that Scot was. He didn't even look unhandsome, despite the scar on one cheek, his unshaven chin, and the dirty work clothes. It would be good enough for the villain in a novel. He definitely had a virile, daredevil air about him. Maybe it was because he was the total opposite of Alexander.

Alexander was a charmer, a ladies man. This Scotsman probably appealed to her so much, because he was nothing of the sort. Alasdair Munro was a total macho, she didn't doubt that for a minute. He had an air of aloofness, and also of some danger. The fellow was so tall, he would tower above her, even with high heels. On the other hand, he also had something vulnerable about him.

A man with a painful past?
As I am a woman with a broken heart?

Unfortunately, Alasdair Munro also seemed to be a total asshole. With swift strides, Lou headed for the tiny grocery, to make some purchases. She tied Doc outside the shop, next to the bicycle, then entered the gloomy interior. It consisted of a single room, dominated by shelves that reached to the ceiling. The old linoleum flooring squeaked with every step. Nonetheless, everything was provided to make a consumer's heart glad. There were no shopping carts. Instead, a selection of baskets in different sizes was provided. Lou took one.

Leisurely, she strolled through the corridors between the shelves, taking in the hodgepodge of wares. Soon the basket was filled to the brim with cookies, chocolate, fudge, tea, coffee, beer, and another bottle of whisky, which she hadn't been able to resist.

Scotland is going to turn you into a drunkard, Lou, her thoughts prophesied gloomily. Under her breath, she answered herself: "Much rather, your screwed-up family!"

At the checkout, finally, she treated herself to an ice cream. Heavily burdened, she left the store, and stowed two of her shopping bags in the basket on her luggage rack. The other two she hung from her handlebars, one on each side. Slowly, she strolled back towards her vacation home, with Doc at her side.

She pointedly ignored Alasdair Munro, who watched her from the seat of an old tractor. It went very slowly. Mostly, that was because it was quite difficult to lick at an ice cream, while balancing a heavily laden bicycle with one hand. More than once, Lou was tempted to just throw the ice cream away.

Finally, she stopped near a large boulder, next to the picturesque lake. She parked her vehicle, and now ate her ice cream with relish, while sitting on a stone and dangling her legs. The sun turned the water a wonderful shining blue. It made her think of Grace's eyes. Hard to believe the girl was really Alasdair Munro's daughter. Alas, she looked so much like her father, he could never have denied her. A loud sigh escaped her lips. Suddenly, a yearning overcame her. Yearning for her children. Frantically, Lou pulled her smartphone from her pants pocket. Once again, there were more than twenty messages in her mailbox. For seconds, her finger lingered over the delete button.

This time, she didn't have the heart to do it, naïve wife and loving mother that she was. As expected, more than half of the messages were from Alexander. He begged her to come back, as everything was sinking into chaos without her, only to call her a disloyal, insensitive slut with the next breath. The other messages were from her sons, Philip and Richard, who outdid each other in their reproaches. Only the last message gave her hope. It was from Tobi, who set her straight, by declaring that she shouldn't even think of returning before the two full months! According to him, her family was totally spoiled, wallowing in self-pity. Otherwise, though, everything was the same as always.

Had she met her Scottish hero yet? He had also talked to her gallerist. Everything was set to have the proceeds of the paintings she had sold transferred to her secret postal account. Her last vernissage had been a surprising success. Almost all of her paintings had found a buyer. His "So. you won't have to starve in Scotland!" let her forget the tears that had already been starting.

Relief spread through her. Alexander didn't know that she had been back in business for years now, with great success. She was painting again, as well as taking the occasional small advertising commission. A significant amount had already accrued to her account. She needn't fear a future without a husband, at least. Suddenly, she no longer felt any yearning for her home, or for Germany.

The Water of Life

This day had cost Alasdair all his strength. It had taken ages to get Grace to go to bed. The girl had thrown a fit, could hardly be calmed down. One of her most painful issues had been her wish for a mother. Outwardly, he had always managed to convey confident composure on this subject, though inwardly was something else again. Felicitas was like a festering wound that wouldn't heal. It wasn't until he had pinned two of the foreigner's pictures above Grace's bed, that she had finally calmed down. It had still taken quite a while for her to get to sleep.

Be damned to that German female!
The animal pictures Grace had drawn with the A' gearmailteach were displayed like a reproach, above the pink four-poster bed he had built for her. For hours, he had argued with his daughter, explaining why he would not accept a strange woman into her life. And, why he wouldn't let an eight-year-old push him into a date.
At first he had tried to deal with Grace's plea matter-of-factly, and, for him, very calmly. Towards the end, however, he had become somewhat irritated, lost control. Which was partly the result of even Marge's conspiring against him.
"It's not as if you have to go to bed with Lou", had been her totally misplaced comment. As if he were so desperate, he needed to get into bed with a vagabond female, who looked at him as if he were the devil's spawn.
Holy Michael, he didn't even find Louise Schulzinger attractive. That hadn't changed in the slightest with her changed appearance.
He had ridden around on his Harley for an hour, afterwards going to the pub on foot. Morosely, his eyes roved over the sparsely frequented public room. In a single draught, he

emptied his whole beer at once, wiping the foam on the sleeve of his checked lumberjack shirt. Both Gordon and Evan kept trying to convince him to join in their game of darts. Glumly, he refused, which led the men to jeer him.

"You afraid, Al?", Stuart jeered, while the rest laughed loudly. Suddenly, the atmosphere changed. The men whistled and puffed out their chests. Rough Gaelic jokes flew. Alasdair would have bet his ass that a woman had just entered the pub. His stomach sank. The impulse to turn and see which woman was almost irresistible. After all, there weren't many women in Kildermorie who could make the lads act so. Next moment, however, that was no longer necessary. He could hear Louise Schulzinger ask about the special of the day. She managed to make herself instantly unpopular, by daring to ask whether the shellfish in the 'fish and chips' were fresh.

Alasdair grinned into his beer. He didn't have to look at the bar to see Duncan Menzies' angry red face. He had seen it often enough to imagine it. Louise Schulzinger seemed to be content with Duncan's answer. At least, he heard her order the special, the house beer and a whisky. From the corner of his eye, he could see her sitting directly at the bar, the dog sprawled at her feet.

Unasked, Gordon joined him on his bench. "Do you mind if we show the lass some Scottish hospitality, Al?", he started, giving him a friendly nudge on the shoulder.

"Should I?", he answered, laconically.

"I just thought, since she's your tenant... I wouldn't throw that one out of bed, I'll tell you", Gordon remarked with a lewd grin, his eyes covetuously on the tourist, scanning her von head to toe.

He couldn't really blame the men. Strange women hardly ever made their way to Kildermorie at this time of year, though their village wasn't very far from Inverness. But there simply wasn't anything to see here but nature. The next moment, Gordon got up, only to stand very close to Louise, who had obviously finished eating.

From the corner of his eye, he could see her taking a look at Gordon's T-shirt and kilt. With satisfaction, he saw Louise put his mate in his place, by pointedly putting some distance between them. Well now, Gordon's T-shirt didn't seem to work on her. It said *I'm no Fraser, but if your hands are warm enough, they can reach under my kilt anyway!* A T-shirt he himself would never have worn, since the female tourists were hard enough to keep off without it, when he was wearing a kilt.

"Smart girl", he murmured into his next beer. His friends insisted on buying the German a new beer, and another whisky. Finally, they all together managed to persuade the clueless A' gearmailteach to play a game of darts with them. Alasdair could see she was feeling ill at ease, in the midst of so many men and the massive dose of testosterone they were exuding. Not to mention that the alcohol was having an effect. Louise Schulzinger was giggling a bit too much, and obviously having trouble not swaying. She was standing with her back to him, and still hadn't seen him. He had to admit, she looked very nice this evening, with her flowered dress that modestly covered her knees. A faded jeans jacket completed her wardrobe.

Granted, the sturdy Doc Marten boots on her feet wouldn't have been his first choice to go with that dress, not to mention that he would never have thought she would wear such in the first place, but, strangely, they suited her. She had tamed her mutilated hair with a broad red ribbon that she wore like a hairband. Alasdair mentally changed his comparison with a Barbie doll. He caught himself looking at her scabbed knee. Annoyed with himself, he rubbed his tired eyes. Evan, who barely reached to Louise Schulzinger's breast, patiently showed her how to throw the darts. Finally, the woman tried it herself, but promptly sank her dart in Stuart's beer.

The men howled with laughter. The tallest of the men then had to search for her second dart, on top of the dart machine. It looked like becoming an hilarious evening. After a further hour, the German woman's darts were at least hitting the board. However, she was now half-drunk, as were the men, whose flirts were getting bolder. Gordon's hands were feeling up Louise's backside a bit too often to suit Alasdair. She was too drunk to put Gordon in his place, however.

Not so good, lass. Not so good!

Doc had long ago taken cover under Alasdair's table, lying across his feet. Again and again, the dog's loyal eyes looked at him.

"She's not my problem, boy", he explained to the dog, while belching audibly. The dog's gaze seemed to say: "Yes, she is. We're your tenants. Please do something, friend!"

Before he realized what he was doing, he had intervened determinedly. "I think Mistress Schulzinger has had enough for today, laddies!", he said loudly and firmly, without singling out any of them, and got up. Resolutely, he freed the swaying Lou from Gordon's embrace.

"You want the girl for yourself, after all, Al? Not a chance. Don't spoil my fun..", Gordon growled, with fist raised.

"Let it be, Gordon. You're drunk. I'm still mostly sober!", Alasdair warned, and held Lou easily, slinging an arm around her slim waist.

"Isn't your bonnie lass!", Gordon protested.

"Aye. But not yours either, Gordon!" Alasdair noted unemotionally. The dog, who seemed unsettled by the argument, came between the two men, growling dangerously.

"….have soooo beautiful eyes, Al", the German slurred, giggling, and buried her face in the crook of his neck, while she stumbled along next to him, with awkward steps. The dim light of the streetlight showed him the swell of her breasts. It was getting harder and harder for him to dislike the woman in his arms.

A litany of Gaelic curses was on his tongue. With an effort, he tried to keep a clear head, and concentrated on bringing Louise Schulzinger back to her bed, without giving in to the huge temptation of landing there himself. "God in Heaven, why do You tempt me so?", he prayed testily. Just in time, he avoided Lou's lips, that were nearing his amorously.

"You 're not a sourpuss after all… don't you like me just a liiiiiittle bit?", she purred. He broke out in a cold sweat, the hairs on his neck stood up. Daingead.

He had to get rid of her, as quickly as possible. His pants were already getting uncomfortably tight. *Damned hussy!*

With no further ado, he threw Louise Schulzinger over his muscular shoulder like a sack of grain. He hurried up the path to the cottage, as fast as his feet would carry him. The German giggled in his ear the whole way, babbling nonsense. This female was driving him crazy! He knew nothing about her, only that she came from Germany and, also, she wore a conspicuous wedding ring on her finger.

A wedding ring on the finger is a reason, not an obstacle! That was Evan's mantra. He himself didn't believe in that saying. Felicitas had been enough to teach him that. He would never sink to her level! Not to mention that Louise seemed to be fleeing from something. No. No, he could not and would not start a relationship with a woman, who would be leaving after two months. On the other hand, maybe he shouldn't be so choosy. Didn't 'married' also mean, there would be no commitment?

He was a man. He had absolutely nothing against sex without commitment. On the other hand, this woman seemed to be a magnet for trouble. Cac. Hadn't he just provoked trouble with his pals? He was sure there would be an aftermath, where he would have to stand a lot of rounds to pacify the men, lest there be a punch-up after all.

This time, he didn't take his shoes off to enter his former house, dirty or not. He steadfastly ignored the creaking floorboards. No light was necessary to find the way to the bedroom. This was his house, just as it had been the house of his parents, grandparents, and their parents before them.

Carefully, he carried Louise Schulzinger, who had buried her slender fingers in his hair, up the narrow stairs, while her lips nibbled at his neck. Once there, he gently put her down on the bed. With a large step back, he was out of reach of her hands. The large, brown doe eyes watched him adoringly. Hastily, he freed her feet from the rough shoes, then lifted the covers and pushed her under them. Again, her slender fingers reached demandingly for him.

O mo chreach!, he groaned silently. Why did he suddenly feel like a moth, looking for a flame to burn in? Why did this woman suddenly attract him so magically?

"You would regret it tomorrow, m' eudail!", he whispered huskily, then clattered down the stairs, as if the devil were after him. Out of breath, he stopped at the end of the gravel path leading to the house, and looked back. The woman wouldn't do anything stupid, would she? What if she had to vomit? He had read too often of cases, where drunks had suffocated on their own vomit.

"Get a hold of yourself, man!", he admonished himself. After all , the German was no teenager. Besides, he was neither her husband nor her babysitter! Unsettled, and uncertain, he ran his hands through his hair, looked back yet again, then pushed his hands deeply into his pockets. With long strides he walked back to Kildermorie.

The next morning showed, mercilessly, what Lou had done to herself last night. Her head ached, and felt as if a jackhammer was hard at work inside it. Her limbs felt twisted, and hurt.

"You're no longer twenty, sweetheart!" she murmured angrily, while asking herself: How in the world did I sleep?

To her chagrin, she could remember everything, every little detail of her binge last night was etched into her memory. Unfortunately, she also remembered Alasdair Munro's strong arms only too well.

Goddammit! Regrettably, Lou also now remembered how she had more or less thrown herself at him.

Dear God, never again whisky!, she swore to herself. Luckily, the fellow had resisted her advances. Alasdair Munro wasn't gay, was he?

"Nonsense!", she murmured. The man had a daughter, after all. But why, then, hadn't he taken unscrupulous advantage of her situation? The strange fellow didn't seem like a typical gentleman to her, though, admittedly, he had saved her from the other men in the pub. Phew, thinking of the chubby guy with the funny T-shirt made her want to throw up. Now she even had to be grateful to that morose, screwy Scotsman, that he hadn't let her do anything, in her drunkenness, which she'd regret. Oh, very well done, Lou! He had carried her in his arms to the cottage and put her to bed, without taking advantage of her.

Anyway, she was a married woman, forty years old, the mother of two more-or-less grown sons. As much as she tried – and even if ten Jamies had come knocking on her door – she was no femme fatale. Even if she had to admit that she had been unhappy for years.

"Oh, Doc. Your mistress may be having a midlife crisis, after all…", she murmured, rubbing her monster dog's ears, while he answered with queer noises of his own. She could always count on her dog, at least. Sometimes, it really seemed as if he was talking to her. Unfortunately, she couldn't understand him.

She felt terrible.

I won't cry. I'll pull myself together, right now!, she encouraged herself silently. It was already after nine o'clock. Surely, coffee and breakfast would restore her to a normal state. After splashing handfuls of icy water in her face, ignoring the dark circles under her eyes, she started out for the kitchen. With a long stride, she avoided the step where she had hurt herself before.

"Ha! What do I have extra long legs for?", she said triumphantly, but took a closer look at the step anyway, planning to come back to it with hammer and nails, if she could find any. Thanks to the extra-long matches she had bought, the stove-top was quickly fired up, without burning her fingers repeatedly this time.

Soon, she was sitting on the already sunny terrace, with the largest cup she could find full of coffee, along with bannock bread and Marge's strawberry jam. It promised to be a beautiful day. At least, there wasn't a cloud in the sky. It was already unseasonably warm, for an autumn day in the Highlands. Lou decided to go to the lake, and bring glorious nature to canvas with pastel sticks. A loud knocking on the door, followed by: "Hello? Lou, are you home?" pulled her from her thoughts, however. Doc began barking joyfully.

That was unmistakably Marge Munro's voice. Heavens, surely Alasdair Munro hadn't tattled about her binge?

"Jesus. I'm not even presentable yet", Lou grumbled, but hurried to the door anyway, letting Marge enter, red-cheeked and grinning broadly, with a young girl with violet hair in tow.

"Good morning, Marge", Lou greeted her, trying hard to seem at ease. Was that a knowing look in Marge's eyes?

I'm sure I'm wrong. She knows nothing. Sons never tell their mothers everything, do they? Unless the fellow is only so taciturn with me?, Lou thought to herself, and tried to interpret the look on Marge's face.

Marge pushed forward the strange girl.

"This is Ellie. She's learning to be a coiffeuse in Inverness. Isn't that wonderful, Lou?", Marge cried cheerfully, gesticulating wildly. She must have seen Lou's incomprehension, because she followed with a conspiratorial "For your hair, lass!", with an amused wink, marching purposefully into Lou's dining room and pulling out a chair.

Dumbfounded, Lou, who had followed her, was placed in that same chair. She gazed at the young girl suspiciously, and swallowed nervously. "You're quite sure, Mrs. Munro?"

"Lass, it's Marge, remember? Anyway, Grandma Evens' hair always looks immaculate, Lou!", she gushed. Lou asked herself: "And just how old is Grandma Evens? A hundred?" On the other hand, she had to admit her self-barbered mop of hair verged on a catastrophe. It could hardly get worse.

Meanwhile, in Germany

"Mr. Schulzinger, I assure you, I'll help where I can. I was secretary to your esteemed father, before you, as you know. I've always taken pride in doing my duty. But this is going too far. Neither the flowers in your house and garden, nor your family's laundry, are any of my concern. I'm no housekeeper, I'm a secretary!", Mrs. Bott explained to Alexander, gesticulating, while leaving through the front door at a good clip.

It closed with an ominous crash. Alexander ran his hands through his graying hair exhaustedly. Two days without Louise, and the whole house was upside down. Nothing at all seemed to work anymore.

The bathroom was full of sweaty, stinking sportswear. Shirts waited to be taken to the cleaners. In the garden, the flowers were wilting in the unseasonal autumn heat wave. Unfortunately, the gardener was on vacation. And Louise, his wife Louise, who usually took care of all that stuff, wasn't here. He had been just as unable to charm Rosalita into taking care of it, as with Mrs. Bott.

"Pa, would you please take my suit along to the cleaners. You could bring the shirts with you on the way back", Richard requested, without batting an eye. He bit into an apple with relish, strolling past.

"Just a moment, son", Alexander held him back by his sleeve. "You can very well do that yourself, my boy. I'm not your servant!"

"But Mom isn't here, and I need the suit tomorrow, because I've been invited to this totally hip vernissage, Pa", his firstborn griped, with an accusing look.

"Save your calf eyes. If you need your suit, well, you know where the cleaner's is. As I remember, you even have a car to get there, my dear Richard. I have work to do!"

Alexander turned on his heel, and rushed up the stairs to his office. At least there, he had peace and quiet. The detective he had sent after his wife hadn't been able to report success. Louise's trail ended at a car rental at Edinburgh airport. Since his fair wife used neither her credit cards nor her smartphone, the detective had no way of finding out just where in Scotland she was.

"Dammit!!, he moaned, sinking into his swivel chair. "Where the hell are you, Louise?", he exclaimed, frustrated. Why had she done this to him? Alexander hadn't slept a wink the last two nights. All right, he was badly hurt, but even if he didn't really think her in danger, that didn't mean he didn't care what happened to the mother of his children.

Did he really see her like that? Just as the mother of his children? But if that were so, why did the thought of her in another's arms torture him so? Was there still any love for her in him at all?

Disappointed with himself, he buried himself in his work. That was what he did best, after all. Work until he dropped.

Opposites attract

Scotland

She must have been crazy, to do this to herself. Why, then, did it feel so good, so right? Lou's once long, blonde hair had made way for a short, light brown pageboy cut. Strangely, she had never felt so much like herself, looking at herself in the mirror.

What she saw there was indisputably she. A thin, admittedly very pale, image of her former self. Tentatively, she smiled at herself. Marge had already left again, with Ellie behind her.

After another huge cup of black coffee, Lou felt as if she could move mountains. Clad in faded, holed blue jeans and her favorite flannel shirt, armed with sketch pad and pencils, she swung onto the bicycle.

She circled a fair way around the lake, accompanied by Doc's joyful barking. The somewhat gusty wind blew in her face. She was unconcerned about rain, though the sky was covered with gray clouds. After all, there was no such thing as bad weather, only unsuitable clothing. She stopped at a pasture full of sheep, leaning the bike against the low wall, which kept the bleating balls of wool from scattering. Nimbly, she climbed over the wall.

Doc followed her, taking no notice of the sheep. The dog simply ignored the bleating animals, and trotted slowly along with Lou, who hummed cheerfully to herself. She imagined how Alexander would have scolded: *Louise, darling. Come out of there this minute. Think of all the sheep dung on your shoes. What if one of those stinking fleabags bites you? Who knows what sicknesses they cause...* Heavens.

He would be certain to throw a fit.

She could almost see him before her, walking up and down along the stone wall circling the pasture. He would probably loosen his tie in annoyance to get enough air. He wore a tie with almost any shirt.

At the lakeside, she found a large boulder. Carefully, she put down the little knapsack, in which she had brought her drawing utensils. Her surroundings were more than picturesque. The riot of colors made her laugh ecstatically. She could imagine fairies dancing in circles, or a kelpie breaking the surface of the lake, which alternated between green and turquoise. Her pastel pencil flew over the pages of her drawing pad, while she alternated between gnawing on her lip and on the pencil in concentration, unwilling to miss a single detail.

Since Doc had never been a hunter, she hadn't noticed him roaming around. She only raised her head when he made his way back noisily through the bushes. Irritated, she watched her four-legged companion approach. "Where have you been, Doc?", she rebuked him. He uttered a piteous whine, which made Lou put down her pad and pencils immediately.

"What's wrong, big fellow?"

The dog came closer. Carefully, Lou felt along his legs and body, looking for a wound. "Are you hurt, somehow? Did a bee, or a wasp, sting you, Doc? Not again?"

Anxiously, she inspected the whining dog's paws, while he tried to squirm out of her hands. He barked at her demandingly.

"Damn. Stay here, Doc. Or talk to me", she hissed, annoyed. She had almost fallen from the boulder on which she perched. Doc bit her sleeve, pulled on it demandingly.

"I guess that means I should come with you, doesn't it?"

Doc answered with a low yelp. Lou put away her drawing stuff in the backpack, and made sure the zipper was closed on her art work, so it wouldn't be damaged, or even eaten. You never knew. On all fours, she clambered down from her perch to follow Doc, who was already running across the pasture.

"Wait for me, you crazy animal! I'm no longer twenty, after all!", she shouted after him.

At least, he waited until she had crossed half the pasture, before running on. Totally fixated on her dog, Lou missed seeing a tree root, and fell sprawling, making the close acquaintance of a saturated part of the pasture. With sheep dung on her trousers, and dirt on her face, she fought back to her feet.

"Bad dog!", she growled. "You'd better have a good reason for the way you're acting, Doc!" Furiously, she stamped on after him. At a decrepit rail fence, which sported a considerable gap, Doc stopped, whining miserably. Gasping for air, Lou stopped beside him. The dog trotted back and forth excitedly. The fence consisted of thin wire, that was connected to wooden palings, of diverse wood and sizes. It seemed to be meant to keep the sheep from falling into a shallow ravine. It wasn't very deep, but the slope was so steep, the animals wouldn't be able to get back to the herd, once down there. Unfortunately, a small lamb was bleating miserably, in that exact place.

Lou stroked Doc's big head calmingly. "Well done, big boy", she praised him. Behind her, from the pasture, a loud "Bahh Bahh" answered the lamb.

"Aha. I guess that will be the anxious mother", Lou murmured. She thought intently. The embankment was, at most, as deep as she was tall. If she climbed down, she should be able to lift the lamb over her head easily, shouldn't she? That should work. A lamb of that age couldn't be all that heavy yet. She herself could find enough handholds on roots to climb back up.

"What do you think, Doc?", she turned to the sheep saviour, who answered her with a loyal look, while hesitantly wagging his tail.

"Good. Let's do it!", she declared determinedly. She was already dirty, anyway. After ordering Doc to stay where he was, she sat on the edge of the embankment, then jumped down boldly.

Unfortunately, it proved to be quite difficult to catch the nimble little lamb. Whenever she got near enough, the little devil broke away. When she had finally caught the squirming animal, she was full of scratches, and soaked with sweat. She also looked as if she had been mud wrestling.

"Goddammit. Since when have lambs been so damned heavy?", Lou groaned. With an effort, she heaved the squirming animal above her head. Hardly had she placed it back on the grass with her last strength, when she felt as if a knife had been rammed in her back. Her legs gave way. Unable to catch herself, she keeled over backwards like a toppled tree. "This can't be!", she moaned, unable to move. From the corner of her eye, she could see Doc, looking down at her skeptically, tail between his legs. She heard a piercing whine.

"It's all right, big boy. Mistress just has a back pain", Lou tried to calm the dog, as well as herself. Her thoughts spun. To make everything perfect, the clouds seemed to have gotten darker, as well.

"Oh great! Why not a nice rain shower as well, Saint Peter? Is that your reward for my good deed?", she grumbled loudly.

The seat of her pants, like every part of her that touched the earth, was soaked, and ice cold. It could take quite a while to recover from a back pain, even when dry and warm. Here, it would probably take at least twice as long. It was no good. No matter how embarrassing her situation was, she needed help. And as quickly as possible.

"Doc? Big boy? Go and get help!", she ordered her dog, hoping he could find someone quickly.

The sky was getting darker quickly. Alasdair could smell the rain coming. He almost fell over his old bicycle, leaning, abandoned, on the wall of the sheep pasture. That was all he needed. He was already behind with his day's work, if he met that cursed German woman again now, he'd never finish before it rained. Resolutely, he turned around, deciding to repair the fence on the upper pasture first.

But he hadn't gone far, before a large, gray bundle of fur shot at him, barking madly, and almost bowled him over. That dratted woman! How could she be so irresponsible, and let a dog roam freely on a sheep pasture? *His* sheep pasture! Luckily, his two collies, Izzy and Sugar, weren't here. They'd have ripped the stranger dog to pieces. Or worse, if those had been Hughie Lewis's sheep, he wouldn't have hesitated an instant, raised his shotgun and killed the dog. Daingead Cac! The dog, with the strange name Doc, acted frantic. Pushed at him demandingly, again and again.

"It's all right, boy. Why are you so excited, Doc?", he tried to calm the animal. In sudden inspiration, he looked around for the German woman. Where in the world had she got to?

"All right, boy. Then show me, where your damned mistress is. Aye!", he told the dog, who immediately started off, purposefully. Doc made for the back part of the pasture, the part where Alasdair had been meaning to repair the fence today.

"A Dhia. She won't have fallen in, will she?", he murmured anxiously, speeding up. The dog really did stop at the large hole in the fence, and whined miserably. Carefully, Alasdair stepped closer. He immediately spotted Louise

Schulzinger, lying at the foot of the embankment, sprawled on her back, amidst muck and leaves. Her eyes were shut. His rage immediately became mixed with concern.

"Mistress Schulzinger. Lou, what the devil are you doing there?", he called down. The German opened her eyes. For just a moment, he seemed to see dismay in her face.

"What does it look like? I'm getting some sun. Get out of my light, Munro", she snapped back. Alasdair snorted angrily, and gritted his teeth.

That woman has a screw loose, somewhere! Without comment, he turned around and left her field of view.

"Munro? Mr. MUNRO?", her fearful cries came to his ears. For a moment, he let Louise Schulzinger wait. Her cries sounded sweet in his ears. Ultimately, though, he felt somewhat responsible for the woman. He stepped closer to the embankment again, so she could see him.

"Aye, Mistress Schulzinger, I'm listening. Let's start again. What are you doing down there?", he asked, with all the patience he could muster.

"I saved your stupid lamb. It had obviously fallen through the hole in your fence. So, I had to jump down to lift the poor animal…"

"That wasn't necessary!", he interrupted the flow of her words, roughly.

"What do you mean, not necessary? If you had repaired your stupid fence, the poor thing wouldn't have fallen in the first place…"

"You're on my land, Mistress, with an unleashed dog. How do I know you didn't wreck my fence yourself, with your escapades?", he upped the ante, though of course he had known of the damaged fence, and was silently annoyed with himself, for not having fixed it long before. The woman didn't have to know that, though!

"You know what, Munro? You can kiss my ass! I'd rather lie here till I freeze, before I'll accept help from someone like you. You..you.. idiot!"

"As you like, Òinsich. Though it will rain soon, lass. Probably quite a bit. Don't say I didn't warn you! I'll just start repairing the fence, here. Should you decide to accept help from an idiot, you just have to ask me nicely!", he answered sardonically.

The dog seemed to follow their words, looking alternately at him and down the embankment at his mistress. Strangely, it seemed to Alisdair he was disappointing the dog, who at least seemed more intelligent than its owner.

Pog mo thon, it's just an animal! And she's a bitchy tourist. Alasdair, however, had his pride.

"Who can understand women…?", he murmured to himself. This A' gearmailteach would see soon enough what her obstinacy brought her. He was in charge here, in any case!

After a while, the heavens opened their sluice gates, just as he had predicted. With great satisfaction, Alasdair heard Louise Schulzinger spitting out water. This stubborn woman would actually rather catch her death than knuckle under. Undecided, he tore at his hair. He was almost tempted to give in himself, when she called for him.

"Mister Munro? Munro, are you still there?", her voice came shrilly to his straining ears. My God. He imagined he could hear the chattering of her teeth, above the patter of the rain.

"Aye, lass?"

"I'm… I'm sorry. Please. Please, would you help me out of here?"

Instead of answering, he slid down to her without further hesitation. Louise Schulzinger's appearance shocked him more than he was ready to admit.

Her clothes were soaked through and streaked with mud. The lips were blue already, as was her recently hurt knee. She had seemed too thin to Alasdair from the beginning. Now, however, she seemed to be skin and bones. *At least you'll hardly weigh anything*, he thought, while his grumble of "Where?" had the German flinching.

Aye, lass. I'd rather be somewhere more comfortable myself! He knew he was avoiding her doe eyes.

"My back....lumbago", escaped through her clenched teeth. His brows rose in comprehension, while his estimation of her age rose.

"Have to carry you. Won't be pleasant", Alasdair explained, as matter-of-factly as possible. Uncaring of the mud, he sank to his knees next to her. Carefully, he felt along her body, pondering how to pick her up with the least pain. She stiffened under his fumbling hands, seemed to be trying to keep a blank face. Alasdair could see her clenching her teeth, while she pressed her lips together. He almost admired her determination to keep from showing any pain.

She stared at him defiantly, not taking her eyes off him for a second. Decisively, his hands pushed through the mud, past the luscious curves of her behind. Knowing it would hurt, he gave her no warning. Instead, he moved as swiftly as possible, acting as if the tourist were a sheep, which he would lift with a practiced hand, and drape around his neck to carry it to be shorn. Of course, he lifted Louise Schulzinger, as carefully as possible, in his arms, since he rather doubted she would find it more comfortable around his neck. The moan, and then the curses she uttered, pierced him to the core.

"Everything all right, lass?", he asked in concern, receiving a hissed "Of course. Never felt better, you clumsy oaf!" in return, which provoked a momentary, unseen grin.

"Good. You're still alive, I see", he answered, laconically, without explaining that she would have to hold up for quite a bit further. Unerringly, he stamped through the mud along the shore. There was no question of climbing the embankment with his burden. He'd have to walk along the shore of the lake for quite a bit, until he could get back to his jeep. The dog followed along stride for stride, though up on the pasture. They finally met back at the jeep. The poor fellow almost burst with joy. Alasdair opened the car door with one hand. He bent in, careful not to hit her head, and swiped off everything lying on the passenger seat.

It wasn't exactly easy to bring the seat to the reclining position, while still carrying his burden. Then, to the accompaniment of her muted sounds of displeasure, he let Louise sink to the seat as gently as possible. By now, he was soaked too, not only from the rain, but also from the sweat that was pouring down his back. He reached for the old blanket on his back seat, and tucked it around her trembling body.

The faded cloth, with the tartan of his clan, complimented her pale face. With difficulty, he closed his eyes, as well as his heart, to the sight. Instead, he let the dog climb in, who gratefully wedged himself into the floor space in front of his mistress. With icy, stiff fingers he started the car, while pushing the button for the seat heaters with the other hand. The jeep roared into motion. Alasdair groped for his cell phone, clamped it into the crook of his neck, next to his ear.

"Doc Carneby? Aye, Doc. It's Al. Can you come to my cottage in fifteen minutes? My tenant, Mistress Schulzinger, has a problem with her back. Yes, I know. No. But she has a bad lumbago. You know as well as I do, that there isn't any other doctor but you anywhere near. Mòran Taing!"

"Thank you!", the German woman next to him whispered, barely audible.

He made no answer. Stared intently at the road.

"Could you stop up there for a moment, please? My… my backpack is still lying there."

Alasdair did so. He found the backpack immediately, put it in the car without a word. He'd take care of the bicycle later. The German woman stared out the window awkwardly. He couldn't think of a single thing to say to start a conversation. Why should he, after all? They were strangers, and this incident wouldn't change that. For his part, he had done everything he could. Doc Carneby would give her one of his special injections, and that would be that. Marge and Grace would be asking themselves, where he was, so late. Besides, he had enough work waiting for him, in the bakery and the café. Playing babysitter to a nuisance definitely wasn't on his program for the evening.

Also, he was pretty tired, actually, totally exhausted. From the corner of his eye, he glanced at the huddled form of the tourist. Why in the world did he suddenly imagine her naked under his tartan? Oh God, what kind of fantasies were these, all of a sudden? Granted, Felicitas had never worn his clan tartan. Not even involuntarily, as the A' gearmailteach did at this moment. How would her naked, pale skin look on this piece of cloth? Finally, the cottage appeared, saving him from his lewd thoughts. She didn't protest, as he picked her up carefully once more, and carried her as gently as possible directly to the bedroom.

Doc Carneby arrived not five minutes later. Alasdair waited near the front door, until the heavily built man had given his tenant an injection.

"I'd only do this for you, Al. Nice derrière that girl has, by the way!", the Doc said, on the way to his van, closing his bag the while.

"Aye, Doc. I know. Just put it on my tab. Oh, and don't

forget the salve I need. Two of the lambs ripped their hooves on broken fencing", he answered curtly, to hide his feelings. God give, that Louise Schulzinger never found out she had been doctored by the local veterinarian!

Teasing is a sign of affection

What in the world had she been thinking? Nothing. That was the only possible answer. That stupid save-the-lamb campaign had ended in a total disaster. Not enough, that that miserable Scotsman, Munro, had ended up saving her, yet again. A total stranger of a doctor had had to free her from her soaked clothes. She had felt more than a little embarrassed, especially with the strange looks the elderly gentleman had been giving her.
Had that really been a doctor of human medicine? She could have sworn that the man, who hadn't even worn the usual white coat, had avoided touching her more than absolutely necessary. And she didn't ever want to think again about that monstrous needle he had injected her with, above her behind.

Dammit! The Highlands are still a bit too medieval for my taste, after all! And no hero from a novel in sight!

This had definitely been one of the worst days of her life. Lou was starving. Even Doc's fur couldn't keep her from shivering with cold. To her chagrin, he also stank terribly of wet dog. If she put her nose near her undershirt, however, she could just get a remaining whiff of aftershave. Again and again, she caught herself searching for that whiff. Trying to preserve it. Goddammit!

In vain, she tried to think about something else than those muscular arms. My goodness, and those broad shoulders… Her thoughts were like a swarm of fish, impossible to catch, even more impossible to stop. The rain pattered on the roof, incessantly. As she was forced to realize, *through* the roof, too. In the outer corner of her bedroom, a single drop of water fell in regular intervals from the innocently whitewashed ceiling. The helpless rage that caused in her now erupted in a loud scream, startling poor Doc so badly that he jumped out of the bed.

"Heavens, I've had enough! God, I just wanted some peace and quiet! And what do I get? A ramshackle cottage. No hero from a novel, instead, a Scotsman I can't get out of my head, whatever I do, and one catastrophe after another! Do I really deserve this, Doc? Dear God, I was never so clumsy before!", Lou ranted at the dog, who watched her with interest, head tilted to the side. At last, he jumped back on the bed. Before she knew it, he had swiped his large tongue fully over her face. Resistance is futile!

"Bad dog! Stop! Don't…. I didn't want drool all over my face!", she defended herself, irritated. Of course, her loyal companion didn't answer her this time, either. Still, as always when she discoursed with her four-footed friend, Lou felt strangely comforted, even calmed.

After turning in place several times, Doc curled up. Immediately, her furry monster began to snore loudly. Since Lou could still hardly move, she had to ignore both the dripping water and the snoring. After a while, in which her thoughts circled around Alasdair Munro, and just how she would kill him, the regular noises lulled her into a refreshing sleep.

Next morning, she felt as if she had been stretched on the rack. Luckily, she could at least fully use her back again. After a huge cup of hot coffee, and a not totally burned egg with toast, Lou went outside with Doc.

The weather today was a mix of sunshine and rain, characteristic of Scotland. Sighing, she pulled her smartphone out of her trouser pocket, looking at the shingles above her bedroom. Somewhere up there, one of those was defective enough to let it rain into the bedroom. There was no help for it but to call her landlord. Sighing deeply once more, she punched his number. For a wonder, she even had a connection for a change. But Lou's run of luck didn't hold. The Scot couldn't be reached. Only his mailbox answered.

"Mister Munro, this is Lou Schulzinger. Not enough that I almost broke my knee, in your dilapidated shack. No. Now it's raining in my bedroom. Oh, and while I'm at it – I'm still searching, without success, for the promised internet connection. Maybe you would be so good as to…."

The shrill beep of the mailbox, ending its recording, interrupted her in the midst of her tirade. This was insufferable! With a huge effort, Lou mastered her rage, barely keeping from throwing her smartphone at the wall. Waterproof, and shockproof, didn't automatically also mean throwproof! A look at the sky told her all she needed to know. Another deluge was coming soon.

"Oh, great. Maybe this time the water will run right down into the living room. What do you think, Doc?", Lou asked sarcastically. Her hand shaded her eyes against the blinding light, while she stared at the roof morosely.

How hard can it be to replace a shingle?, she thought. Determinedly, she marched to the shed, squirming through the wide crack left by the door, into the gloomy interior. She found the ladder immediately. She found a bucket with shingles, by almost falling over it, while transporting the ladder outside. Hammer and nails were a different story, though. Only after looking through what seemed a hundred emptied tin cans, standing in rows in a man-high, tilted rack of shelves on one of the walls, did she find what she sought.

There, between fishing lines, potting rubbers, rolls of wire, and other odds and ends, she found, by feel, some rough, rather long nails and a large hammer, which missed falling on her foot by a hair. After carrying everything outside, she took the hammer and nails, putting them in a rusty bucket, which she had emptied of water.

"At least you're not really a dumb, helpless blonde, Lou", she murmured to herself, self-satisfied. The wooden ladder was rather heavy, not to mention monstrously awkward. Probably caused by moisture and/or bad storage, the ladder was also somewhat warped, which, together with the uneven ground at that point, made it impossible to position it optimally. Lou broke into a sweat. Uneasily, she asked herself if what she was doing would be the right thing for her ailing back.

"What's the big deal about climbing a ladder, or pounding in a nail? I don't have to lift anything heavy, or twist around like a contortionist!", she tried to put a good face on what she was doing. Before stepping on the ladder, she tried to reach Alasdair Munro again. No luck.

"Oh, what the hell. It can't be all that hard!"

Carefully, testing each creaking rung, she climbed the rickety ladder.

Alisdair had had a tiring night. Not enough that Grace had cried herself to sleep again, thanks to some problem at school that she wouldn't tell him about, no matter how much he pleaded with her. No. He had had an argument with Marge, who had heard that he had called the vet to Louise Schulzinger. In a town with only two streets, nothing stayed secret long. His mother had actually accused him of mistreating the foreign lady. And he had only been trying to help. She said he was acting like a jilted suitor, and that he should rather look out for his daughter.

Why in the world did his mother think he was a Don Juan? He, of all people, who usually avoided any contact with women? And, of course, she had started in on the old litany: "Girls of Grace's age need a mother. Aren't you tired of being alone, Al? I can't believe God wants a strapping fellow like yourself to live like a monk. It's been eight years now!"

This accusation had followed the other, almost in the same breath, never mind the contradiction. His own mother! The straw that broke the camel's back had been Conner, though. Conner Munro, his father. Who, with his long gray braid of hair, looked like a cross of pirate and Father Christmas.

"Your mother is right, son. You're supposed to be a grown-up. So act like one!"

Furious, he had locked himself up in the bakehouse. Worked out his rage kneading bread dough, until only leaden emptiness was left inside him. What in the world connected him to this German woman? Why the devil wouldn't she leave his thoughts? The more he tried to avoid her, the more they met.

Tiredly, he rubbed his face with his floury hands, sank, exhausted, on one of the stools scattered in the bakehouse. Since last night, he had felt an uncomfortable pinching in his own back, which kept reminding him of what had befallen.

He had to admit, he had been wrong about Louise Schulzinger. She wasn't bitchy, nor did she throw her wealth around. Though she obviously possessed it. He was no expert on expensive designer fashions, but he knew what they looked like. Her clothing on arrival, and her manners, made him certain she came from a wealthy background.

"Pah. That's something, at least, I learned from you, Felicitas!", he growled gruffly, and wiped away any further thought of his ex-wife. "What does someone like me want with a tourist? Another broken heart? God, Al. Assuming that bonnie lass would fall in love with an ugly guy like you… You'd never be able to hold her here, in this godforsaken place! Don't kid yourself, Alasdair Munro. She'd run for it, just as Felicitas did! You cannot, you will not, do that to Gracie!", he told himself. But somehow a stale taste was left, and a feeling he was lying to himself.

After spending the whole night without sleep, working on overdue work in the bakery, he saw himself, at nine o'clock in the morning, confronted with another problem. The wedding cake of his friend Cormack Fraser and his fiancée, Emily. He had, at first, refused to do his friend this favor. Unfortunately, neither he nor Cormack had the money to order a cake from elsewhere. So, this cake would be Alasdair's wedding present. With an effort, he pushed aside everything else, concentrated on forming innumerable delicate red roses, with their accompanying green leaves of fine green marzipane. He and Felicitas had never had a cake. His ex-wife had shunned his sweet baked goods, as well as bread, or rolls.

"My giant, that ruins a woman's figure! Surely you understand, Ro?", he remembered her honeyed tones. "Ro", or "My giant". Only she had called him that. Strange, that it had taken him so long to see the things about Felicitas that his parents had seen at once.

Damn. He couldn't form the roses properly. It was almost, as if the lopsided flowers were a symbol for how much he hated weddings, and everything to do with them. Furiously, his fist pounded the already finished marzipane leaves. All right, today had only been for practice, but in a week, he'd actually have to bake the cake and, especially, adorn it. God, Cormack would kill him if he botched it.

He didn't hear Louise Schulzinger's message on his mailbox, until late in the forenoon. At first, he thought her furious voice meant that she had found out about the vet. But that wasn't it.

"So it's the roof again..", he mumbled tiredly.

Sighing, he rubbed his eyes, before taking his waxed cloth motorcycle jacket from the hook, resignedly. He suddenly felt uneasy. Since he needed a diversion anyway, he brought his baby, his Harley, out of the garage.

Something made him drive faster than he usually would. Shortly, he arrived at the vacation home of the German lady. The deep drone of his Harley had hardly been silenced, when a piercing cry for help, along with the miserable howling of a dog, reached his ear.

"Oh God. What has that crazy female done now?", he groaned, while putting down his motorcycle helmet and sprinting up the path to the house. He saw her from a distance, hanging from the roof gutter. Louise Schulzinger. She must have tried to replace the defective shingle herself.

"That suicidal female!", he spat, exasperated. He guessed the ladder had fallen. At least, that's what it looked like. She had at least managed to hook her arms into the gutter and hold on. Now, it looked as if she was at the end of her strength. Speed was of the essence.

"What the hell do you think you're doing up there, lass? I doubt the internet connection is any better up there. Not to mention that you're ruining my cottage," he scolded, while already reaching for the ladder, and keeping his eye on the woman.

"You...you... there's nothing left to ruin of your cottage, and besides, you weren't to be found, were you? You miserable Scot!", Louise Schulzinger shot back, while her feet scrabbled, searching desperately for a hold.

"See here, lass. I don't think you're in a very good position to argue with me, just now", he answered coldly. For just a moment, he gazed at the long, svelte legs, which were again clad in short, far too loose dungarees, which allowed interesting insights. His gaze rested on red-and-white checked underpants.

My God. What a view! Alasdair was glad Louise Schulzinger

couldn't see the look on his face, which he was sure was rapturous.

"I'm putting up the ladder again. Feel carefully for the highest rung with your feet", he ordered. After a few seconds, the woman had secure footing again, but made no move to climb down. He was losing patience rapidly.

"What are you waiting for, lass?", he barked gruffly.

"I...ah... have a slight problem here, Munro", she stuttered, meekly. "Could you, maybe... climb up here?" Her question sounded so unsure, that he looked her up and down, alarmed. Had she hurt herself somehow? Without further thought, he moved, not stopping until he was right behind her up at the gutter. Carefully, he placed his feet outside hers on the same rung, and looked over her shoulder. He was very careful not to press against her sweet rump, which wasn't easy, with the two of them on a not very stable, ancient ladder.

"What's the problem, lass?", he murmured, while trying not to inhale her scent too obviously. Damn. She smelled really good. Across her tilted head, and the sweaty short hair that curled slightly near her neck, he looked at her arm. She had actually managed to replace the defective shingle, even fixing it in place with the correct big nails. For that, and her intact fingers, he had to give her credit. Which he would never say aloud, of course! Alasdair had feared she might have bruised one of those delicate fingers with the hammer. She was a woman, after all. But Louise Schulzinger's problem was a different one: she had hammered one of those large carpenter's nails right through her shirt, and hadn't been able to remove it on her own.

"Good work, lass", he laughed, amused. "I hope it wasn't your favorite shirt!"

"I don't think that's funny, Munro", she snapped back.

He could see how she wrinkled her cute little nose in annoyance, on which, as he could now see from up close, myriads of tiny freckles were sprinkled. He hesitated, and received a suspicious look.

Aye, lass. I guess a man can't fool you for very long…

Unfortunately, this didn't seem the right situation for a flirt, both of them standing on ancient wood, which could give way at any moment under their combined weight. It seemed he had better act quickly. Somewhat reluctantly, he ripped the cloth of the shirt away from the nail. Slowly, he began climbing down, while she followed him, keeping some distance. At the foot of the ladder, for her safety, and also because he couldn't help himself any longer, he put a hand on Louise Schulzinger's enchanting backside.

She responded at once with an indignant snort.

"Hands off! I can climb down a ladder by myself, thank you!"

Alasdair cleared his throat, but didn't seem convincing even to himself. Having reached the ground, the woman gave him a forced "Thank you!", and sank strengthless to earth, right where she was. He looked at her under lowered lids. Once convinced that she was only exhausted, he retreated.

"By the way, you can find an internet connection at my café any time, lass. You could try your cell phone, next time, aye!" Whistling, with hands deep in his pockets, he sauntered off. Amused, he noticed there was no comeback from the woman, who he suddenly found quite attractive.

Meanwhile, in Germany

"He won't talk to me about his sister", Alexander struck the tabletop, indignantly.

"Did you ever talk to each other, Alexander?", his wife's best friend asked calmly. It took all his strength not to explode, or scream at the plump woman with the unsightly braids. If he wanted to find out where Louise was from Debbie, he needed tact. Which wasn't his strongest suit.

"Listen, Alexander. I don't know what you expected from this meeting. I don't know where Lou is, and even if I did know, you would be the last person I would tell. And…"

"But Debbie, I…"

"Don't interrupt me! I just hope Lou can find herself. That she can finally begin to live again, which she certainly can't in the golden cage you've put her in, dear Alexander", Debbie accused him.

He pinched his own thigh to remain calm. "Aren't you exaggerating a bit, Debbie? Look. I love my wife. We've been happily married for twenty-two years, after all." *You only got a second-string lawyer, who's ugly as sin!*, he thought, but instead conceded: "Maybe we made some mistakes. All right. Maybe I made more mistakes than Louise. But I want to make that right! Can't you, her best friend, help me out a bit? Come on, Deb!" he pled, using his nicest smile.

"Forget it, Alexander. What you love about Lou is what you made of her. Namely, a bleached-blonde Barbie doll. I'm just happy she didn't have plastic surgery for you, too. You, my dear, are the pits. Men like you are first-class assholes. I just wish Lou had never fallen for your charm", she confronted him.

He would have loved to wipe the insolent grin from her face with his fist. But he wouldn't let himself sink that far. He had never hit a woman, and he wouldn't start now.

"You don't have to help for my sake. Do it for our children. Deb, you're a kindergartner.

You know what children of divorced parents have to endure. Emotional wounds!", he pleaded.

Horrified, he saw the car keys already in Debbie's hand.

"You simply don't understand anything, Alexander. Not a thing! Your children are 17 and 21. They'll weather a divorce better than you will. Better get used to the thought that your ego is going to get a slight bruise!", she said sweetly and cheerfully.

"You can't just leave, Deb", he exclaimed, incredulous.

"For you, Alexander, I'm still 'Mrs. Lauser'. You're not one of my friends, to call me 'Deb'", she answered, and left him sitting there.

Thank God, the news that his wife had run off hadn't reached his friends yet,.

"God dammit. What have you done to me, Louise", he mumbled.

He didn't leave the restaurant till after his third martini.

The detective agency still hadn't been able to find out anything new. Louise's rental car alone was enough to make his heart race with fear. A Jeep Cherokee. A vehicle that was much too large for his wife. He felt sick when he thought that his wife hadn't driven herself in twenty years. Scotland, driving on the left side, huge car, and Louise. His Louise. That combination couldn't end well.

She still hadn't used her credit card. "Where the devil did you get the money for all that?", he murmured musingly. By now, he had even had the few hospitals in Scotland checked. Without result, which was of course good, in a way.

He had spent nights searching through Louise's papers, and found a separate bank account, and the name of her gallerist. His oh-so-loyal, innocent wife had gone behind his back. "You'll pay for that!", he growled, hurt. For reasons he could not understand, she had not only been able to place some of her painfully embarrassing pictures in that gallery, but even, seemingly, to sell them for a good price. Without his knowledge. God alone knew who hung such trash on his wall. Just thinking of half naked bodies, drawn by his wife, before drooling men... No.

This was an unforgivable breach of faith. Alexander had even gone so far as to visit the gallery himself. Appalled, he had left it again, after the gallerist had refused to discuss how to most effectively close down his wife's source of income. It was none of his business, and she couldn't discuss her artists with him, the woman had told him, icily. He was almost certain she was one of those bull dykes. He hadn't been able to find out anything more. What he had already found out, though, was more than enough. His pride was hurt. Hurt more deeply than he was ready to admit to himself. What he didn't know, yet, was whether another man was involved. Lost in thought, he played with his iPhone, at last dialing Louise's number again, though without much hope.

An excursion and other embarrassments

Scotland
What a humiliation. Why did all these ridiculous things happen to her, all of a sudden? She hadn't been so clumsy before coming to Scotland, had she? Why now? And why the devil always when that grumpy Scotsman was nearby?
"Goddamittohell! You almost broke your neck, Lou", she scolded herself, while poking her finger through the rip the nail had left in her shirt. When she closed her eyes, she could still feel Alasdair Munros big, muscular body behind her. For a moment, she had thought she would simply faint, had had to control herself not to lean back against him, his breath in her ear. Luckily, she had managed to avoid that, at least. If she ever fell for someone, it would only be for someone like the hero of that novel, the one she adored. On the other hand, there were no such men. Not even she was naïve enough to actually believe in such heroes. Only, what was she doing here, then?
Cozy, idyllically sited cottage in the midst of the Scottish Highlands. Warm. Including electricity & water. Internet access available. Access to village. For rent.
She could still see the advertisement she had found on the internet with Debbie – and which she had ultimately answered - before her eyes. And where had she landed? In a better shack. Of course, she could mostly do without the World Wide Web. But, to keep in contact with her gallerist, and any customers, she needed access to her E-Mail account.
      She certainly wouldn't use her Master Card. She knew her husband's habits all too well, and was certain he would already have a detective, or maybe one of his police friends, looking for her. She felt a little like in the film with

Julia Roberts: Sleeping with the enemy. Of course, Alex had never used violence. If he had, she would have had a reason to leave him much sooner.

Unfortunately, her situation couldn't really be called romantic. Sighing, she stood, wiping the dirt from the seat of her pants. After a large mug of black coffee, with a sinful piece of chocolate, she decided on a walk along the lake to get her head straight. A light rain had started. With a temperature of at least 24 degrees centigrade, she estimated, it was unpleasantly muggy. "And this is supposed to be autumn", she murmured, kicking at stones. Doc followed her unhurriedly. The big dog ignored the cooling rain as easily as she did. Alasdair Munro's sheep pasture came into sight. She gave it a wide berth, with a strange feeling in her stomach. At least there was nothing to be seen of the owner. Lou felt no need to meet that fellow again so soon. God in heaven, she hadn't the slightest explanation for all the screw-ups she made near that ruffian. On the other hand, she suddenly felt as strongly attracted to the man as if he were a magnet.

"You're married, Lou. Married, and mother of two children. Jesus, Louise, you're too old to be so maudlin!", she scolded herself, with fists balled. Annoyed, she growled loudly, answered only by the bleating of the peacefully grazing sheep. Everything seemed so typically Scottish, as if it were from one of those travel brochures about the wild beauty of the country, which she had fallen in love with as a young girl. Her collection consisted of no less than 46 photobooks and 12 brochures. The lake came into view. Greyblue water lapped in little waves against the boulders that pushed into the water. Suddenly, tears came to her eyes, which she fought against doggedly. How had her life gone so terribly wrong?

She wrapped her arms around herself, and followed Doc

along the stony shore, circling partway around the lake. The small pebbles and rough sand under her sneakers crunched with each step, almost as if she had snow under her feet. They stopped at an old tree that had fallen into the water. Tired, Lou sank to the mossy wood. The play of colors on the water tickled the artist in her awake. In her thoughts, she was already choosing the correct pastel chalk. A welcome distraction for her heart, which felt like a block of ice. Birds circled above her, carolling. Doc bounded joyfully along the lake, chasing an insect.

What's wrong with you?

Inside her was pure chaos. She didn't know whether she wanted to laugh or cry. Why in the world couldn't she simply have a quiet, relaxed vacation? Coming to Scotland, she had fulfilled a long-held yearning. She wanted to finally experience the mysticism of this country for herself. To capture the magic of its colors on her canvas. Lou had come here to find peace and quiet, away from everyone and everything. Hadn't she? But that didn't seem to be working at all. Now that she thought about it, she had been lying to herself. Watching some ducks landing elegantly on the surface of the lake, she talked to herself again: "You ran for it, Louise. You ran as fast as your legs would carry you. From your problems, from your spoiled sons, from your husband. Not to mention your feelings…"

Lou's loud sigh mixed with the ringtone of the cell phone in her pocket. *Nothing else matters*, by Metallica, sounded loudly. Without thinking about what she was doing, Lou picked up.

"Thank God!", she heard the relieved voice of her husband. The reception was so good that she looked nervously over her shoulder, to be sure Alex wasn't standing right behind her.

"Louise, do you have any idea at all how worried I've been?

Honey, where are you? Are you all right?... Louise, are you still there?..."

Of course she was still there, he should be able to hear her breath, if nothing else. What a stupid question. Only, she somehow couldn't get a single word out. How many nights had she dreamed of such a situation. Had thought up snappy rejoinders, had planned how she would react. Now, when she had the opportunity, nothing would come to mind!

"Louise? My God, honey! I'm appealing to your reason, here. You're the mother of two sons, who need you, dammit! Do you have any idea what I had to endure because of your midlife crisis? Do you ever think of me? How many women get a huge party, with string quartet and everything, for their fortieth? Hello? Louise? Stop this bullshit at once! Do you hear me? Louise, you can't treat me like this! If you have another man… Do you?", Alexander screamed through the telephone. She could hear the fury in his voice. Could see, in her mind's eye, how he loosened his tie to get enough air, with his typical gesture. She was sure he was already bright red in the face. Strangely, it didn't bother her. It left her almost completely indifferent. She was disconcerted to realize that she had thought of Alasdair Munro, when he had accused her of having another man. That didn't bother her conscience a bit.

"Louise, you're ruining our marriage, and if you do that, if you…. Listen, you slut.."

At this point, she should really have answered something, should have defended herself against his bizarre accusations. Why did men always immediately think there must be another man involved? Instead, she heard herself say, without emotion: "What marriage? Ours? That has only existed on paper for years now, Alex!"

Spontaneously, she wound up and threw the blaring

smartphone, from which loud screaming could be heard: "You can't do this to me, you … slut.." into the lake with all her strength.

Polluting the environment. Hope no one saw me!, shot through her head. Something plucked at her pants leg. With stiff, trembling fingers, her eyes still on the spot in the lake where the water was now still again, she tried to pat her dog, but her hand found no fur. Astounded, she took a step back, saw the affronted gaze of Grace Munro. Gesticulating wildly, the girl repeatedly pointed at Lou and the spot where she had just sunk about 500 Euros.

The girl seemed to have observed her long throw clearly, and it seemed she wasn't enthused by it. Placatingly, Lou pointed at her lips, prompting the girl to read her lips. Grace paid no attention. Her eyes blazed angrily as she stamped her foot. She pointed at the ducks, who were circling peacefully, and pulled faces, letting her tongue hang out, rolling her eyes and swiping her finger across her throat. The meaning was clear enough. "I know, Grace. Yes. Yes, you're right. The ducks could die through my smartphone. Terribly stupid of me", she said, forming the words as clearly as possible with her lips.

Grace put her hands on her hips, stamping her foot once again. Oh God, she looked just like her father. Grace looked at her challengingly, describing further water denizens who would die through her environmental sin with theatrical gestures.

"Heavens, Grace. All right. Calm down, girl", Lou capitulated. Not knowing what else to do, she took off her shoes, socks, pants and sweater under the vigilant gaze of the girl, then waded courageously, clad only in brassiere and slip, into the cold water.

"Oh God, it's cold! Just like her father. What did I do to

deserve this, that Munros are swarming all over the place!", Lou cursed quietly. She needed all her determination to wade out far enough into the cold water. At least the water where she had sunk her smartphone only reached to her chest. Unfortunately, said water, which had looked so clear from the shore, was here more of a murky sludge, opaque for anything more than a handsbreadth. She grimaced disgustedly. The water had looked much more inviting from shore. No. This definitely wasn't the place to put one's head under water, at least without a mask and snorkel. Unfortunately, though, Lou had no other choice than to do just that, if she didn't want to fall out of favor with Grace. The girl might even tattle about her misfortune to her father.

She had to dive.

"Damned Munros!", Lou hissed. No amount of encouragement helped, though. Pure fear spread through her. Her trembling was not only from the cold. Pictures of all kinds of sea monsters floated through her head. "This isn't Loch Ness, Lou. Calm down, damn you!", she whispered to herself. But weren't there supposed to be Kelpies in every Loch? It was no good. The water plants around her shins felt like tentacles or icy fingers, curling around her ankles, pulling at her. Weren't there also dangerous water nymphs? The Scottish fairy tales suddenly seemed all too real. The algae-covered stones under her feet didn't help things either, several times she slipped on them and almost fell.

Naturally, there wasn't any hero nearby, either, who could have saved her if necessary. Feeling blindly, she searched through mud and detritus, while holding her breath. It seemed an eternity until, in spite of her numb fingers, she actually managed to retrieve the device from the deep. Even then, she felt certain she had been incredibly lucky to find the phone at all.

Gratefully, she sent up a quick prayer of thanks.

Grace smiled at her with lifted thumb. She was frozen. After making it back to the shore, she spoke beseechingly to the girl.

"I'd be very grateful, Grace. That is, if you could keep this accident, I mean, this foolishness, to yourself. Please. I'm very embarrassed. Your father and I are having enough trouble already…", she explained, as matter-of-factly as possible.

Grace smiled, held up crossed fingers.

"You swear it? That's what that means, isn't it?"

The girl nodded firmly. She felt a weight fall from her mind. After dressing quickly, wet as she was, she said goodbye to Grace at the road, and made for her cottage as quickly as she could. She needed a hot bath so she wouldn't catch a cold, to top it all.

For the next few days, she actually managed to avoid Alasdair Munro. Just the opposite with Marge Munro. The older lady was seemingly determined to keep her from starving. She continuously provided Lou with bread and baked goods, even pushing jars of fresh-cooked meals on her every day.

Grace, or rather now Gracie, was another surprise. Despite their linguistic problem, the girl was soon dropping in every day, or else sat waiting in the old swing chair behind the cottage. More often than not, the girl did her homework with Lou, now. Often, though, they just sat together on the lakeshore, drawing or painting.

The girl had natural talent, with an enchanting feel for colours and shapes. Lou's heart melted when she saw how painstakingly the girl handled the expensive pencils, totally absorbed. Did the Scotsman know about his daughter's talent? Probably not. She couldn't imagine the grumpy fellow being pleased that his daughter was seeing Lou regularly. On the other hand, they weren't doing anything wrong. In fact, Marge seemed pleased to have her granddaughter doing her homework with Lou. Where was the harm?

Alasdair had really tried to keep away from Louise Schulzinger. But somehow, God seemed to have other plans for the both of them. Whatever he did, however much distance he put between them, the German constantly crossed his path. At first, he had dismissed it as coincidence, told himself it didn't bother him. Louise Schulzinger was a tourist, neither more nor less. And he was used to tourists, after all. Every year, a number of them came searching for the isolation of the Kildermorie Lodges, and the beauty of the Highlands. Not for nothing did he have another side-job, as a tourist guide. He regularly drove tourists to Urquhart Castle, on Loch Ness, or to the Culloden battlefield, with his Mercedes bus.

So what was so different about this German? He couldn't answer the question. Just as he couldn't say when he had started to secretly watch the foreign woman. In the beginning, it had only been out of concern for Grace; at least, that's what he told himself. He had soon noticed how often the girl met with the German lady, but hadn't done anything, believing that problem would soon solve itself. Grace wasn't like other children, after all. She was deaf. He hadn't reckoned with Louise Schulzinger, though. Astonished, he had realized that the German didn't let the language barrier disconcert her in the least. Maybe that had made the difference? He remembered one special moment clearly. Lou had been explaining to Grace intently, enunciating clearly, how to draw something or other. At least, that was what it had looked like to him, watching from a distance. Grace had become so enthused, she had danced around the German like a little tornado.

For just a moment, it had seemed to him that Louise Schulzinger was shining like an angel, in her pleasure and happiness. From that moment on, he was lost. Suddenly, he saw her with totally different eyes. The artificial blonde with high heels had made way for a doe-eyed brunette, in jeans and sneakers. Lou, as his mother and Grace called her, attracted him as the lure on the fishing line attracted the salmon. Only, the salmon lost his life.

Alasdair had herded the cattle from the lower pasture to one of the upper ones with his father. On the way, his father had called his attention to the two figures sitting peacefully under one of the oaks, drawing. "Finally, a woman who knows what to do with herself", Conner remarked, with a nod toward them. "Good for the girl, the woman is, aye."

"I don't know, mo athair. Grace will be devastated, when Lou goes back to Germany", he answered curtly, so his father wouldn't guess his feelings.

"What's wrong with you, mo mac?"

Alasdair gave Conner a bland look and a shrug. Without answering, he herded the cattle on, calling orders to Izzy and Sugar, the two border collies. He didn't dare pay any more attention to Grace, or Lou.

"Don't you do your tour tomorrow?", Conner needled him further, unimpressed.

Alasdair already knew what the old man had in mind. "Aye", he confirmed.

"I'm sure Lou would love it, even if she's not one of your typical tourists", Conner remarked.

He knew exactly what his father was trying to say. The typical female tourist expected the Scottish cliché. A heroic, handsome Scot in a kilt. That Scots only wore kilts for special occasions, and that none looked like Mel Gibson, or Gerard Butler, made no difference to them. Alasdair also wore his kilt on these tours, to uphold his image as a Scot, being both driver and tourist guide. Annoyingly, some of these Scotland-crazy ladies halted at nothing! Quite often, he had to defend himself against importune hands that strayed under his kilt. He'd just like to know whether they tried that on the kilt-wearing Pakistanis or Indians in Edinburgh, too. After all, there were hardly any real Scots left in Edinburgh. Was the German also one of those ladies, who only came to Scotland to find a Scot like those in their romances? He was no longer so sure that she was really that shallow, or whether he had simply put her in the same category as all those other ladies in his thoughts.

"Why don't you invite her?", his father had asked. The actual invitation, however, had come from his mother. Without regard to him, or any feelings he might or might not have, Marge had invited the woman. She had even recounted to him, with pride, how long she had taken to persuade Louise Schulzinger to go along on the excursion.

Of course, he had had no intention of doing so himself. He was a simple farmer, with a mountain of debts and a daughter. Louise Schulzinger, on the other hand, was a married woman with, he suspected, a rich husband. But, even assuming she wasn't already married or otherwise committed, what would a woman like that want with a crotchety fellow like himself? He wasn't stupid enough to have hopes of any kind, where a woman like Louise Schulzinger was concerned.

Still, there she was, sitting jammed between two fat Americans in the back of his minibus. Unavoidably, right in his field of vision whenever he used the rear view mirror. Which was a necessity, when driving a minibus full of tourists in the

Scottish Highlands. Amused, he saw how she twitched guiltily each time their eyes met in the rear view mirror. Lou looked incredibly sweet, trying to avoid his gaze, while not knowing where else to look. She was obviously uncomfortable between the two men, but had chosen to sit there, rather than next to him in the front passenger seat, much to his chagrin. Svetlana, one of the married Russian women, sat there instead. That lady didn't make it easy for him to remain polite. Repeatedly, Svetlana's eyes roved covetuously over his kilt, resting on his naked knees, until that nakedness began to seem lewd even to himself. He was starting to feel as if he were on display in a meat market. Sometimes he asked himself why the devil he had ever taken this job as a tour guide. *Because it's fast, easy money you need desperately!*, he answered himself.

Louise Schulzinger was refreshingly different than all the other lady tourists he had met before. No wonder she attracted him so. He could deny it how he would. He liked her more than he was ready to admit.

Once again, his gaze rested on her tall, slim figure in the rear view mirror. She was looking out the window, spellbound. An enchanted smile played around her lips, erasing the melancholy which he so often saw on her face. She was really the absolute opposite of the two Russian couples, or of the two Americans, who were travelling without their wives. While the Russian women had chosen high-heeled sandals, their men wore flip-flops. Lou, on the other hand, wore green Chucks on her feet. Her dungarees flapped around her long legs, making them look unintentionally sexy. The same couldn't be said of the legs right next to him, with pink, high-heeled sandals on the feet, poking out from a too short miniskirt and, what's more, bobbing up and down wildly. He would never understand why tourists ignored all the well-meant advice in guidebooks and from tourist informations. Sturdy shoes, layered and waterproof clothing, were consistently advised there, but too often the advice fell on deaf ears. In Lou's T-shirt, that could be seen under a faded open jeans shirt, the green of her shoes was repeated. A light raincoat she had bound around her hips, as well as a faded baseball cap, completed her outfit. She was better equipped, he was sure, than all the other tourists taken together. Without having looked into her backpack, he was sure what he would find there. A pad and various pencils. He also knew, from Marge, that it included a bottle of water from Highlandspring, and a steakpie. The steakpie he had baked himself that morning, without knowing for whom. Marge had only said it was ordered. Of course, knowing would have changed nothing about how he made it.

It had started to rain lightly, and the wipers were squeaking monotonously over the windshield. Drich, this sort of rain was called, which was accompanied by some wind. Not too bad, but uncomfortable. Alasdair was pretty sure none of the Russian women would go wandering around the Culloden battlefield in this weather. Regrettable, as he felt a childish glee at the thought of seeing those pink sandals sink deeply into the moor. Before his inner eye, he saw Louise Schulzinger again, on the day of her arrival, sinking clumsily into the muck in her high heels. As if she had heard his thoughts, their eyes met again in the mirror. He had to control himself to keep from jerking the steering wheel.

Daingead. Concentrate, man!, he scolded himself silently, avoided looking in the mirror again. Had she noticed the slight swerve of the bus?

Svetlana's gaze still rested on every bit of naked skin he showed. He tried not to sigh loudly.

Pog mo thon, I almost feel naked!

In a few moments, they would arrive at their destination, Culloden Moor. He turned on the microphone, still studiedly ignoring Svetlana, who hung on his lips, as he started telling the tale of the events of April 16th ,1746, the blackest day in Scottish history, when Jacobite hopes were finally dashed in battle, on that very moor. As always, he prettied nothing up, but neither did he dwell on the horrible details.

As usual, the glum silence of the tourists lasted exactly to the moment when they drove into the visitor's parking. Then, they were already laughing loudly again, or discussing whether there would be a good T-shirt shop. It was always the same. Only the German woman stayed quiet, didn't look at him, but stared inscrutably at the visitor's centre.

After his tourists, all but Lou, had had their pictures taken with one of the employees, who was clad in a Dragoon uniform, he had quickly absented himself.

Too often, he had to pose for such photographs himself, which he hated passionately.

Today, he didn't feel like it. He needed some time alone, to master himself and his feelings. Tired, he strolled into the tea shop, where he allowed himself a hot coffee. After that, he watched Lou with interest for quite a while, as she followed both the Jacobites' path and that of the English, pacing the whole distance twice. At last, he lit himself a cigarette at the exit to the moor.

"I thought you were going to quit, Al?",

he heard a teasing voice next to him.

"Aye, Kevin. I did. But you know how that goes, sometimes…", he shrugged, while giving his friend a light.

"I get it. Got a really special group again."

Kevin grinned broadly, nodded towards Svetlana, whose heels clattered loudly through the exhibition, heading for the tea shop.

"Aye. You said it. Didn't even take a look at the battlefield, did they?", Alasdair confirmed, shaking his head.

"No, they didn't. But the bonnie lass with the short hair isn't bad. Nice ass, sexy legs. Right now, she's having old Annie explain all the field medics' utensils to her. And she even asks after the details, without fainting."

Kevin's voice sounded admiring, while his eyes followed Lou with open interest.

Alasdair followed his friend's gaze. The German lady had bent down to old Annie, who looked like a gnome next to her. There were at least two heads difference between the two women. Alasdair could see Lou, gingerly picking up a bone saw. Her face showed no disgust, merely a mix of curiosity and concern. She seemed to feel watched, and looked around. Strangely, he felt caught in the act, and drew behind a wall.

"You like her, eh?", Kevin commented, with an amused undertone.

Alasdair made no answer.

Kevin quickly put out his cigarette, as Lou was heading toward the counter with the audio-guides.

"Aye, work calls", Kevin joked, and winked at Alasdair conspiratorially.

Alasdair could see his friend begin flirting with Lou, which needled him a bit. She still hadn't seen him. She seemed to be following Kevin's explanations very closely. Nodded several times. Laughed at his jokes, while leaning casually on the counter. *Now, don't you get jealous!*, he cautioned himself. Lou had an infectious, winning laugh. Alasdair wondered why he hadn't noticed that before. *Because you're only interested in women for bed, and this one doesn't fit the pattern! Don't kid yourself, Al, Felicitas has killed the capacity for love in you!*

Annoyed with himself, he ran his hand through his damp

hair. He let himself sink limply against the wall at his back, and exhaled with a loud sigh. Meanwhile, Lou marched out on the bleak paths through Culloden Moor, the device at her ear, and with the umbrella from her backpack held over her head. She was obviously absorbed by the voice of the audio-guide. The fine rain, which soaked everything sooner or later, didn't seem to bother her at all. He could see her putting her head back every now and then, putting aside the umbrella, to look at the clouded sky. He imagined how the fine rain dampened her face, how she licked the raindrops from her lips...

God, Alasdair! Stop it right now!

He wondered whether Louise Schulzinger was superstitious. Because, just as he had expected, she was totally alone out there, if you didn't count the spectres of the past, of which there were an abundance here.

It had been a mistake to come. Lou knew that all too well. Alasdair Munro had greeted her in a kilt. Instead of glum, as she knew him, he had been quite gallant, answering the questions of the other women patiently, and bravely enduring their importunate hands. She had almost felt pity for him. Lou had blushed at his answer to one of the Russian women's questions, who had, of course, asked what a Scot had under his kilt. She found the pushy women downright embarrassing.

"Nothing but Scotland's future!", Al had said firmly, and looked at her with a piercing glance. He had seemed to ask silently: "Do you want to check, lass?" She still imagined she felt his piercing blue eyes, dancing with humor, resting on her. Why did she suddenly feel attracted to Alasdair Munro, as if he were a magnet? The farther she stayed from him, the closer she came to him. The Scotsman had a hold on her.

Stole into her thoughts. Influenced her deeds, without doing anything.

Squeezed as she was between the two Americans in the bus, their eyes had met in the rear view mirror, again and again.

"Ha. What else can he do? He needs to watch the traffic in the rear view mirror, after all, Lou. So he has no choice, and you're just sitting in his line of sight, that's all", she told herself silently.

She tried to ignore her heart, which started beating faster at the mere thought of the name 'Alasdair'. Damn, this fellow turned her upside down. He wasn't at all her ideal of a Scotsman. No. Munro was just about the opposite of a hero, such as Jamie. Why had she let Marge talk her into this excursion?

"Al has a free seat in his bus anyway, lass. Let Scotland's sad history be brought home to you!"

That's what she had said. And Lou had thought, since she couldn't get an excursion to the Outlander scenes from one of the local travel agencies, she'd at least get to see some of Scotland this way.

Alasdair Munro hadn't asked why she drove with him, instead of booking an Outlander tour. She could see the question in his eyes, though. Just as she could see his dislike of fans of the series in his face. In fact, Alasdair Munro had a face she could read like a book.

Of course, she hadn't mentioned that his bad internet connection, and the missing cell phone reception, had made it impossible for her to book such a tour. And, when Marge had been nice enough to offer to watch Doc, too, she had had no more arguments left. What was the big deal, anyway? Nothing, really. If only she didn't have such a strange feeling in her stomach.

"*What devil got into you?*, her thoughts screeched. To be sure, she hadn't wanted to drive herself, especially not with that monster of a jeep. And, of course, it was an opportunity to see some more of Scotland and its history.

It had started to rain, just as they were starting out. Not strongly, but persistently and uncomfortably. She had still taken the earliest opportunity to flee from the bus and his proximity. Her beating heart hadn't slowed down until she reached the interior of the Culloden Battlefield's visitor centre. As expected, it was a sad place. She followed the Jacobite's route twice, the same for the English. She watched the documentary film alone. Standing in the middle of the square room, she watched the battle scenes with wildly beating heart, frozen in terror. She felt as if she had truly landed in the middle of the battle. Though she knew, of course, that the film was staged, she had the feeling her heart would stop beating from fear. After leaving the little cinema and calming down a bit, she had listened to the explanations of a little old lady in a historic costume, about the terrible medical conditions of that time. It had been bad enough reading of them, but to see the terrible instruments before her was something else again. Despite the disgust she felt, Lou listened attentively to the descriptions and the knowledge of the likeable Scottish lady.

Curiousity had finally even brought her to pick up a rusty bone saw, and look at it more closely. She felt lucky that she didn't live in that time any more.

She wouldn't have lasted two days in that age. Suddenly, she no longer found that epoch romantic any more, either. She was actually glad to escape the visitor's centre, even though the young man who had explained the audio guide to her had done his best to make her laugh.

It seemed to her the heavens were crying for all the dead,

who had found their last rest on the moor. Her baseball cap and the thin raincoat weren't enough to protect her from the steady rain. She was already soaked through. But it wasn't the cold, which she felt in her bones, that bothered her the most.

Still, she didn't turn back, refused to flee to the security and warmth of the tea-shop. Instead, she took her small umbrella from her backpack, followed the paths through the moor with firm steps. While listening to the sad story told by the audio-guide, she gripped the handle of the umbrella tightly. Without meaning to, she started to cry silently. She cried for all the dead, as well as for her failed marriage. She felt very small and lost among all the white and red banners waving in the wind. She went on step by step, took in all the many details of the Culloden Battlefield.

The Spring of the Dead, the monument to all the fallen, and, of course, the thatched cottage.

A weathered gravestone stopped her. *Munro* was still easily legible. Were ancestors of Alasdair and Marge buried here? A twist of dried flowers lay before the gravestone. Only now did she realize that she was totally alone.

Suddenly, the cloud cover broke, showing blue sky, and a few stray rays of the sun shone on the weathered stone. "Rest in peace", she whispered and started back. She had stayed too long on the moor, quite forgotten the time. According to her watch, she wouldn't even have time for a coffee or tea.

"Goddammittohell!", she cursed, annoyed, and hurried back to the parking lot with long strides. She arrived just in time to see Alasdair Munro defending himself, with a forced smile, against Svetlana, who seemed to want to get in his pants, or rather, his kilt. It seemed she actually meant to check what the Scotsman had under his kilt.

Maybe it was because she didn't like the Russian woman. Or maybe it was because Munro was doing his best not to be unfriendly, while also trying to keep the woman away. Afterward, Lou couldn't say what had made the difference. She was usually a quiet, peaceful person, who liked to keep out of matters that didn't concern her. Anyway, she strolled casually toward the two, closing her umbrella, then opened and closed it quickly several times, right in front of the Russian woman. A veritable flood of accumulated raindrops showered Svetlana, who jumped aside with an indignant cry.

"Sorry!", Lou mock-apologized, while winking at Alastair slyly. She had to bite her tongue to stop herself from giggling childishly. Cursing loudly in Russian, the woman sought solace from her husband, who immediately gave Lou the evil eye. Before he could do anything more, however, the Scot pushed between the angry Russian and her. Alasdair held the door for her considerately, and nodded at the front passenger seat.

"You might as well save me completely, lass", he whispered conspiratorially in her ear, which immediately brought her goosebumps.

Oh God, why is he so charming all of a sudden?

The Russian woman gave her a drop-dead look, but followed her anxious husband into the back of the little bus. With a "Catch!", Alasdair Munro tossed her a towel, which she took gratefully. She peeled off her dripping-wet raincoat and took off the baseball cap to towel her hair as dry as possible. Meanwhile, Alasdair explained to his bus group that he was putting on the heater, so they could all get warm again. He also told them they would be taking the route through Inverness, so they could see some of the city. Their starting point at Loch Ness would be Urquhart Castle, which they could tour, but they could also go boating on the largest

Scottish lake, by water volume.

"I heard Loch Lomond is the largest lake of Scotland", Svetlana contradicted him flippantly, almost as if she wanted to take revenge on him.

Oh oh. This could get interesting. Under lowered lids, she waited for Alasdairs reaction, which came immediately.

"Well, that's almost right, Mistress. Actually, I said Loch Ness is the largest lake in Scotland *by water volume*. In terms of surface area, of course, Loch Lomond is the larger of the two", the Scot answered calmly, while again winking at Lou.

"There's a nice song, by the group Runrig, called 'Loch Lomond'. The lyrics are based on a sad story", he explained didactically, looking at Lou the whole time.

"1745, after the second failed Jacobite uprising, two of Bonnie Prince Charlie's men were captured. One of them was freed, and took the High Road – the road over the mountains home – the other was condemned to die by hanging, taking the Low Road – the path of the dead through the underworld. I'll put on a CD with some very nice Scottish traditionals."

She could have listened to his explanations for hours. It was the pronounciation, that rolling 'R'. It actually caused a strange prickling throughout her body.

While the sad strains of the bagpipes to 'Loch Lomond' sounded, Alasdair started the bus. Lou didn't dare look at him, fearing her face would betray how badly he confused her.

In her head, she repeated the same sentence again and again: *You're married. You're the mother of two sons, Louise! Married. MARRIED! Even if things* are *going to shit with you and Alex.*

That was a damned good reason. But was it also really an obstacle? The story of Loch Lomond, combined with the sound of the bagpipes, made her ready to cry. Chilled to the bone, she pressed herself into the seat.

"Cold?", he asked anxiously. She nodded uncertainly, watched as the large calloused hands which, as she had cause to know, had a pretty good grip, pressed the button for the seat heater. With an effort, she tried to banish the pictures from her head which those hands called up. Dear God, she could almost feel those hands on her body again, as when he had saved her from the pasture. In a panic, she felt her cheeks growing uncomfortably warm.

Please, please don't let me blush, she prayed silently. "Won't take long", the Scot murmured laconically, and reached to the side. Next moment, he tossed her the blanket with the Munro tartan, which she already knew well. Lou thanked him with a cautious smile, which he answered with a friendly nod.

It was hard to concentrate on the traffic. Again and again, Alasdair was tempted to look at Lou, who sat wrapped in his blanket on the passenger seat. The sweet lips were formed into a reverent 'O' at the sight of the Inverness streets, but let not a sound escape. Her hair stood out wildly. Louise Schulzinger was a sight for sore eyes, but seemed unconscious of it. Repeatedly, he felt a pang at how well the red-and-black tartan of his clan, of which the blanket was made, suited her.

But maybe he was just feeling smug, because Mistress Unapproachable had smiled at him for the first time, even winked at him. Or, maybe he was just getting strange at his age of 36 years.

You haven't had a woman at your side for far too long, Al. So now you're out of your depth, flirting. Guess you're rusty!, he told himself silently.

They left Inverness by one of the numerous bridges. He automatically took the road to Urquhart Castle. Meanwhile, the rain had gotten worse, as had the wind. Well, that certainly didn't bode well for Loch Ness. From the loudspeakers sounded the warm voice of Dougie MacLean, singing 'Caledonia'.

Alastair wasn't surprised that the visitor's parking at Urquhart Castle was mostly deserted. After all this rain and mud, he would have to give the bus a thorough cleaning. Daingead! He made sure to drive as closely as possible to the round dome marking the entrance to the ticket booth, as well as to the visitor's centre of Urquhart Castle itself. Everyone, including Lou, vanished quickly inside, out of the rain.

After parking the minibus, he would usually have taken his midday meal, and had a short nap. Last night, with an extra work shift in the bakery, hadn't really left much time for sleeping. The loud babble of voices, as well as the many questions of the tourists, not to mention defending against brash female hands, had totally exhausted him. Furthermore, he hated wedding cakes, since his marriage fiasco, and thinking of the miserable thing, which he had promised to make, almost drove him crazy. Today he couldn't get to sleep, despite his exhaustion. Nor did he feel hungry. What was wrong with him, all of a sudden? He wasn't usually such a sissy.

Was she already sitting in the cinema, watching how Urquhart Castle had changed over the centuries? He doubted Lou would be sitting over coffee and scones. Before he realized what he was doing, he had already bought a ticket. As if of themselves, his legs carried him down the broad steps, winding down in a spiral. He was met by bagpipe music in the background, as well as by some tourists, who were browsing typical Scottish souvenirs. There were Nessies in all colours and shapes, as well as tea, shortbread, and a number of different whiskies, grossly overpriced, in his opinion. Everything to warm the heart of the tourist was available.

A friendly voice announced over the loudspeakers that the film 'Urquhart Castle through the centuries' would begin in a few minutes. His eyes searched the room for her. For a moment he felt a pang, because he couldn't find her right away. Then, however, he saw her right in front of the cinema. She was standing at the display cases which, as he knew, showed finds made at the castle. Lou seemed to be reading something, looking intently into the display case, gnawing at her lip. A Dhia, that looked tempting. He couldn't stop staring at her lips. Would they taste as sweet as they looked?

Unsettled, he leaned on the wall, forced himself to look somewhere else. Dammit, what was wrong with him suddenly? Why did his blood run so hotly when he thought of this woman? God. He had so many commitments. Besides, as a single father, up to his neck in debt, he was anything but a good catch for a lover. A woman like Lou deserved better. Not a small farmer, with matching manners. So, why couldn't he simply go back to the bus, and act like he usually did?

Why did this A' gearmailteach make him sink into an emotional chaos? Something about her affected him, affected him so much that he couldn't defend against it. She brought out a part of him he had thought lost. Alasdair knew what he was doing wasn't right. It was absolutely clear to him that he would have to pay for his feelings toward this stranger, and sooner than he would like. His heart had been in shards for the last eight years. He simply couldn't believe that this bonnie lass, of all people, would be brave enough to cut her hands on it and save it.

Just as he knew that, when she at last left him, nothing much would be left of the pitiful remnant of what had once been a heart, only ashes. He was already burning like a torch, and the reason for that was just strolling leisurely up to the cinema. She still hadn't seen him. He followed her at a short distance, his gaze on her swaying hips. He ignored the looks of the various ladies around him, who all stared fixedly at his bare knees unter the kilt.

Just don't encourage any of them by eye contact!, he thought to himself. Lou sat in the last row of the little cinema, which was considerate of her, tall as she was. The Americans from his bus sat in the very first row and waved to him exuberantly. He gave them a friendly nod, but also sat in the last row, though not right next to Lou.

He wondered whether he wasn't being too bold. He didn't aim to embarrass Lou, or himself, by kissing those desirable lips, here in the dim light of the Urquhart Castle visitor's cinema. Even though he suddenly needed all his willpower to withstand that temptation! With an effort, he tried to follow the film. Not enough that he was dead tired, or that he knew the film by heart, no, he could hardly keep his eyes from her.

Maybe it would never have gone so far, if Marge hadn't practically pushed him at her. "Don't be so stupid, Al. Lou is an enchanting bonnie lass. I think you should really show her some of the beauty of your native land, to make up for the faults of your cottage!" The words of his own mother, no less.

"The devil. Faults…", he grumbled silently.

To his chagrin, he had to agree with his mother. He really had glossed over some details in his advertisement. Suddenly, the memory of red-white checked underpants flashed in his memory. He was sure he hadn't uttered a sound, but he could feel her questioning gaze on him. She had seen him, then. Of course she had, he hadn't been hiding, after all, and neither was she blind. All quite normal, then. So why did he suddenly feel like a miserable excuse for a Romeo?

Watching the screen fixedly, he wondered, glumly, whether he was blushing yet. He suddenly felt uncomfortably warm, shifted his legs nervously, pulled down the kilt, so he wouldn't show too much knee.

After the end of the film, they both stayed seated for a moment, letting the pushy tourists go by.

They both looked out the large window, whose curtain had disappeard with the end of the film, and which gave a breathtaking view of the ruins of Urquhart Castle. Now he could no longer avoid her doe eyes, which mustered him frankly.

"Long time no see, bonnie lass", he joked, giving her his most charming grin.

"Doesn't this get boring for you, Munro?", she asked back, with an innocent smile on her face.

Damn. Look at me like that, and I'll kiss you regardless!, shot through his head. "Och, it's long since I've been in here."

Her eyebrows rose sceptically.

"It's lonely out there, today. Thought you might need a guide. Just as a thank you for saving my virtue, aye!", he hurried to say seriously.

She reddened slightly and snorted, amused. "If you're virtuous, Munro, then I'm a nun", she answered dryly. He breathed a sigh of relief. The German lady seemed to take his eccentric humor in stride. Grinning at each other mischievously, they got up and left the cinema together.

They took the door directly to the outside, with Alasdair

letting her go first. Like a gentleman, he even held the door for her. Unfortunately, the Scot was proving more and more to be an attentive and nice man, and thus a danger for her heart. Lou was aware that the few tourists present were staring at the Scot admiringly, some talking behind their hands. She was certain that his kilt, or rather, what was under it, was the subject of those discussions. She was actually embarrassed, at least for the moment, to also be female.

She flinched momentarily at a cool gust of wind that intruded under her jacket. The Scot next to her seemed totally impervious to the weather. Well, he was used to such capers by the weather, after all. Didn't they say that there were four seasons in Scotland, all on the same day?

She examined his rugged face from the corner of her eye. The stubble of a three-day beard gave him a raffish look. This man's Celtic blood was not to be denied. It took her an effort to stop watching the guy and turn to the spectacular view of the ruins of Urquahart Castle.

It was situated at the end of the hollow they were heading for, right on the edge of Loch Ness. Alasdair had been right, they were just about the only ones on their way to the imposing ruin. The rain had lessened to a slight drizzle, almost imperceptible. To make up for it, the wind pulled at them. On Loch Ness, waves piled up in a colorful medley of gray, green, and a blue so dark it was almost black. It wasn't hard for Lou to imagine the large head of a sea monster named Nessie, emerging from the unquiet surface. Maybe she shouldn't have perused her Scotland guide books quite so much. At the moment, at least, she wasn't really keen on some details, like the corpses of suicides never coming back up, for instance.

"Did you know Loch Ness is the largest lake in Scotland, going by water volume?", the Scot tried to make conversation.

"Yes. You explained that in the bus!", she answered. She refrained from asking since when they were on a first-name basis, admitting to herself that she liked to hear him talk.

She still attributed that to the typical Scottish pronunciation of the letter 'R', but knew very well that it was just as much the timbre of his voice. That was very deep and thus very male.

They walked past the old catapults with their menacingly large balls of stone, finally crossing a wooden bridge over the moat. From above, she heard the sound of bagpipes, playing a familiar melody. She looked for the instrument and its player, but couldn't find him, until Alasdair showed her.

"He's up there, in one of the rooms with an intact roof", the Scot explained, while leading her back a step with a hand on her arm, onto the wooden bridge, where they could see through the broken wall to where the Scot, complete with kilt, coaxed such wonderful sounds from his instrument.

"The song he's playing is called *"The Parting Glass"*. It's one of the Scottish Traditionals", Alasdair explained.

Lou nodded respectfully. Apart from themselves, there were hardly any tourists left in the riven castle ruins. The wind almost knocked the baseball cap from her head, which she had pulled down over her face, to keep it hidden as far as possible from Alasdair's gaze. Happy to find some protection from the gusts of wind, they fled into the tower to the left. A spiral stair of latticed steel wound upwards. Some meters above, a narrow corridor was illuminated, which a small sign identified as a dungeon cell

Alasdair was already on the stair, waiting for her. She followed him, keeping her face bland and trying not to look up, lest she see more than was good for her peace of mind. Somehow, Lou couldn't shake the feeling the damn Scot knew exactly what he was doing. Was the miserable fellow checking her reaction? He actually seemed to relish her embarassment. He stopped to look at the dungeon cell more closely. She followed suit, also looking at the penned-in figure of a life-sized doll, that had been put in the dungeon cell as an illustration.

"Looks pretty cramped", she remarked.

"Aye. I can think of more comfortable surroundings", Alasdair answered, leaning casually against the stony castle wall so he could see better. In the dim light of the tower, he suddenly looked incredibly handsome and masculine. She barely managed to keep from staring at him, like one of those almost drooling female tourists.

Oh my God, Louise!

Shocked at herself, she fled, pushing past his body on the stair. The smell of his aftershave, and the momentary touch of his muscular breast, almost made her stumble.

Get a hold of yourself!, she scolded herself silently, while concentrating on her feet, taking the rest of the stairs step by step. This arrangement wasn't much better, though. She thought she could feel his lustful eyes on her behind.

Once reaching the top, she was confronted by a breathtaking view of Loch Ness that made her forget all else. The wind pulled at her, sometimes even taking her breath away, making her forget the rain. That was all unimportant, though, as the view was more than worth it. Before a new gust could rip the baseball cap from her head, she took it off and faced into the rain.

"You seem to like storm and rain, lass", she heard his amused voice from behind her.

"You don't, lad?", she answered pertly. His deep laugh gave her goosebumps again, and she turned her heated face into the wind on purpose.

"Somebody's done their homework. Aye, liking it would be an exaggeration, but I guess it simply doesn't bother me anymore."

A few minutes later, Lou followed Alasdair back down, where they strolled through the ruins together. They hadn't gone far, before the clouds suddenly broke, letting the first rays of sunshine of the day through, which dispelled the rest of the rain.

"That's what I like so about my country. We always have all seasons in a day. That leads to such moments as this", the Scotsman explained, while she followed the silent prompting of his pointed finger. Enchanted, she watched the rainbow that spread its shining colours across the now sunlit waters of Loch Ness.

"Incredible!", she exclaimed.

"Aye!"

Only seconds later, a new cloud had veiled the sun and the rainbow disappeared. Since the weather had now become a bit more clement, the first tourists were pushing into the ruins of Urquhart Castle. She followed Alasdair to the rear section of the walls. The tall man strolled to a bronze plaque, where he waited for her. *The Great Raid of 1545 / The MacDonalds Takeaway Menu* was written there. Fascinated, she began to read.

"The old kind of 'fast food'", he remarked with an urchin grin.

"Heavens! How did they transport all that? 3377 sheep, 2355 cows, 2204 goats, 371 horses and, mind you, two oxen. Not to mention the poultry and grain",

Lou uttered incredulously.

Alasdair shrugged. "Other times, other skills, aye. Let's go a bit further, before they reach us",

he answered with a disapproving look at Svetlana and her

husband, who were nearing with unsteady gait and gasping visibly. Lou stayed, her eyes fixed on the deeply sunk heels of the Russian woman. She was unable to tear herself away from that absurdity, until the Scot had had enough. With a mumbled "They're not getting on my bus like that!", he took her briskly by the sleeve of her jacket and pulled her along.

Unconsciously, her hand nestled into his. Large, rough fingers gripped hers warmly and firmly. Lou felt sure she could say good bye to her hand if he should press really hard.

They began to ascend the steps to the next level of the ruin briskly. Once there, they simultaneously let go, both embarrassed and slightly out of breath.

Almost as if they had done something reprehensible.

Lou's heart pounded. She didn't dare look at the Scot, instead let her gaze roam over the lake into the distance.

What in the world had that been?

Had she just imagined that moment?

"I'm glad you traded your high heels for sneakers, lass. Very sensible", Alastair tried to bridge the embarrassing silence between them.

Pull yourself together, you stupid bitch!

"Thanks. I, um… I'm sorry, I didn't mean to…", she stuttered, avoiding his inscrutable gaze.

"Aye. So am I. I hadn't meant to pounce on you right away", he said, with a look that seemed to say: "Not until later!".

Before she could answer the seemingly hurt Scot, he pointed with his chin toward the bus. "I've got to get back, lass", he growled glumly, and left her standing.

Her rejection had truly seemed to hurt him. For a moment, she was too confused to react. But the moment passed. Before she knew what she was doing, she was already running after the tall man. What should she do, when she had caught up? Falling around his neck was out.

"You're married, Lou. Married and totally screwed", she groaned, knowing her heart had already gone another way than her head. At least the daily jogging with her personal trainer had been good for something. Only a few minutes later, she had caught up with Alasdair, without being the slightest out of breath. He was strolling, seemingly deep in thought, to the bus. Why didn't he see her? Was he ignoring her on purpose? Annoyed, Lou buried her fingers in the linen of his shirt, forced him to stop.

"Listen, Alasdair. I'm really sorry, I hadn't meant to hurt you. I... " Eyes as deep blue as Loch Ness shining in the sun stopped her from saying another word.

Before she could dodge, he took her hand as if it were the most natural thing in the world. Softly, he brushed his finger over her marriage ring. "I know you aren't free, Lou. This ring might not be an obstacle for many a man." He laughed sadly. "Once, before Gracie, I might even have been such a man. Today I'm a different man, however. I don't know who you're running from, Louise Schulzinger. Just let me give you a piece of friendly advice. No matter how fast you run, Lou, it won't be fast enough or far enough. Nor will it be the solution to your problems!"

"I don't see what business that is of yours, Munro", she exclaimed, affronted, and pulled away her hand. She had to clench her teeth not to burst into tears immediately. Alasdair Munor had jolted her. Even more, he had her dead to rights, as if he had read in her heart. She felt attacked, pierced to the core. The Scot had put into words what she still didn't really dare think. The thought of the naked truth of her marriage to Alexander, suppressed for years, pained her. Hurt her. She had lived a lie, an illusion perfectly crafted to show friends, acquaintances, even her husband, how perfect their marriage was. The wall of lies she had built around herself and her heart all these years was falling, because a total stranger was throwing her into emotional turmoil. What more could happen, if he touched that wall with deeds, instead of only words? Lou could already feel the walls trembling. Everything was tottering since she had come to Scotland. No. She should never have let things go this far. Helpless, naked as a newborn, that's how she felt. She no longer had firm ground under her feet.

She found no answer for him. No adequate defense found its way through her trembling lips. She couldn't look at him, fearing to lose control of her tears, or her body, which yearned for a strong embrace. He was still watching her. She could feel it.

Every millimeter of her skin seemed to burn under his gaze. Silently, she walked to the bus ahead of him, waited until he unlocked the door, then immediately fled to the passenger's seat, where she froze.

"I didn't mean to offend you, lass", the Scot murmured in his deep voice. She could feel him waiting for her response. Determined not to let anything show, clenching her teeth, she looked back at him.

"I'm right, aren't I?", he began.

She nodded hesitantly.

"I knew it. You don't look like one of those females who run after the myth of a romantic hero, only to find there is no such thing in real life."

"Thank you very much, Mr. Female Connoisseur", she murmured sarcastically.

„I only ask myself, what kind of husband just lets his wife go off to Scotland for two months…"

Lou flinched, caught, and quickly turned her face toward where the other tourists were nearing the bus.

„Let me guess. He doesn't know? Your husband doesn't even know where you are, right?", was the last thing the Scot could ask, before the sliding door was jerked open and a bunch of cheerfully babbling tourists flooded in. Their conversation ended. During the whole drive back, she could feel his questioning gaze rest on her every now and again. But she didn't return his glances, and she didn't speak to him. Bewildered and introspective, Lou bit her lips, letting her eyes roam over the landscape passing outside the window.

Germany

"Why can't you tell us where she is, Uncle Tobi? I don't understand. We're all worried about Mama. I'm sure you know exactly where in Scotland she is!", Philip accused his uncle. The soulful look that accompanied it put a begging dog to shame.

"That's why you showed up here, Flip. Not Richard, or your useless father", he riposted ironically.

Philip, whom Lou and himself lovingly called Flip, had always been different than his arrogant brother, Richard. Probably because he didn't favor Alexander, but had received more of Lou's characteristics. Thus, Tobias had not been surprised to see the 17-year old at his door. He had probably even played truant from school, so he could come visit the unloved brother-in-law.

"Pa says she has a lover. I don't believe that."

Annoyed, Tobias ran his hand through his short curls. "I should have known he'd think that. Flip", he said, "I can reassure you on that. That would have been simplest, but Lou doesn't have a lover, and she doesn't have a midlife crisis. Your parents have problems, Flip. Problems which neither your father nor your older brother want to acknowledge. And no. No, I don't have the slightest idea where, exactly, she is in Scotland. She didn't tell me, and, honestly, I didn't ask her!"

There were tears in Philip's eyes. "I didn't have time for her on her birthday. Maybe it's because of that...."

"Flip, your mother isn't one of those women who run away when things get complicated. She'd never go because of a little argument. It's not your fault!", he interrupted the agitated boy.

"He hired a private detective to find Mama. Papa, I mean.."

Tobias laughed without humor. "That sounds like Alexander."

"His old school chum with the police refuses to tap the GPS coordinates from Mama's rental car, Pa said. It seems that's a pretty new Jeep, where that feature is built in."

Tobias rolled his eyes in frustration. "Why can't your father just leave her alone? I think my sister knows exactly what she's doing, and why she's doing it. She just wants some time to think."

"I wanted... well, I thought, if you knew where she was... could you call her? She won't answer my calls. I'm worried that Papa will get those GPS coordinates after all. Richard is supposed to fly to Edinburgh, just in case, and I thought..." Philip shrugged.

"You thought I should stick my oar in, so there's no trouble?", he deducted aloud, while giving his godchild an admiring look. The boy had courage.

Philip nodded, and bit his lip nervously.

Oh yes. You really are your mother's son, Tobias thought to himself.

"I do understand there's not really much you can do, Uncle Tobi. But I thought, since Papa can be such an ass, and Richard..."

Strictly speaking, he should have agreed with his godson; after all, he couldn't stand Alexander, and the feeling was absolutely mutual. But he was reluctant to call his brother-in-law an ass. "Well, Flip, maybe I should agree with you, but I can't. Yes, your father acts like an ass sometimes, but I think that's because he never understood that your mother loved him before she ever knew of his rich family. She didn't marry him for the money. Your father never really understood that. Lou was best in her class at the art academy. Your mother was an ace at her job in advertising. That's how they met each other, by the way. Did you know that?"

Philip shook his head and looked at him, curious.

"Lou created the advertising slogan for your company. Soon after they met, she was pregnant with Richard. Your father asserted himself against your grandparents. He married his girl, even though she was beneath him socially.

Everyone was against it. True love, just like the romances Lou reviews for that blog." He sighed loudly, ran his hand through his hair again.

"You know, Flip, I believe in destiny. Let things play themselves out. If Alexander thinks he can get Lou back by travelling after her, and pestering her – well, let him try. Neither you nor I will be able to stop him!"

"I think I'd better fly with him, Uncle Tobi. You never know what Richie will get up to."

How to get flour dust to explode

Scotland

While the tourist were thanking Alasdair for his lovely tour, Lou disappeared into the café to retrieve Doc. Before Alasdair could look for her, she was already on the way back to her cottage. Once there, she luxuriated in a hot bath, and then opened a bottle of Scottish fruit wine. Gazing idly into the crackling fire, she pondered her screwed up life once more. Could you destroy something that didn't really exist anymore? Wasn't her marriage now only habit and duty toward her sons? At last, she fetched her well-worn copy of "Outlander" and, armed with a large bar of Cadbury Caramel Chocolate, began to follow her hero through the Jacobite Highlands.

Though she had already read the book ten times, she hadn't been able to stop and had seemingly fallen asleep over it. A loud knocking on her terrace door started the new morning with a bang. Though she pulled the blanket over her head and showed no reaction, the noise continued, even escalated to an obnoxious hammering. Sleepy-eyed, she peered over the blanket's rim.

She recognized Grace Munro, who waved at her, beaming, and pointed at a basket in her other hand. Doc was already scratching at the door and wagging his tail. Yawning, she left the warm cocoon of her blanket to let the girl in, while letting Doc outside into the garden at the same time.

As if it were the most normal thing in the world to visit strangers early on Sunday morning, the girl skipped past her purposefully to the dining room table and put down her basket there. Excitedly, she began talking with her hands. Of course, Lou couldn't understand a word – after all, she didn't know sign language. Luckily Grace, as almost always, had her pad and pencil with her to communicate. The next words were enough to set Lou cursing silently.

"*Papa is coming to…*" was written in her best hand.

What was this? A Sunday breakfast? Had the Scot sent his daughter ahead, so Lou couldn't say 'no'? And, of course, he had to pick a morning when she looked like a train wreck. Overwhelmed, Lou left Grace standing, and hurried to her bedroom to find something suitable to wear. That dratted guy had put one over on her. What did he intend? Did he mean to urge her to call Alexander, and reconcile with him? Or did he want to apologize for his clumsy remarks?

While pulling pants and dresses at random from the wardrobe, she realized she didn't even know what the weather was like. Warm or cold? Pants or dress? Dammit. She probably just had too large a selection. Minutes later, her bedroom looked as if a tornado had hit it. At last she held her red dress in front of herself, but threw it on the bed with a snort after looking in the mirror. No, that would really be too overdressed. Goddammitt. Since when did she care so much about her outfit?

"I'm acting like a lovestruck teenager", she scolded herself, and finally chose comfortable clothes, namely a faded jeans and an oversized sweatshirt.

Stop making more of it than it is, Lou. It's just a breakfast raid. No more, no less, she admonished herself silently. She just managed to brush her teeth, wash her face and run a brush through her hair. A knocking pulled her from her sleepy image in the mirror, whose cheeks still showed the indentations of the Highland Saga she had fallen asleep on. A minute later, Alasdair Munro stood in her vestibule. He watched, amused, as she stumbled hastily down the stairs.

"Not so fast, lass. Those steps merit some caution," he

warned. "Madainn mhath. We thought there's nothing better on a sunny Sunday morning than a Scottish breakfast", he greeted her and raised the basket, from which the delicious smell of freshly baked rolls came, toward her to confirm it.

Before she could answer, Doc pushed past her to greet the Scot properly.

"Umm, how nice….", she answered cautiously.

Grace had already decked the table. A bouquet of fresh field flowers stood in the middle of the table, and colourful napkins enhanced the simple white porcelain. To hide the turmoil inside her, and give her trembling hands something to do, she fled to the kitchen to put on water for the coffee. In her rush, she burned her fingers again, while lighting the gas flame.

It didn't help that Alasdair watched her from the door-frame, where he leaned nonchalantly. At least he seemed not to have noticed her clumsiness.

"I wanted to apologize again for my words yesterday, lass. They were out of place.", his deep voice sounded behind her.

She immediately got goosebumps again. Nervously she looked for the girl. He didn't miss her look. Casually, he answered her unspoken question. "Gracie is in the garden with Doc for a bit. That's ok with you, isn't it?"

She nodded desultorily, while trying to swallow the big lump that had suddenly appeared in her throat. Promptly, several large drops of boiling hot water fell on her fingers.

"Ow", she hissed.

With two strides he was at her side, took the kettle from her hands. "I'll do that. Cool your fingers, else you'll get blisters", he told her. They were so close together that their bodies could hardly avoid touching in the little kitchen.

"Wow, lass. Everything ok. No reason to get nervous!",

he breathed into her ear on purpose, as she made a little jump to get away from his sudden nearness. That made her bump her hip painfully against the kitchen cabinet, and his hoarse laugh almost made her heart stop.

"I think you're a bit too sure of yourself, Mr. Charming", she uttered pugnaciously.

"Maybe. Or maybe not!", he answered impudently. She couldn't help rolling her eyes.

"So you're not mad at me? Peace?"

"That depends on what you pull out of that basket of yours, lad", it was her turn to be impudent.

He laughed again. "Just let me fry some bacon and eggs, aye. This kitchen is too small for two who don't want to touch", he answered with a sly wink that immediately made her blush. She had no answer to that. Oh my God. What in the world was going on here? Why did she feel as if she were on a darn date?

"So you ran away from your husband?", he asked her conversationally, the dishtowel hanging casually over his shoulder. Desperately, Lou tried to catch her breath. Made her eyes turn away from the hairy, muscular breast she could see through the two open buttons of his checked shirt. The fellow seemed to have a weakness for checked shirts.

"No, I didn't. I took a time-out", she heard herself answer confidently, while taking up his former place and leaning, more casually than she felt, against the rough wood of the door frame. She distracted herself by staring at the tattoos that were bared by his rolled up sleeves. Heavens, she hadn't noticed those before. At the same time, she asked herself why she was telling a total stranger these things. Surely that wasn't normal? Besides, her marriage problems were no one else's affair.

What's wrong with me?

"So. A time-out. Is that what they call it in Germany?", he returned, eyebrows raised and waiting for an answer. Simultaneously, his hands were scrambling the eggs so skillfully she couldn't tear her eyes away.

"And where is Gracies mother?", she returned with a look that said: If I'm going to tell you my secrets, I demand the same of you! For a moment, his features hardened, but then he grinned broadly.

"Okay, lass. Point for you. The woman who birthed Grace, my ex-wife Felicitas, left us two days after the birth. A baby and a poor farmer didn't fit into the career of an aspiring actress. Even when, after three months, it turned out that Gracie was deaf, she didn't come back to us."

"That's horrible! How could she do such a thing?" escaped her.

"Och, I gave up asking that long ago. We agreed on the divorce very quickly. Your turn again", he prompted her.

"My husband cares more about his company and the office than me. Even when the children got older, he didn't like me working again. But since I like to stand on my own two feet...."

"Do you still love each other?"

"Um...I.... I don't know..."

"Excuse my bluntness, lass. But you're still wearing his ring, after all."

He gave her a strange, challenging look. She immediately felt cornered, almost as if she were a lamb and he the wolf. Damn, she could hardly tell him the stupid ring had grown into her finger over the years.

"Why did you never let Grace have an operation? There's a kind of hearing aid for the deaf nowadays. Or isn't that possible, with Grace?", she skillfully, at least in her estimation, directed the questioning away from herself.

A frown played about his lips. He was freshly shaven, and for a moment her gaze rested on a little cut on his cheek. Had her question gone too far?

"Aye. It's called a cochlear implant. An operation is risky, and I didn't want… I couldn't risk losing Gracie", he answered with a deep sigh, his gaze on his hand, which was pushing the mass of eggs back and forth in the cast iron skillet with the spatula.

"And maybe I was just cowardly. I regret very much that I put my ego above Gracie's future. Aye, Gracie is eight now, and a cochlear implant means at least three years of audio training…", he shrugged. His honesty touched her deeply.

Lou had to hold herself back, the impulse to simply take the Scot in her arms and comfort him was almost overpowering.

Abruptly, he turned around with skillet in hand.

"Breakfast is ready…"

"Okay. I'll… I'll get Grace", she interrupted, stuttering.

"No. Sit down. I'll get her myself!"

Lou couldn't look him in the eyes. Cowed, she sank into the nearby chair. Sinuously, like a great cat, he moved out onto her terrace.

Only a couple of minutes later, Doc rushed in, followed by Grace, who sat down right next to her, beaming with joy.

Lou couldn't say what was worse, that the girl sat next to her, dangling her legs cheerfully, or that she couldn't understand a single one of the words she formed with her hands. In any case, Alasdair was now forced to sit opposite her. She didn't like the expression on his face at all.

"So, Gabaldon, lass?", he murmured in amusement, watching her closely. He must have seen the book, still lying on the floor. She returned his gaze pugnaciously, which resulted in them both reaching for the same roll. Their fingertips touched. Lou felt as if she had been struck by lightning. She could see how Alasdair's eyes slitted and grew dark.

"Why not?", she growled sourly.

He grinned, unimpressed, while biting into a bacon roll with gusto. "I've read it myself", he said through the mouthful. "It's not bad. Some of the history isn't exactly right, but still better than most authors. Is that Jamie your image of a Scotsman?", he asked, munching, and watched her closely.

What did he expect her to answer? Desperately, she searched for a good riposte, but nothing would come to mind.

"Now, that bit about putting over the knee... just between you and me....really?"

Oh my God!

Now she was less than ever able to answer him. Overwhelmed, she stared at the play of muscles on his forearm, which made the tattoos play almost like a kind of moving pictures, as he buttered another roll. Her hand was still outstretched in the air, reaching for a roll of her own. Lou knew she was blushing furiously, knew as well that she was biting her lip indecorously. She felt the heat gathering in her face.

Alasdair Munro wasn't just playing with her, he was flirting shamelessly. He knew exactly what her silence meant. Amused, he bit into the new roll. She finally managed to get one for herself. Despite her trembling fingers, it landed on her plate. Meanwhile, some honey had dripped on Alasdairs large hand. His tongue emerged from between his sensual lips. Without taking his eyes from her, he licked the honey slowly and provocatively from his fingers. The heat in her body increased, shot from her cheeks down to her knees. Lou was certain that, if she had to get up now, she'd fall over like a rotten tree.

"Aye. Who can understand you women? On the one

hand, you're against any violence. On the other hand, you flock into that movie, *Fifty Shades of* whatever… Would you like it, if I put you over my knee…?", he started.

That was the moment she embarrassed herself totally, by breaking into gales of laughter. The breakfast, the whole strange situation with the tension between them, Grace seemingly acting the part of chaperon. It was all totally absurd and surreal. Lou laughed so hard, she could hardly get a breath.

"Oh my God….", she gasped out, chortling, unable to avoid the Scot's piercing blue eyes, who watched her with arms loosely crossed over his chest, looking amused.

" 'Al' is quite enough for now, lass. And, for my part, I could well imagine giving your sweet bottom the occasional swat…"

She interrupted him, still laughing, by by giving him an offended push on the shoulder.

"Dream on, Munro!"

"Oh, don't worry, lass. That I can do easily!", he joked. There was still a strange tension between them. Almost as if a single spark would be enough to set them both aflame.

After washing the dishes together, they went to take a walk along the lake, with Doc and the girl.

"About the internet connection, I was thinking I'd reserve the back table in the café for you. The reception is best there. If you want, I'll also refund part of your rent", he said casually, while skipping one stone after another skillfully over the surface of the Loch.

"Oh, that's nice of you! Sure. I'll gladly take the offer about the table. But I don't need a refund. It's okay", she said quickly, so he wouldn't notice she was watching him covertly.

The sleeves of his shirt were still rolled up. She could make out a wolf, as well as several celtic tribals, among the tattoos. Were the whole arms, or even his whole body, tattooed? At least he had no visible piercings, except a small silver earring.

The rest of the way, they talked about all kinds of things. Lou couldn't remember when she had last had such an engrossing conversation with a man, without having to consider every word carefully. Alasdair was totally different from the other men in her life.

The more she got to know him, the more she liked him, and the way he looked at things. He seemed never to hold back his opinions, said right out what he thought. Not to mention his not wearing a suit and tie. His clothing consisted of jeans, checked shirt and battered laced boots. He didn't care about mud spatters on his pants, or the paw prints Doc left on them, when he retrieved the stick Doc threw for him.

The few rays of sun the clouds let through made his short hair shine light brown. She couldn't find a single strand of grey in his hair. She was absolutely certain, though, that this man wouldn't dye his hair. The one thing Alasdair Munro was not, was vain. The piercing blue eyes shone warmly, as he watched his daughter run around with Doc like a small tornado. That made his somewhat rugged face less hard. Handsome, he was not.

Even after he had been gone for a while, she imagined she could still feel his gentle good-bye kiss on her cheek, smell his tangy aftershave.

When she thought of Alasdair Munro, she felt a flutter in her stomach. She had to look the truth in the face. If another man could throw her emotions into such turmoil, without even having kissed her, or gone to bed with her, then that could only mean she no longer loved Alexander. Wasn't it ironic, that the name Alasdair actually meant nothing else but Alexander, if you translated it? No matter how she looked at it, the fact was, she was well on the way to falling in love with that miserable Munro. A man she would have to change her whole life for. All for a man wholly four years younger than herself. In her head, she could already hear Constance and the others gossiping about her: "Imagine, Louise had such a bad midlife crisis, that she found herself a younger man, and what's more, a farmer from Scotland. Isn't that disgraceful?"

On the other hand – would she ever know whether her marriage and her love for Alexander were over, if she didn't risk it now?

"Since when do you care about other's opinions? When did the confident Lou turn into a timid mouse?", she scolded herself.

22 years of marriage weren't exactly chicken feed. One couldn't remain unchanged. She had never been one of those women who wanted to rule the home, but neither were the absence of all affection, not to mention of a sex life, what she desired for the rest of her life.

She found several missed calls from her gallerist, and a voice mail, on her smartphone. That afternoon, she spontaneously picked up her laptop and put Doc on his leash. With the laptop under her arm, she set out to take Alasdair up on his offer.

On a Sunday afternoon, there was quite some activity in Kildermorie. Hordes of strangers had suddenly appeared, and strolled along the lakeside. Even the café was crowded. Marge was busy, but greeted her with a cheerful: "Oh Lou, nice to see you!"

Lou almost felt guilty, as she explained the reason for her visit. Marge waved it away with a smile, though, and pulled

Lou past the counter and into the back, Doc and all. She found herself in a spacious corridor , with a heaped desk on one wall, complete with telephone, fax and computer.

"Here you have the best internet connection, and you're also away from all the curious looks and the noise", Marge explained with a wink. "Just make room for yourself, darling. Oh, and if you're looking for Al – he's in the bakeroom. You can't miss him, just follow the loud curses, aye!"

Her face must have shown her incomprehension clearly. At least, Marge felt compelled to murmur conspiratorially, behind her hand: "I'll just say: wedding cake!"

Wedding cake? She suddenly had a huge, aching lump in her stomach. Was the damned Scot getting married? Why hadn't he said anything? She rolled her eyes. Just as she was falling hopelessly in love with the fellow. On the other hand, it was small wonder that such a magnificent man was taken. At least he wasn't gay, as she had feared in the beginning. She had probably groaned aloud, because Doc looked up at her from where he had made himself comfortable under the desk at her feet, alarmed.

"You have no right to this man, Louise. After all, you're still married and have a wedding ring on your finger", she murmured, annoyed, while she once again pulled at the ring, which she couldn't get off her finger, no matter how much she wanted to get rid of it. The golden ring with the large diamond had grown into her finger immovably. She needed a distraction. Right now. Pondering fretfully, she plugged in her laptop and started working. After doing some overdue reviews, she looked at her mails. Her gallerist, Alicia, had actually managed to sell all her paintings. She also already had a new date for a vernissage, should she, as her gallerist rightly supposed, come back with a suitcase full of new pictures from her time-out. She also had a disquieting message for Lou, though. Alexander had somehow found out about her bank account and the pictures she had sold. He had pressured the gallerist badly, even threatened her. Luckily, Alicia hadn't let Lou's husband impress her.

Lou was almost certain that Alexander had engaged the detective agency that sometimes worked for his company to find her.

Typical. Alex was a control freak. He had to control everything and dominate everyone at all times.

The piercing bang of a slammed door, followed by some rough curses, which she couldn't quite make out, tore her from her dark thoughts. Doc wasn't interested, he was sleeping, sprawled out as far as possible in the confined space under the desk.

She rose, determined to find the reason for the noise and, at the same time, satisfy her curiosity about Alasdair Munro. Several dull thuds in a row made her flinch. What the hell was the fellow doing? Cutting the cake with an axe? The first door she came through led into a room that was obviously a storeroom, filled with myriads of tin cans, as well as flour and grain sacks. Three of the four walls were covered with shelves from floor to ceiling, filled to the brim. Various sacks were stacked against the fourth wall.

A new spate of curses sounded through a door that was ajar. Hesitantly, she opened that further and gazed into the heart of the bakery – the bakeroom. It consisted of a single large, light-filled room, with several tables, shelves, and two huge ovens.

A wide row of windows, with a continuous workbench running underneath, illuminated the fine flour dust thrown into the air whenever the Scotsman, obviously incensed, hit the dough in front of him with his fists. He had his back to her and didn't seem to have seen her yet. Admiringly, her eyes rested on his broad back, muscles delineated under the snug black T-shirt that was full of flour.

On one forearm she could see the name "Grace" as a tattoo and recognized the Midgard snake.

Is black the right color for a bakeroom? What other muscles are hidden under that T-shirt..?, she asked herself. Next moment, with a furious cry, Alasdair wiped everything before him from the table. Flour, dough, as well as several jars, all crashed to the floor, some of them breaking. Lou cried out, startled, and tried to dodge backwards, which the door behind her prevented painfully. The Scotsman turned to her, then froze.

"Lou?"

"Sorry, I didn't mean to just barge in here, but I heard you all the way outside and I thought…I..", she babbled in a rush to hide her nervousness, which had her blushing again. This man just looked too good, standing there in that black T-shirt, on which she could now distinctly read "AC/DC". Even the white apron bound loosely about his hips, and the flour in his face and hair, somehow gave him a raffish look.

By now he was wearing a pleased, impudent grin. He also had that dark, predatory look in his eyes again that immediately made her knees weak.

"You must have a terrible impression of me, lass. I think I'm the one who has to apologize", he answered, extending his hand toward her. "I had… well, have… a problem here…", he tried to explain, while she took the offered hand and suddenly found herself right in front of him.

"Hmm… wedding cake, Marge says. Yours?"

For a moment he just looked at her, flabbergasted. Then he broke into a gale of laughter. "Ha ha… good one, lass! A Dhia. Mine..", he gasped for air and slapped his thigh, which made the flour on his apron rise in a cloud.

Stunned, she allowed their fingers to interlace.

"I just thought, because…. because..", she desperately searched for an explanation she could give.

"Well,…", he said. His fingers, seemingly on their own, boldly pushed a strand of her hair aside, while he continued darkly. "It's the wedding cake of my best friend. It's supposed to be my wedding present. Baking it is no problem, and I'd even manage to decorate it somehow. It's just these goddamned little marzipan roses and hearts, aye. They're driving me crazy! Anyway, I've been practicing for days. Without much success, alas! The wedding is in less than a week", he explained, twisting one of her longer strands around his finger provocatively.

Oh God, I'm going to faint!, she thought desperately.

He was now leaning back against the table, legs crossed casually at the ankles. They were only a handsbreadth apart.

Lou couldn't stop looking at his full lips. The bastard knew it, too. Was playing with her again. He licked his lips sensually, showed his white teeth. Suddenly she realized that they had been silent for far too long already.

No. No. No, this isn't good. Not good at all, I'm about to ravish him!, Lou moaned silently, frustrated at her own feelings. With an effort, she pulled back from his hands, took a step back. He watched her in obvious amusement.

"We.. this… Stop it, Alasdair!", she stuttered.

"What do you mean, lass?", he asked innocently.

"You know exactly what I mean, Munro!", she answered firmly, but with her voice trembling audibly.

Dammit!

"Okay. I'll stop, before we do something we might regret later", he promised soberly, though his gaze seemed to say something else entirely. "You can't mould, by any chance, can you?" He looked at her hopefully, while sweeping the chaos on the floor together, and disposing of it.

"Mould?"

"Yes. With marzipan. You're an artist after all, aye. Maybe that's more in your line than mine. Would you try? For me?", he pleaded, with a desperate roll of his eyes.

"You ham actor", she answered, laughing.

"I'll get on my knees before you, if I have to, lass."

Oh my…. Anything but that!, she thought desperately. My God.

This guy was driving her crazy. It seemed to Lou she could almost actually see the sparks flying between them. Wasn't flour dust supposed to be explosive?

"All right, I'll try. Though I have to warn you, I've never tried anything like that before. Not even with plasticine."

Before she knew it, he had tied a white apron just like his around her hips with a practiced hand. She listened to his instructions with interest. He had opened a book with instructions for the forming of marzipan flowers, as well as hearts and other decorations. They worked side by side. After Lou had replicated several of the examples from the book, she tried some creations of her own. Alasdair seemed more than happy with her results.

"Aye. I knew you'd be better at this than me. You're saving my neck, Lou", he praised her.

Every now and then, he helped her, putting his hands over hers, hiding them completely, to knead new powdered sugar into the marzipan mass. She was only too conscious of his body behind hers. A scene from the movie *Ghost* came to her mind, in which the two protagonists and a potter's wheel had played a large part. This situation seemed to her to be at least as illicitly erotic. His breath brushed her ear, the nape of her neck. His masculine body touched hers innocently.

Without meaning to, she reacted to him. She had goosebumps all over. She couldn't resist any longer. She sank against him. Felt his warmth through her clothing. Smelled the tangy, fresh scent of his aftershave. His breath quickened audibly, matched her own.

"Not a good idea", breathing heavily, she tried to bring the situation under control, as his lips brushed her ear tenderly.

"No. Not a good idea", he murmured, agreeing, turned her to face him.

"We… we shouldn't do this", she whispered haltingly, but was already burning under the sensual look he was giving her.

"No. I guess we shouldn't…", he whispered hoarsely. One of his hands wandered slowly, as if waiting for her to stop him, upwards along her flank. Full of desire, it cupped her cheek, while his other hand rested on her behind, pressing her demandingly against him. Her head screamed silently: no!

But it was far too late. Her heart and her body had already decided otherwise, and showed her desire for this man. She was hopelessly lost. Lou could see the same desire in the Scot's dark gaze. Her cheek nestled against his hand, while his thumb stroked her lips gently. As if of themselves, her lips opened and she nibbled gently at his finger, without taking her eyes off his. He tasted of powdered sugar and the almond of the marzipan. A hoarse groan came from his throat, and his groin pushed her against the edge of the table.

"A Dhia, I can't resist you…I just can't", he breathed apologetically, before pulling out his thumb.

She just managed a "Neither can I… I want you!", before his lips had taken its place. As if he had just been waiting for that admission, he plundered her mouth with such skill that she felt the heat spreading through her would immolate her. She couldn't help answering his kisses. Passionately, she buried her hands in his short hair. She hardly noticed as Alasdair once again wiped everything off the table. Neither the crash of bursting ceramics, nor the clatter of pastry wheels, rolling pins etc. was important. Only the two of them existed. Next moment, he lifted her and sat her on the table without interrupting their kisses, which became ever more passionate and demanding. Of themselves, Lou's thighs twined around his hips, while her hands were already pulling the AC/DC T-Shirt out of his pants to wander upward along his stomach caressingly.

Alasdair couldn't remember when he had last had such feelings for a woman. Had he ever? There was no question of stopping now. The touch of her body, the feel of her fingertips groping gently over his skin, her dancing tongue, had him in goosebumps all over. His ears were hot, his heart was about to explode, and he was afraid he was going to come into his now much too tight pants. She was the wife of another, and he despised himself for what he was doing here with her.

Only, how could he stop, when her every touch stoked the passion deep inside him, seemed to be answering his own desire? How to escape, when reason no longer had the upper hand? In her eyes and the small sounds she uttered, he found the same fire that was burning in him.

I want you!, she had said.

No woman had ever said that to him before.

Now she was here, here with him. Now, at this moment, this wonderful woman belonged to him, never mind what tomorrow might bring. He wanted her. Burned for her with every fibre of his body, of his being.

She almost ripped the T-shirt off him and it flew in an arc to the floor. Her eyes scrutinized him openly for a moment, then her bold tongue left a trail of kisses across his hairy chest, while her legs pulled him even closer.

Tempted, his hands pushed under the loose sweatshirt and grasped her breasts possessively, stroking the erect nipples.

"Oh God, mo cridhe. I can't stop", escaped him, hoarse with passion. His fingers were already opening the buttons on her jeans.

"You don't have to… Al", she answered, out of breath.

A moan escaped her, as his fingers dipped into her wetness. He could hardly believe how ready she was for him.

It seemed as if he had been waiting all his life for this woman, as if they already knew each other intimately. A moment later, they had both hastily struggled out of their pants.

They fell on each other like hungry wolves, merged in a whirlpool of passion and emotions, only to find each other again, like one body, one heart, and one soul. He had never experienced anything like it, not even with Felicitas.

Alasdair couldn't remember later how often they had made love. No place in the bakeshop had been safe from their passion. He had no thought for hygiene rules, nor for sudden visitors, or even spectators through the windows. All that mattered were he and Lou. He couldn't get enough of the sight of her naked body. Everything about it tempted him. He was besotted. Intoxicated by every centimeter of her skin, he wanted to memorize every little birthmark, even the small blemishes, like scars, stretch marks, or what little cellulite there was. Memorize them, so he would never forget them. For this enchanting creature in his arms was not his, was not his wife. Inevitably, she would return to her rich and, almost certainly, better-looking husband, leaving him with a newly rebroken heart.

And he? Well, he would armor his feelings again, probably

for years. How long would it take, for him to be able to give himself to a woman again? Now, at this moment, he wished Louise could love him, love him for the man he had once been and could never be again. His mother had told him of soul partners, of the one special person who fit like no other.

He had never believed that Marge could be right, that there could be one special woman for him. Why had fate brought them together, only to rip them apart again? Didn't he deserve joy and love? It was hard enough for him to forget the problems weighing so heavily on him. With Louise, however, everything suddenly seemed so easy, so simple. Everything was full of life and colour.

They might have continued forever, and he might have further deferred his anxieties, if Doc had not suddenly burst in and interrupted them.

Germany
"Mrs. Bott, is the flight booked?", Alexander barked at his secretary. He looked terrible since Louise had vanished to Scotland. He had cut himself badly while shaving. He was chain-smoking again, and drank too much in the evenings. No wonder he looked like hell. He couldn't abide his own reflection in a mirror anymore.
The pitying looks of his employees made him even more angry than he was already. It was all her fault. Louise, whom he had given everything. Louise, who had trampled on his feelings, had left him.
Just thinking about how she had embarrassed him before all the birthday guests, by not attending, made him hammer angrily at the keyboard of his computer, ignoring the terrible feeling in his stomach. Alexander wasn't eating enough, nor was he sleeping enough. His thoughts kept circling around his wife. Unfaithful. Was she unfaithful to him? He was con-

stantly being asked about her. Everyone wanted to know how she was. He was so sick of all the questions, not to mention the comments of his own mother.

"I told you so. I told you, she's beneath you. But you wouldn't listen to me. A peasant like that just isn't a good match for the only son of the Schulzinger dynasty!"

If he closed his eyes he could still hear Beatrix Schulzinger, his widowed mother, scolding.

"Mrs. Bott, I asked you something", he growled grumpily, which made that fiftyish lady, who had just reentered his office with a tray in her hands, flinch, startled.

"Of course, Mr. Schulzinger. I've already answered you twice. Flight and hotel are booked as you wished. The man from the detective agency will be waiting at the airport for the young Mr. Schulzinger", she said.

"I've taken the liberty of bringing a slice of your favorite cake, and a Latte Macchiato. Mr. Schulzinger, you should really eat something!", the good Mrs. Bott urged him, with an anxious look on her face. Mrs. Bott had already been the secretary of his father, and Alexander had more or less inherited her with the company. She understood him like no other woman in his life, even Louise. She had always been a kind of surrogate mother for him.

Beatrix had always been Beatrix. He would never have dreamed of calling the woman, who always looked as if she had a broomstick for a spine, "Mother". She would probably have sold him if it had been profitable enough. Had it been a kind of rebellion that had made him marry the good-looking young art student, Louise?

He thanked Mrs. Bott curtly for the latte, and hustled her out before he lost control.

" A Schulzinger doesn't cry. A Schulzinger is above that!", he heard Beatrix commanding again. Tiredly, he ran his hands through his grey hair. Everything was ready.

The detective agency Osanowic had procured the GPS-data of the rental car Louise was driving. It seemed she was in a hicktown in the middle of the Scottish Highlands, just about the last place he would have expected. It was out of the question that he fly there personally and make her come back. In any case, he was probably the last person on Earth who could persuade her. That's why he had drafted Richard to do so.

The 21-year old had refused vehemently, but Alex knew how to make him accept that important role. Louise was more likely to come home for her children, at least, for one of them. That was his hope, anyway. And once she was here again, he would soon cure her of all this nonsense. He was pretty sure of that!

Today was Sunday. The flight was on Wednesday evening, he had taken a cheap one. After all, Louise's escapades had cost him enough money already. Early in the morning of the day after their arrival in Edinburgh, the Osanovic employee would drive up with Richard, and fly back the following day. He himself had no time for this crap. After all, he had a company to run.

Emotional Chaos

Scotland

It had taken them ages to restore the chaos in the bakeroom. Neither Lou nor Alasdair could meet the other's eyes properly. Did the Scotsman already regret what they had done together? She could feel the hidden looks he gave her under lowered lids. Again and again, when he wasn't looking, she did the same, watched him. She couldn't get enough of watching his supple movements, the play of his muscles under the snug T-shirt, and on his tattooed arms. She could still feel the heat pulsing in her body.

Finally, there was no more tidying to be done. Alasdair strolled towards her leisurely, one eyebrow lifted in amusement. He bit his full lip thoughtfully, which she had to admit totally turned her on. She counted to ten silently.

"A penny for your thoughts, lass?", he asked quietly, and ran a finger along the contours of her face.

"Do you regret it?", the crucial question escaped her.

"What kind of man do you think I am?", he asked rhetorically. "No. No, mo cridhe. I regret nothing. Do you?"

Tears came to her eyes. He noticed immediately. Lou could see his features hardening for a moment.

"I... I should regret it, shouldn't I? After all, I've just been unfaithful to my husband with you. So…so I should regret it…", she said, her voice agonized, while her hand groped for his, and pressed it anxiously. She couldn't raise her head to look him in the eyes. Would she see contempt or even disgust in them? With an effort, she made herself continue disclosing the truth. A truth which, once uttered aloud, would leave no way back. Then she would have to face her demons.

"But I don't.. I.. you must think I'm a terrible person and

that…", the words fell from her mouth clumsily. Alasdair wouldn't let her continue. His dizzying kiss closed her trembling lips. At last, he pushed her back gently.

His eyes seemed to see directly into the darkness of her soul. "If I thought that of you, mo cridhe, I'd have just fucked you, not loved you with body and soul. If you really had been just a slut, looking for a stereotype Scot for one night, Lou, I'd have used you. Used you and forgotten you the next day. I swear to you, by all I hold holy, by the name of my daughter Grace, I'd never have let you into my broken heart", he whispered insistently, while his hand on her chin forced her to look at him.

"Felicitas didn't leave much of me whole. I was alone for seven years. It wasn't all bad, don't get me wrong, lass. I had some women, whom I'm not proud of. But that was just sex, and had nothing to do with love."

Lou stood still, gulping under his harsh words. What in the world was she doing? Her attempt at putting a good face on things was failing. The Scot seemed to notice, at least.

"I'm sorry, lass. I'm not used to having serious conversations with women any longer. You'll have to be patient with me", he tried to explain, with agitated gestures, as if he felt her uncertainty.

"Marge gave me some good advice at the time: You can't break what is already broken! Now, I have hope that she was right!", he said simply, and took her hand.

Was it really so simple? You can't break what is already broken? Was that true of her marriage to Alex, or was she just desperately looking for an excuse to justify her infidelity?

Her hand felt good in his. Her hand didn't feel small or lost. No. This large hand held her safe. Like the glow of the sunset in the sky, she suddenly saw a glimmer of light on the horizon of her loneliness. The yearning for a fresh start was growing increasingly stronger.

Alasdair bridged the embarrassing silence between them by gripping her hand more firmly and pulling her along.

"Come along, lass. I'll show you my dreams", he murmured, as if that were a special promise. They left the bakeroom, going through a narrow, somewhat warped, wooden door from the corridor to reach another, smaller corridor. Hand in hand, they ascended the stairs, which were carpeted in the same friendly green as the bordure of the wallpaper. They reached a sort of vestibule, from which some more doors, and further stairs, went on.

Alasdair opened the first door on her side. This led to a bedroom with an enchanting view. At least, Lou supposed it would be a bedroom, as the walls were bare. The floor was laid with dark cherrywood boards. There was a passage, missing the door and its frame, but giving a view of a bathroom in an early stage of construction, with only a toilet already installed.

"I used to dream of turning this house into a Bed & Breakfast", he explained, and pulled her to the window to show her the garden. There were glorious old apple trees, as well as a mix of diverse vegetables and flowers. A country house garden, as if from a picture book. Exactly the kind of garden Lou had always dreamed of. She loved gardening, found it relaxing. Unfortunately, she had never been able to convince Alex of it.

Think of all the dirt under your fingernails! Louise, that's work for servants!, she could hear him say, in memory. *Besides, it's a waste of time*, he had grumbled. Before she knew it, she was afflicted with a gardener, sometimes even several of them. Her nice, wild garden idyll was turned into a precisely styled trendy garden, in which no blade of grass dare be out of place.

Admiringly, her eyes wandered over the plants distributed over the lawn in pots. There were little statues and decorative stones dotted all over the garden.

"It's simply….wow… I can't find the words, Al", she whispered reverently, her eyes glued to the garden. His cheek was lying on her hair. She almost felt she could feel his grin.

"Aye. There it is, mo cridhe. Could you say that again?", he asked gravely.

"What? That the garden is wonderful?", Lou turned to him, perplexed.

"No…" He cleared his throat in embarrassment. "No.. my… hm… my name. I haven't heard it in a long time, at least not like that."

"Alasdair, Al", she murmured adoringly. Before they could start devouring each other with kisses yet again, however, they heard loud steps on the stairs, followed by barking, and snippets of Gaelic.

"I'm afraid we have to go save my friend from your dog, lass. Come on!"

At the foot of the stairs, they were greeted by a very amusing sight. A red-haired man was standing on the seat of the chair where he had fled, the same chair Lou had used previously while working on her laptop. Doc had taken position before the chair, baring his teeth and growling so ferociously that the stranger's hair was literally standing on end.

"Down, Doc", she scolded the big dog, who looked up at her loyally.

"Cormac, how's the view up there? What brings me the pleasure of your company?"

Without hesitation, the big Scot sauntered over to the still growling dog, stroking his ears quite unconcernedly. While doing so, he skillfully pulled him a bit away from Cormack by the collar, allowing his friend to climb down from the chair.

"Since when has the devil moved into your house, my friend? And who is this enchanting lady?", he began, shaking his head and moving away a few feet.

Alasdair laughed quietly.

"This is Louise, um, my tenant." In spite of the sharp disappointment she felt at being introduced as "my tenant", Lou forced herself to a friendly smile. Looking bewildered, the Scotsman smiled back, and offered her his hand for a firm handshake.

"Oh, so you're the German who rented Alasdair's cottage, right?", he asked.

"That's me."

"Louise has been good enough to help me with your wedding cake, Cormac", Alasdair explained.

A cheeky grin appeared on Cormac's face. "Aye. Has she? Lucky for me! I was beginning to be afraid I'd have to do the decorating myself", he explained to her mock-seriously, which Alasdair commented with an indignant snort.

"I'd like to bring Louise along to your wedding, if I may. I'm sure weddings in Germany are somewhat different from ours", he answered.

What was happening here? Why wasn't she at least being asked whether she wanted to go? Why was he treating her like just another acquaintance in front of his friend? Alasdair Munro was acting like a total macho. To make things worse, before she could stop herself, she heard herself saying distinctly: "I'd love to come, Alasdair". *Dammittohell, Louise. What are you doing?*, she groaned silently. She couldn't even stop the stupid grin she was sure was pasted on her face. Dammit, she had been unfaithful to Alex with a macho. Worse, she was falling in love with a man who, it seemed, could be quite an asshole.

The two men seemed to be trading odd glances. It seemed to Lou as if they were conversing silently. In Cormac's face, at least, she could read the thoughts all too clearly: *What's going on with you two?* seemed to be written in neon letters across his features.

Since Alasdair had some things to discuss with his friend, he sent Lou along to see some more of the house alone. *This is your chance to get out of this, while you can! Get your ass in gear and run as fast as you can, Louise!*, her thoughts screamed at her. Instead, she again did something totally untypical for her. She obeyed.

Bemused, she strolled slowly through the top floor, inspecting each of the five unfinished guest rooms. Worse than that, though, she was already furnishing them in her thoughts. My God, what was wrong with her? Each room was more beautiful than the last. She had the strong suspicion that Alasdair had run out of money to realize his dream.

Another thing we have in common, unfulfilled dreams!

"Oh Al, I'm so sorry!", she whispered softly into the empty room that the sinking sun was painting orange. Alasdair was a man who hitched up his sleeves and tried to do everything himself. Was that what fascinated her so about him? Whenever she thought of his muscular chest with the tattoos, strange feelings ran through her, and it wasn't only her heart that started pulsing wildly. Unsettled by her feelings, she tried to direct her thoughts in other, less emotional directions.

To renovate, you needed money, she mused. That, her Scotsman didn't seem to have. Alasdair and Alexander weren't only physically totally different. Alexander had money enough. Whenever Alexander Schulzinger snapped his fingers, five lackeys not only jumped, but asked how high they should jump. Alexander was a cool, calculating person, who seldom allowed himself feelings, and even more seldom showed them. And yet, she had fallen in love with him, not his money. Just when had her feelings for him disappeared?

Uncertain. Lost. That's what she felt at the moment. The carousel of her emotions whirled inside her with such dizzying speed that she feared to lose herself. Hesitantly, she forced herself to walk on, step by step. The old floorboards, visible under a number of worn rugs, accompanied her with creaks and groans.

Marge and Conner Munro seemed not to live here. Lou found herself in a small living room, in which she immediately felt at home. It looked almost like her own old living room, the one she had lived in before meeting Alexander. Shelves of books reaching to the ceiling took up almost all the walls. An oversized, mended leather couch stood in the middle of the room. The only modern item was a large flatscreen TV that had been integrated into one of the bookshelves skillfully. Everywhere on the shelves were framed pictures of Grace, Grace as a baby, Grace in the sandbox, or Grace on the shoulders of her father. What there wasn't, however, was a picture of her mother.

Next, she found his bedroom. This was also stuffed with books, filling more shelves all around the large bed. She found only one thing jarring, the large mirror on the ceiling above the bed, the sight of which made her blush.

I had some women, whom I'm not proud of. But that was just sex and had nothing to do with love, Alasdair's voice repeated in her head.

To divert her thoughts, she took a closer look at the bedframe, which had also been turned into a resting place for reading material. She bent to look at one of the magazines and found, to her surprise, that they were farming and motorcycle magazines, though she also found some Playboy magazines. And why not? Alasdair was a man, not a saint. A worm-eaten wardrobe, a rocking chair piled high with clothes, and a massive desk, completed the furniture.

Grace's room, directly opposite, gave her a little pang. Someone, she supposed Al, had, somewhat clumsily, tried his hand at painting clouds and star constellations on the ceiling. All furnishings were lilac- or rose-colored . A small dressing table with a mirror, and a matching wardrobe on ornate legs, revealed that this was a young girl's room. There was a large stuffed unicorn on the bed, and some of the pictures they had drawn together hung on the wall above. Lou's heart jumped for joy as she discovered the elephant with which it had all begun, clearly marked with a red A+. Grace had talent, that was obvious. You didn't need hearing to draw.

How could a macho also have such a soft heart? The Scot seemed a really strange man.

Through another door, Lou found a bathroom, whose appointments made her giggle with her hand over her mouth. *Heavens, what kitsch* shot through her head. For a man with Alasdairs appearance, this was really a bit too much. A brick-built shower, tiled in dark blue, with a ceiling of LED-lights, reached by an oriental-styled archway. One wall was adorned with a washbasin formed like a seashell, standing on a pedestal, and with a huge mirror behind it, bordered by hundreds of mirror shards in bright colors. Sand-colored terracotta tiles on the floor, and walls of splintered natural stones that, together with real seashells, formed ornaments, completed the fantasy from Arabian Nights. Admiringly, she brushed her fingertips across the seashells.

"So he's an artist, too", she murmured approvingly. My God! Every time she thought of him, she felt like a teenager, butterflies in the stomach and all. For the life of her, she couldn't remember when she had last had this feeling.

"I like your laugh", came an amused voice from behind her. Caught, she turned to him. His piercing blue eyes looked at her, full of desire, which made him look incredibly sexy. Nervously, Lou bit her lip.

"I'm asking myself, lass, just what is it about my bath you find so amusing? Or is it more the thought of what I could do with you in this watery oasis...", he murmured, and came nearer. Too near. Lou could feel herself blushing again. Suddenly, her legs felt rubbery. His voice made the swarm of butterflies in her stomach flutter wildly again. She gulped, but didn't try to avoid his index finger, which, once again, traced the contours of her face in slow motion.

He stroked gently over her lips down to her chin, followed her neck down to the collarbone, between her breasts down to the waistband of her jeans. There, his index finger hooked in, and pulled her against his muscled upper body with a jerk.

"Whatever shall I do with you, A' gearmailteach", he murmured hoarsely. Her answer was silenced by his skillful soft lips, which made her want more, once again. More of this man.

God in Heaven, this guy can kiss!

Before she knew what was happening, he was pushing her body further into the bathroom with his own. He noticed her resistance. "Tell me a little about your German customs. Are *Lederhosen* something like our kilts here?", he began to divert her, but kept pulling her along. As he seated himself on the rim of the bathtub, she landed on his lap.

Now it was her turn to hold down laughter. Alasdair actually thought those were typical for Germany: *Lederhosen*, *Dirndl*, *Sauerkraut* and cuckoo clocks. The usual cliché. Lou set him straight. Those were traditions from specific regions and had nothing to do with everyday German culture, with the possible exception of Sauerkraut, which some people did like to eat. It was no more universal fare, however, than Frenchmen eating snails every day, or Scots haggis. And the famous *Lederhosen* were traditional only for certain regions in Bavaria, mostly Alpine, and no self-respecting German from, say, Hamburg, would be caught dead in one. She told him about some of the other German traditions. He found the Bavarian *Fensterln* very interesting (courting a girl under her window) and asked her to make Swabian *Spätzle* for him sometime (a special kind of noodles). She promised to do so, but forgot to mention that she couldn't cook, nor that she hadn't the slightest idea where to get the requisite special *Spätzle* press here in Scotland. As it turned out, Alasdair didn't like haggis, though he knew how to make it, as he explained to her.

His fingers wandered on their own while they were talking, dipping teasingly under her loose sweatshirt. Who knew where that might have led, if a piercing scream hadn't suddenly reached them from downstairs. They flew apart, startled.

"What..?", she started.

Alasdair shook his head, mumbling reluctantly in Gaelic, while already hurrying to the stairs. She had only been able to understand something like "That's Gracie… something's upset her…". Undecided, she wondered what to do. Finally, she decided to follow the Scot.

The sight that greeted her in the almost abandoned café wasn't pleasant. Alasdairs daughter Grace was out of control. Like a dervish, the girl whirled through the room, toppling chairs, pulling cloths off the tables, so that several vases were already broken on the floor. The few customers left in the café were fleeing hurriedly outside. Fascinated, she watched the man's hands, that had been wandering over her body so tenderly just a few minutes ago. Now, they were dancing wildly in the air.

It seemed that father and daughter were having a spirited discussion. Of course, she couldn't tell exactly, but she had seen a lot of sign language lately. Doc was also suddenly back, pressing against her shin and whining.

"The girl just needs a mother to confide in", Marge snorted next to her, disapprovingly. A flood of gray hair had escaped her bun, while her cheeks were reddened from work and she was drying her hands on her apron. Lou avoided the awkward topic by asking: "What are they arguing about?"

"Well, they're not really arguing. Rather, they're discussing certain things Grace is hiding from her father, as well as us", Marge explained, hastily reaching for a broom.

"Grace is just as stubborn as Al. I'd really like to know how long things can go on like this…", the older woman scolded, while pushing past Lou.

Indecisively, she stood where she was, only to be almost bowled over the next moment by a tearful Grace. As if that weren't enough, her stupidly loyal dog followed on the girl's heels. "Stop! Here, Doc!", she exclaimed, cursing, but he took no notice.

An apprehensive look at Alasdair showed him tearing at his hair. Suddenly, she thought of Richard. Even today, when he was 21, she had no close bond to her oldest son. How often had she asked herself what she had done wrong in his upbringing. She could see the same question unspoken in Alasdair's face. That didn't calm her, though. On the contrary, she didn't wish even more problems on him than he had already. She watched as Marge flinched at his look, and closed her mouth without saying anything. "Not a word, mo màthair", he growled at her.

Moving past Marge, he pushed Lou outside without a word. She gave Marge an apologetic shrug, who nodded understandingly in agreement.

"Hmpf!" As if she didn't have enough on her plate with her own problems and her feelings for this screwy guy! Why couldn't she just leave? Unfortunately, she was old enough to know all too well that it was impossible to run from problems. This damn Scot had woken something in her that had been buried deeply. Feelings that she feared more than desired. It was too late, though! Whatever she tried to tell herself – the truth was, she had fallen head over heels in love. She couldn't go back into the shell she had hidden herself in for years. Except in novels, she had all but forgotten love, had forsworn it. Well, but it seemed love had not forgotten her!

So, Louise, what has it come to? You've been unfaithful to your husband with a macho, casually fallen in love with a man who lives in a dead-end village in the middle of nowhere. Goddamittohell, Lou. This guy brings you even more problems than you had already!, her conscience told her darkly.

He didn't let go of her, nor did she try to flee. She just couldn't do it.

After a detour through the kitchen, they sat with two bottles of beer in hand on the roof of the veranda, which could be reached through his bedroom. Skillfully, he opened her bottle, using the rim of a roof tile. He handed it to her without looking at her. For a long while they sat, companionably but silently, staring into the enchanting garden, or sipping at their beers. Such a long time, that Lou thought she would go crazy, at the side of this strange man.

"You shouldn't have involved yourself with me, lass", he murmured bitterly. The dark timbre of his voice gave weight to his words. Lou almost choked, froze.

"I'm not the man for a woman like you, aye", he explained. "Maybe it was a mistake, with us. Don't misunderstand me. It was wonderful, but... I don't think feelings are enough... I've been alone too long, Louise."

His words spread like burning acid in her stomach. This was exactly what she had been afraid of. So, she wasn't good enough for him. In the end, he had just used her like one of his floozies.

"You regret it...", she started, while her fingers gripped the neck of the bottle so tightly she was afraid it would break.

She heard a sad laugh. "Regret? Are we back on that subject? If it were only so simple, a Dhia, Lou. The truth? You want to know the truth?", he exclaimed, with eyes that were now the sinister blue of a stormy sky.

She gritted her teeth defiantly, nodded.

"I regret nothing we did together", he said fervently, looking deeply into her eyes.

"What I regret is letting it go so far between us. You'll go back to your old life..."

"No, I...", she tried to object, but he wouldn't let her.

"Yes, lass. Go back to your husband, your sons, and your job. I'm not good for you. I'm a nobody", he interrupted her, in a tightly controlled voice.

"Why do you say such things, Al? Why are you pushing me away?", she whispered, in a voice full of tears.

"Because you deserve the truth. This is the truth, mo cridhe, even if it hurts. Leave my life, lass, before it's too late."

She hated herself for letting him see the tears running freely down her angrily reddened cheeks. "All right. If that's what you want, I'll go. I'm sorry for you, Munro. I was crazy enough to believe I actually meant something to you. My mistake. It won't happen again." Carefully, with legs that felt as if they would stop obeying her any instant, she got up. "At least I was well serviced. You had a lot of stamina. That's what they say about the Scots, don't they, lad?"

The ice in her words dismayed even herself, as she poured the rest of her beer over Alasdair Munro's head with a false smile.

She climbed from the veranda roof and ran out of the house so quickly, she never even heard him call after her.

A Scot at the window

The first clear thought he managed was: Dearg Amadain, cac! He had blown it. Barefoot, and with a shirt dripping with beer, he had tried to catch up with the German. In vain. The first woman since Grace's birth who had pierced his armor, who had made his heart sing, and he had pushed her away. Angrily, he threw the beer bottle against the wall, where it burst in a shower of glass. It was better like this. Better for Louise. Then why did he feel so guilty? Why did the thought hurt him so much that she now felt herself used, that she was sitting crying in his cottage?
"What an asshole you've made of me, Felicitas", he whispered into the evening. He cursed the missing 'E' in Lou's rental inquiry for the cottage. How could he even think for a moment, that a woman like Louise would stay with a man who was up against the wall financially.
The guest rooms of the Bed & Breakfast had been his last chance. But fate had sent him foot-and-mouth disease. Horrendous veterinary bills had exploded his rescue plan. Alasdair Munro stood on the edge of ruin.
Armed with a fresh beer, he went to the garage where his baby, his bike, stood. Reverently, his fingertips brushed along chrome and metal. Caressed the broad leather belt. His shirt sleeve polished the brooch on the fuel tank cap. As expected, he had already found several buyers for the motorcycle.
He couldn't hold back the tears anymore. Sobbing helplessly, he slid down the wall of the garage to sit on the ground. Would it never stop? Couldn't fate be on his side just once? In torment, he buried his head in his arms, imagined Lou holding him, whispering loving words to him. Love and comfort. He saw again her tears, felt the hurt he

had done her with his words. His bonnie lass had paid him back in the same coin. Her words still gnawed at his ego.

"At least I was well serviced. You had a lot of stamina. That's what they say about the Scots, don't they, lad?"

Her words ran through his head in an endless circle. Sleep was out of the question. Alasdair tossed and turned in his bed. He had again needed a whole hour to persuade Grace to go to sleep. What the hell was going on with his little girl? At eight years old, she was still far from puberty, wasn't she? He was used to her not letting him help her. But Marge and Conner? Yet even they couldn't find access to the girl. Suddenly, she would no longer let anyone close. She would confide in no one, and he didn't like that at all. How could he help her, if she wouldn't let him?

Her teacher could also make no sense of her behavior. There were no problems at school, she had told him.

Should he make himself ask Lou to talk to his little girl? The German woman seemed to be the only one to still somehow connect to Grace. On the other hand, his problems wouldn't get lessened by that, since Lou wouldn't be in Scotland much longer, he was pretty certain of that.

Besides, what had happened between them wasn't so easy to just undo! He wasn't the right man for a woman who was so beautiful, she could easily pose on a catwalk for a some famous fashion label.

Damn, he shouldn't have thought about her, and her soft body. He should have kept his hands off her, dammit! Now he was hopelessly lost. Whenever he closed his weary eyes, he saw again her wounded doe eyes, watched the swaying walk of her long slim legs. He still seemed to feel the sweetness of her soft lips against his, feel how she had willingly followed his movements as he had taken her on the counter of the bakeshop, so full of passion, so full of desire. It seemed he could still hear her quiet moans of passion as they had continued to make love on the floor, slower but also more tenderly.

„Dearg amadain!", he groaned in frustration. Annoyed, he rolled out of bed. "Stamina…. Damn woman." Shaken to the core, he took a cold shower. Unfortunately, that didn't help much. Before he knew what he was doing, he had put on fresh jeans and a T-Shirt. The front door closed behind him softly. He hadn't had so much to drink that he couldn't go for a ride on his baby.

The Harley Davidson 74 Knucklehead was quickly pushed some meters from the house, so the sound of the motor wouldn't wake Grace and his parents. Without a helmet, he let his wet hair stream around his ears in the slipstream. For a whole hour, he rode about randomly, not even knowing where he wanted to go. Like a bad joke, he ended up in front of his own cottage without consciously intending it. There was no light. Lou was probably sleeping peacefully. Was she dreaming of him? He didn't dare give a single thought to what she might be dreaming of….

A Dhia, what was wrong with him? He couldn't allow himself to fall in love with her. His heart was much too scarred for a forbidden love.

"She's dreaming of cutting off your balls and roasting them in a skittle. And she has every right to do so", he castigated himself. Restless, he left the bike standing, but walked in the other direction, to the Loch. Once there, he spent some time skipping stones over the smooth surface of the water, while pondering himself and the life he led.

Late the same evening, she sat before the crackling fire, whisky in hand and looking into the flame musingly. Her smartphone had shown even more messages and missed calls than the days before, which was probably due to her having had uninterrupted reception for a while in Alasdair's café. Unfortunately, more than half of them were due to Alexander. Each of those messages made her feel guilty. Maybe she was simply too honest to have an affair. Didn't all those people who strayed have consciences?

She hated the thought that Alexander was suffering because of her. Heavens, she wasn't like Constance, who would sell her own grandmother for her career. Maybe she should have put on her beer goggles for that horrible guy in the pub? She wouldn't have cried any tears over that one, that was for sure! No, it had to be that miserable Munro. What did a woman like her want with a man like Alasdair? Not only was he younger than her, he probably had women lining up for him.
"He's an asshole, and not worth thinking about!", she encouraged herself, and raised her cup full of whisky to her favorite book: „Slàinte mhath! Thank you, Ms. Gabaldon, it's your fault I'm in this sticky situation now!", she slurred. But wasn't it unjust to blame an author for her own childish behavior? After all, she had only brought the yearnings of women to paper, given them a body and some character. It wasn't Alasdair's fault he couldn't live up to that heroic image. Honestly, though – which flesh and blood man could ever measure up to the Jamies, Mr. Darcys or Christian Greys? None.

On the other hand, it could have been much worse. She could have ended up tied to a bed with zip-ties. Good, consensual sex was, she had to admit, the much better alternative.

"Be damn..damned to alllll mennn. Another ..hup.. whisshki to that.."

Doc was looking at her queerly. But maybe it just looked that way because the room was beginning to spin.

"Ooopss… too much whisshki…"

At least now, she wouldn't have to admit her miserable cooking skills to him. After what had happened, he could forget about their date for the next day. She had no intention of cooking for that bastard now. Though it would have been easy for her to poison him. It was just a pity about the ingredients, which she had bought for exorbitant prices in the little village store. Oh well, it hadn't been the right cheese anyway. Maybe she could use that for something else. Her search for the right dough for *Käsespätzle* on the Internet had also been in vain.

She took a look at the sketch of Alasdair on her pad. She had caught his likeness well. Too well. Seconds later, the sketch was crumpled into a ball. That didn't stop a tingling from spreading all over her body as she thought of him, though.

"Forty. You're … hup… forty, not a teen…", she scolded herself. More crawling than walking, she dragged herself to her bedroom, where she had to put out a leg to keep the bed from spinning like a carousel, thanks to the amount of alcohol she had consumed.

Alasdair didn't stay long at the Loch. Lou kept running through his confused thoughts. He felt terrible. Had he destroyed their relationship, before it had even begun? Soon, he was sneaking around his own cottage like a restless predator, looking for some sign from inside, which wouldn't come. The stars in the sky shone lavishly on him, almost as if he were standing in the spotlight of their ridicule. Loser. Idiot. Lousy lover, they seemed to call to him. He hadn't felt this shabby in all his life.

Gazing at the front door, he scraped his shoes nervously on the dirt-crusted wooden boards. What the hell was he doing here? He could hardly just put the key in the lock and walk in, even if that was what he had been about to do.

„Dearg amadain." Retard, he cursed himself. That had been a really stupid idea. If he scared Lou to death, she certainly wouldn't offer him a place in her bed. Suddenly, the scales fell from his eyes and he saw clearly. He, Alasdair Munro, the betrayed Scot, who had armored his heart against anyone wearing a dress. He, who only brought women to his bed for casual sex. Of all people, love had smitten him, and now it was making him a laughingstock. Not bad enough that he had fallen in love in the first place, though that was absolutely the last thing he needed. No. The pile of shards that was his heart had picked a married tourist from Germany, of all people. A woman he had already explained to, in exhaustive detail, why he was absolutely the wrong man for her. How stupid could you get?

He fled with long strides, but didn't get farther than the edge of the property, where he stopped, gasping for air. Louise Schulzinger surely wasn't the right one for him, was she? But what if she was? What if she, of all people, was brave enough to sift through the shards of his heart? Would she persevere, regardless of cuts? Not leave him? What if Louise tried to heal him, for the sake of the man he had once been? Would he ever know, if he was too cowardly now to fight for her? He wasn't the only one with inner demons. Louise had her own.

"Oh, come on, Alasdair. What decent husband would let his wife move to a desolate spot like this for months?", he encouraged himself.

"None that has all his marbles! I certainly would never have let a woman like Louise go!"

Decisively, and with firm steps, he went toward the old barn. It was out of the question for him to find sleep this night, unless he could get forgiveness for his words. So, he would try that strange custom from Germany, or was it Bavaria? Whatever, something about a window. Well, he would try it, even though it would be a tight fit for him through the tiny, crooked bedroom window. But maybe it would impress Lou enough that she would listen to him asking for forgiveness. "Or else she pushes you off the ladder. Ha, that's if you don't fall all on your own!", he grumbled to himself.

The old ladder from the barn under his arm, he went to work. Admittedly, he felt a bit queasy, as the ladder had seen better days, and besides, he felt a bit ridiculous with what he was doing. The bedroom window looked even smaller close up. He hoped Lou delivered him quickly.

Ten minutes later, his idea seemed more and more stupid, as the object of his desire would not hear him. All his knocking, hammering, or shaking the window was to no avail.

Nothing moved inside, except for the dog, who watched him skeptically, wagging his tail. Where in the world was Lou? Had something happened to her? Was she hurt? One question after another shot through his head, while the old ladder creaked ever worse under his weight and he wrenched at the window. Maybe he should rather be thinking about his own neck, he thought.

Another possibility would be to simply bash in the window. On the other hand, buying a new window, one specially fitted what's more, wasn't exactly the cheapest alternative for someone who's back was already to the wall financially.

Next moment, he almost lost his balance as the sleepy face of his bonnie lass suddenly looked at him from inside. Just in time, she reacted by pulling open the window and removing the annoying glass between them.

"What the hell are you doing, Munro? Have you gone crazy?", she snarled at him, making no move to let him in.

"I wanted to… well… I admit this isn't exactly optimal.."

With an angry "Forget it!" she slammed the window shut again. He just managed to save his fingers, but that made the ladder sway alarmingly.

„Daingead, cac!", he hissed. Knocking at the window, he pleaded: "Louise, Lou, please listen to me!"

The window jerked open again. "Somehow I can't think of any reason to, Munro. Strange, isn't it?"

"Please. I fuc-… fouled up, okay? No question about it. I told you, I've lived alone for eight years. At least, without a woman and… Say, have you been drinking?"

Lou's attempt to close the window failed, as he had already stemmed both arms in the wooden frame.

"That's none of your business, is it? Besides, I'm sober again!", she growled at him.

"For someone who's sober, you have quite the breath! Whisky, I assume?"

"You're boring, Munro. I don't feel like any more discussions in the middle of the night with you, of all people, Mr. Expert Womanizer. Excuse me!" Wagging her hand, she tried to shoo him away. Unfortunately, that didn't work, even if he had wanted it to, as he felt another rung break under his feet at just that moment.

"I made a mistake, lass. I thought if I denied my feelings for you, they'd go away. If you feel anything for me, Lou, then let me in now, before I fall. I promise not to do anything you don't want!" Not a second too soon, he squeezed through the narrow window, while the ladder fell apart under him. He thankfully availed himself of her helping hand, never taking his gaze from her tear-stained eyes.

He had felt somewhat queasy at thinking of Lou in his house. Or rather, of her in this bedroom, with the bed in which he had begotten Grace on Felicitas. Now, however, he could hardly take his eyes from her. His heart wanted to jump from his chest jubilantly as he saw her clad in his own T-shirt. A red Guns'n'Roses T-Shirt he had looked for in vain for the washing. It looked incredibly good on her, but barely covered her shapely behind. Her short hair was bristling in all directions, and there was a worried look on her face.

"I thought I'd try that thing with the window to apologize and..", he tried to joke. It was an attempt to distract from his rubbery legs, and also to calm Lou. She was still slightly drunk, he could see that from her uncoordinated movements. "But maybe I should have used the door, if I had suspected how much I had hurt you!"

He never saw the slap coming, which she gave him with her free hand, before throwing herself in his arms, almost making him lose his balance.

"Tell me that noise wasn't the ladder collapsing!", she cried accusingly, while pressing herself against him.

"Umm..", he cleared his throat uncertainly.

Her whole body was trembling. "You stupid idiot", she scolded, appalled, as if she already knew the answer. "You could have fallen! Do you realize that!"

He had no difficulty holding her hands, to stop her from hitting him again. Well. She was right. Trying to be romantic after one had hurt the other badly wasn't such a great idea. He regretted having used the ladder now. If he hadn't been lucky, he might be lying with broken limbs or, worse, a broken neck, under the bedroom window. It looked as if his apology had gone totally wrong. On the other hand, she seemed to be anxious about him. A feeling of warmth spread through him. Did she feel more for him than he had thought, after all?

"Hey, lass. It's all right. Could you calm down please, aye?" He let go of her hands, but cautiously took a step back. A bit of caution was seldom amiss. Lou looked at him apologetically.

"I'm sorry, Al. I didn't mean to hit you... But that was really the craziest idea I've ever seen. My God, if you had fallen... You could have broken your neck!"

Her voice was almost inaudible, she spoke so quietly. She had called him Al again. He loved hearing her use his nickname so tenderly. She had no idea what she did to him. Entranced, his eyes wandered along her sweet body, resting at last on the twin pistol barrels of the Guns'n'Roses T-shirt, which met exactly between her breasts. At the thought that he had been wearing this very T-shirt, which was now barely covering her enchanting body, just a short time before, he suddenly felt even hotter than he was already. He cleared his throat loudly, to get his voice, as well as other parts of his body, under control again.

"Aye. I have to admit it wasn't the best idea I've ever had. It's just that I couldn't think of any other way to get you to listen to me. I wish I could plausibly explain how it happened, that I hurt you so badly yesterday. As you can see, I'm not a man of many words, nor am I much of a romantic... what I said wouldn't let me rest. I drove to the Loch, wandered around and... well, I hadn't thought that this thing with the window would be so hard."

He was really doing his best to explain his motivations, without making a complete fool of himself because of his emotions. Which, to be honest, wasn't exactly easy.

It seemed, though, that she had seen right through him, at least she looked as if she knew all his secrets, with that little quirk of her lips.

Dear God, how could I fall so hard for this woman?

Unable to resist, he moved closer to her, reached with his index finger to touch that entrancing corner of her mouth, then following it to her warm, soft lips. She made no move to hinder him. Instead, she gave him a cheeky smile, while inserting her own index finger in the waistband of his pants and pulling him to her, just as he had done the day before.

Daingead, lass. You learn quickly!

"That wasn't in proper style, though, Mr. Scotsman. A Jamie would have climbed in here gallant in a kilt", she teased him quietly.

"Aye, that may be, lass",

he admitted, smiling in amusement, "but I thought one of us should have the pants on, and that's not you at the moment, mo cridhe", he explained, while his hand could no longer resist the temptation, and cupped her bare bottom under the T-shirt teasingly.

"Point for you, Munro!", came hoarsely from the mouth he now neared to kiss. In the blink of an eye, everything had become simple.

He no longer gave a thought to what had happened eight years ago in this bed, nor to Felicitas. All that mattered were Lou and himself. It was as if their bodies were giving each other long forgotten answers to something they had both been searching for desperately for years, but had only found this night.

After they had made love, he finally managed to ask the questions that had been torturing his soul.

"Why me, of all people, lass? All I can offer you are my hands, my stubborn head, and a broken heart. Any money I ever had, my ex-wife got. I'm a terrible catch for a lady like you, Louise. Not to mention my deaf daughter, who hates her father… So, why me, Lou? Why would you want to stay with me?"

The sudden silence between them was unbearable. Cold, leaden fear weighed on him. Her answer came slowly, haltingly, yet it was all he had hoped for.

"Because you are you, Alasdair. You see me. Not the rich wife. Not the artist or mother. You see me. Without make-up, with all my scars, all my faults. You give me the feeling I'm myself again. That's why I've fallen in love with you!"

Nothing in the world could have been more beautiful than Alasdair's face as he understood what she had just revealed to him. For herself, it was also a revelation. Up until this moment, she hadn't been certain about her feelings for the Scot. After all, a straw fire also burned brightly for a short time, but in the end it was gone completely. Was she really capable of leaving everything behind for a new love? Maybe it was simply because she hadn't been this close to a man for over five years.

Alasdair looked happy, sitting there. His long legs sprawled loosely, his eyes seemed to see all the way into her soul.

"Oh Al, what do you want with someone like me? You have a well-toned athletic body, and you're fully four years younger than me. I have stretch-marks, a slack stomach and I don't even want to mention all the grey hairs.. Why don't you get yourself a pretty girl of your own age? They must be crazy about a well set-up man like you," she tried to relieve the seriousness of her words with a joke. She heard a sarcastic laugh.

"A Dhia, Lou. Are you joking? You're not really worrying about a piddling four years, are you? I assure you, I'm not! Besides, I'm neither under age nor retarded. We're both adults, and knew what we were doing. I like the battle scars of your pregnancies. You shouldn't be ashamed of them, rather carry them proudly! I don't understand who convinced you you're not beautiful. Your husband? If that's so, if he doesn't love you as you are, then the man doesn't deserve you, Lou! Besides, I hate tarted-up women, just as I hate the ones who wouldn't have anything to do with an ugly guy without a penny in his pocket, who's also a single father!"

That last sounded so bitter, she felt compelled to wind her fingers around his to make him look in her eyes.

"You're not ugly, Al. I think you're masculine and attractive. I can also find no fault with your competence as a father. In fact, you're just the wonderful father an enchanting girl like Grace deserves. Anyone who says differently is just blind", she whispered firmly.

"About my husband…I…I don't want to talk about him. If you really loved a woman, Al, no matter what she looked like, would you… not… for years… I mean…", she stuttered, embarrassed, while feeling her cheeks grow warm, signaling a revealing blush.

Alasdair looked at her in obvious shock.

"You didn't have sex anymore?", he exclaimed. His hand pulled her closer into a firm embrace.

"That explains your lack of confidence, mo cridhe", he whispered into her hair. "Your husband is an even bigger idiot than I had thought. I'm so sorry, Lou."

Gently his lips touched hers, whose trembling betrayed how hard it was for her to hold back her tears. He kissed her tenderly, until she finally responded. Heated, and with swollen lips, they finally left off after a good long while.

Lou tried to memorize this moment, take in every nuance of his face so she could later reproduce it on canvas or in her sketch pad. Would it really be possible for her to go back to Alexander after this affair? Back to a life without love, to continue playing her ordained role in their family charade? She couldn't help moving closer to the man at her side, drew her fingers over his muscular chest and laid her cheek on his shoulder again.

"Felicitas turned me into a nervous wreck. I used to do guide tours in the historic quarter of Edinburgh. That's where we met. Since our divorce, I haven't set foot in the city. I've never felt so whole, and full of life, with any woman but you!", he confessed to her, before they both finally fell asleep.

The next morning began with a knot of arms and legs, in which she had lost all feeling. Alasdair had buried her completely under his body. Lou tried to keep breathing softly, so she could watch him in his sleep. The peaceful sleep gave him the appearance of an overlarge boy. The first hairs of his beard were already sprouting on his cheeks. She was so immersed in watching him, that she didn't immediately notice he was already awake.

"And how did I do yesterday, lass?", he teased her, his hands buried in her hair.

"Oh, you're awake…"

"Am I? Or maybe I'm just having an especially sweet dream. I'm not really sure just now", he answered her with amusement and sparkling eyes.

"A good B plus, if you really want to know, Munro", she retorted cheekily, just to pay him back. His eyebrows shot up! "What? Only a B?"

"Plus", she retorted gravely, though she had to bite her lip to keep from bursting out laughing.

"A B? Hard to believe…", he growled next to her, while his hands were already moving on her naked body with expert skill. Prickling heat spread through her whole body.

"So this is only a B plus, mo cridhe?", he whispered, his fingers teasing the tips of her breasts maddeningly.

A sensual moan escaped her involuntarily. Bastard! His lips followed his fingers, which were now moving to the pulsing wetness at her center.

"Just a B, aye, lass", he breathed in her ear, which he was nibbling on. His exciting hardness pressed flatteringly against her backside. Lou's ears seemed to be glowing, just like every inch of her skin which the damned Scot was touching.

"To the devil with the plus, mo cridhe. I'm going for an A", he let her know hoarsely, before he tongued the rest of her body into flames skillfully. Alasdair Munro knew exactly what he was doing. This man made her burst into fireworks!

Lou was hopelessly in flames, exploded at his first thrust. But that wasn't enough for the Scotsman by a long shot. Teasing unbearably, stroking, exciting her with every last thrust, he drove her out of her mind completely. He drove her higher and higher, until they reached the highest peak of lust and love together and exploded.

"Now don't say that wasn't an A with a damned plus!", he exclaimed, gasping for air.

"No. A B with two Plus, Al. An A plus wouldn't be only for me", Lou answered quietly, gaze averted, so he wouldn't see the tears in her eyes. Controlling herself with difficulty, she slid to the edge of the bed, taking the coverlet with her, and tried to get up.

"Lou?"

His arm around her hips stopped her escape.

"Did I do something wrong, mo cridhe?" His voice trembled a little, sounded anxious.

She couldn't stop her loud sob.

"Look at me, lass. Everything is okay. There is nothing you need to be ashamed of with me, my bonnie lass. Nothing you need be afraid of. I'm here, Lou!" He drew her closer carefully, turned her averted face so he could see her. Tenderly, without another word, he kissed away every one of the tears running silently down her cheeks.

"It's just, I… I don't remember when I last felt so, so…" Lou couldn't say the word "loved" aloud, because if she did that again now, then she would reveal her most inner self to Alasdair, and she couldn't allow that. Not yet. But even that didn't seem to matter to this man, this incarnation of her dreams. He simply closed his strong arms around her trembling body, cradling her with gentle movements, as if she were a small child. She had never wished more fervently to be able to just let go.

But she couldn't do it. A quote from Constance went through her mind: " The mistake most women make with adultery, is that they aren't just unfaithful with their plumbing, but with their heart, soul and mind!" That certainly wasn't true for all women, but in her case, it hit the nail on the head. She had screwed up totally, had let a man into her heart who furthered her yearning for a fresh start.

Soon after, she stole off to the toilet, wrapped in the coverlet to cover herself.

"Why are you suddenly hiding yourself from me, lass?"

"Because…. Do you really have to know everything, Alasdair Munro?", she defended herself, but froze in place uncertainly.

He laughed softly. "No, only about you. But, since I've already seen every inch of your beautiful body, I have to ask myself, what's wrong with you all of a sudden?", he asked, in a tone of voice that made it clear he meant the question seriously.

Braver than she really felt, she let the coverlet fall and posed for his admiring gaze. "Better?", she exclaimed sarcastically.

The wide grin from ear to ear she earned would have been enough for her, but the hoarse: "Aye, mo cridhe. I never had a better view!" had the butterflies in her stomach fluttering so violently that she almost walked into the frame of the bathroom door. God in heaven, how did this guy know exactly how to get to her?

"Goddammittohell, why can't I resist this man? What's wrong with me?", she scolded her reflection that looked at her with reddened cheeks and swollen lips. As much cold water as she threw in her face by handfuls, it didn't help a bit. Darned. All through her body, the hormones were boiling like water in a kettle.

Decisively, she climbed into the bathtub, turning the shower progressively colder, while she leaned against the cool tiles with her eyes closed. She knew he was there, though she hadn't heard the door or any other sound. Nonetheless, she could feel him standing in the tub behind her, though he didn't touch her. Yet. His body radiated warmth. Even when his hands braced themselves to left and right of her, he left a space between their bodies.

"I could have told you that a cold shower wouldn't help with us two", he breathed confidingly in her ear.

"You don't say. And how do you know that so certainly?", she answered the man, who drove her crazy yet again by leaning against her suddenly, so he could adjust the temperature.

"Aye. I tried that myself, before I drove here to you", he confided, beginning to spread shower gel on her back with circular motions of his hand.

"Let me guess, Al. We won't be getting out of here in a hurry, will we?"

His answer wasn't given in words.

Suddenly Mrs. Munro

Despite a lack of sleep, yet again, he was so cheerful that his father looked at him in some irritation in the bakeshop. Conner had not, though, said a single word about the easily visible love bite on his neck, which he wore like a trophy. For the first time in his life, he believed in fate. Even Grace's dim mood as she got on the bus, which took her to school at Inverness, like every morning, couldn't make him despair.

Instead, he swore to his daughter that he would persuade Lou to accompany her to school some day soon, even though he still didn't know why a woman should be able to help Grace with her unvoiced problems better than he. Was she in love, too?

All his thoughts on this morning circled around the woman who was healing his broken heart. Had she found her breakfast yet? He had tiptoed out, so as not to wake her. He had almost fallen over the dog in the living room, who had left them when they couldn't keep their hands off each other. Moving quickly, he had set the table for her, had made coffee, and put it in the old thermos. He had cut the last rose from the garden, and placed it in a glas on the table as a decoration. A Dhia, this woman even managed to make a romantic of a cranky guy like him! A wide grin transfigured his face.

A B with two plus, because an A isn't for one alone, he heard her say in his thoughts. Actually, her confessions had already gotten under his skin. Louise Schulzinger hadn't ever said the three special words. That hadn't been necessary, though. He'd have to have been blind to miss what was in her enchanting doe eyes, and interpret it correctly. Every one of her tears told him more than he needed to know, more than he had ever dared to hope.

After doing his baker chores, he had returned somewhat later to put freshly baked buns on the table. As promised, this time he had used his key and come in the door, though taking the precaution of bribing Doc with a large fresh bone from Gregory, the butcher.

The weather report had promised fine weather for today and the next day, but cautioned that regional changes were possible. He was used to the constantly changing four seasons in one day, had been so all his life. Luckily, Lou also seemed inured to the changeable weather.

After a visit to the lower pasture, on an impulse, he brought his baby out of the garage again, though he had been meaning to finally ready it for a buyer instead, after the ride last night. Reverently, his fingers stroked chrome, steel and the old leather of the Harley Davidson. As always, he lingered at the ancestral belt, then polished the plaid brooch that was fused to the filler cap with his shirtsleeve.

Whenever he thought about all the blood, sweat and tears invested in this wonderful machine, tears of frustration came to his eyes. His baby was as good as sold. Any Harley Davidson rider would sell his grandmother for a rarity like a 74 Knucklehead. None of them could know the true worth of the machine to him, though. The decision to sell it hadn't been easy, but he didn't really have any other choice. Too many open bills had to be paid. This might be his last ride with this machine. Maybe Lou would like to go on a little ride, over to Ranoch Moor and Glen Coe? At this time of year, there weren't quite as many tourist busses on the road. She loved the Scottish scenery, and the valley of Glen Coe was very picturesque.

His old leather jacket would doubtless be far too large for her slim upper body, but he was sure she would gladly trade stylish clothes for the feeling of freedom and the slipstream on the motorcycle. Maybe it was egotistical of him, but the only thing that could make the last ride on his bike even better, would be to share the feeling of freedom with the woman who had managed to wake his hope for a better future. Even now, just thinking about her, his heart started pounding wildly. Lost in thought, he leaned against his machine

The morning had gone by on wings, as usual. Grace should be finished with school soon. Lou was surely already waiting at the school, as she tended to be overpunctual. Did she already regret having let him persuade her to this strange excursion? What in the world had Grace done, he asked himself for the hundredth time.

Lou had spent all morning at the shore of the Loch, paying no heed to the raindrops which came and went. Alasdair, as well as the Scottish landscape with its magical, always changing light, had provided a real artistic boost. She had already finished her third sketch. Elated, she packed her utensils, then changed and delivered Doc to Marge.

She couldn't deny being somewhat apprehensive about being alone with Grace. Would the girl be able to make her comprehend everything? She didn't know sign language, nor had she anyone along who did. She just hoped Grace's problem was one she could actually help with.

"Dear God, please let me find the school and a parking space right away!", Lou prayed aloud. Inverness wasn't exactly a small town, and her having to cope with the huge Jeep, as well as driving on the left, didn't exactly make things easier!

Luckily, she had started out early. For seemingly the tenth time, she ended up in a one-way street leading by Inverness Castle. Impulsively, she turned into a large parking lot beneath the castle hill to turn around. This didn't seem to please the parking attendant at all, though, as he came running up, gesticulating wildly. Angrily, the old gentleman explained that she had just driven into his parking lot through the exit. He wouldn't let her back out, but made her turn around, under his instruction, regardless of the narrow space available.

Grinding her teeth, and soaked in sweat, she made it back to the one-way street. In the square before Inverness Castle she stopped for a bit, hugging the wheel and taking deep breaths. It almost seemed as if the statue of Flora MacDonald was watching her disapprovingly from its pedestal.

She finally managed to reach Grace's school a half hour later. On rubbery legs, and with ruined coiffure, she left the teacher's parking lot, praying she wouldn't get a ticket. The school bell rang piercingly, while hordes of students were already flowing over the wide staircase outside the old Victorian building. For a school for the deaf, it was anything but quiet.

Lou found Grace almost immediately. She was standing next to a petite woman above the school stairs, and was waving to her to come over.

The unknown woman gave Lou a friendly smile.

"Ah, you must be Grace's mother. My name is Fiona Lewis, I'm Grace's homeroom teacher!"

Lou barely managed to keep her features under control. What the hell? "I…um… I'm pleased to meet you, Mrs. Lewis. Louise..um.. Schulz… um… Munro", she stumbled, trying to put a good face on this strange situation. Grace gave her a cheerful grin, as if there was nothing out of the ordinary.

"Grace has her writing tablet along, I'm supposed to tell you. Oh, and before I forget, if you're interested, I can recommend our sign language class. It's really not so difficult to learn, and with a bit of practice your language difficulties will be a thing of the past", Grace's teacher explained.

Heavens, what had Grace been telling her? Alasdair's daughter seemed to be a crafty little devil.

"Oh. Thank you, Mrs. Lewis. That's very kind of you", she answered, while piercing Grace with a drop-dead look her sons knew all too well. Unfortunately, it showed no effect on the girl. Lou couldn't say what she preferred, to drop dead immediately herself, or to disappear into some hole and not come out until this farce was over.

God, how embarrassing!, she screamed inwardly.

"Gladly, Mrs. Munro. You wouldn't believe how happy I was for Grace and her father when the girl told me about you. Grace is such an intelligent, talented child. I think it's admirable of you, Mrs. Munro, that you're doing so much for Grace, even though you have no experience with the deaf."

Mrs. Lewis either loved to talk, or she had too much time on her hands. In any case, this embarrassing conversation seemed to last forever. Every time the woman called her "Mrs. Munro", Lou's heart almost stopped. She felt like a fraud. Though she also felt somewhat flattered. Louise Munro. Actually, a nice combination.

"I'm very glad to have met you, Mrs. Munro. Will we see you at the next parent-teacher conference?"

"I... Oh, I'm honestly not sure whether Alasdair, um, my husband, won't want to come instead. About the class, I may contact you, possibly. Thank you, Mrs. Lewis. Have a nice evening!", she quickly said her good-byes.

. She fled with long strides to the jeep, pulling Grace along by her sleeve. There she pushed the girl roughly onto the passenger seat, and didn't dare to breathe freely until she had slammed the door behind her.

Angrily, she scolded Grace: "What the hell were you thinking, Grace? Are you crazy? Your father will kill us both if he finds out, missy! I…. goddammittohell", she exclaimed, exasperated, and took a deep breath, ready to continue scolding the girl, but stopped when she saw her horrified face. Big tears ran down Grace's cheeks. The mouth formed a silent 'O'. Dear God, the girl looked terrified! Lou had forgotten that Grace could only read lips if one spoke clearly and face to face. She had just done neither.

Distraught, the girl pulled her tablet from her bag jerkily. "You don't want to be my Mommy?", she wrote in a childish hand. Tears of shame shot into Lou's eyes. She almost cried herself, so touching was that sentence. Though she couldn't quite rid herself of the feeling that Grace knew exactly how to manipulate her. Shaken, she took a deep breath and pulled herself together. Finally, she turned to the girl and said, enunciating each word clearly:

"I didn't say that, Grace. But don't you think it's a bit early for that?"

"You don't love me?"

"Oh Grace, that has nothing to do with it. Of course I love you!"

"Why don't you want me, then? Because I'm deaf?"

"Dammit, girl, don't say that! I love you just like you are!"

"But you love Daddy, don't you? So what's the problem?"

If it were only as simple as you think, in your childish imagination!, her thoughts protested silently. "Oh Grace, those are things you can't understand yet. I can't explain it to you…"

"I thought you could tell her that you're my Mommy now. That she'd go! But you don't want to and I don't know…". The rest of the sentence was smeared by a flood of tears.

Lou felt alarm bells go off. What the hell did the girl mean?

She pulled the sobbing girl firmly into her arms and hugged her tightly.

"Who am I supposed to tell that to…", she whispered into the girl's hair, then pushed the girl away and said it again into her face: "Who am I supposed to tell that to, Grace?"

"The woman."

"I don't understand. What woman, Grace?", she repeated, ignoring the icy lump in her stomach.

"The one who says she's my Mommy!", the girl scrawled on the tablet in an almost unreadable hand. Not that, too! It just couldn't be! Didn't she already have more problems than she could handle?

It took half an hour for Lou to coax the story from Grace, how Felicitas Munro, Alasdair's divorced wife, had stolen her way back into her daughter's life.

It seemed the woman had lain in wait for Grace in front of her school, with an interpreter in sign language along. She had bluntly introduced herself as Grace's biological mother, and claimed her father had forbidden all contact. Which, Lou guessed, was probably true. She couldn't believe Alasdair would welcome this meeting, if he knew of it.

Secretly, the woman had lain in wait for Grace again and again, taking her to a café beneath Inverness Castle to persuade her with cake and ice cream. Though Grace had voiced her annoyance and unwillingness time and again, the woman would not leave her alone. That was probably why Grace had enlisted Lou, to avoid escalating the situation. God forbid, if Alasdair learned of the affair, all Hell would break loose! The girl had placed all her hope in the new woman at the side of her father.

Dear God, she couldn't leave the girl in the lurch now! Besides, she had good reason to be concerned how Alasdair would react to the return of his hated ex-wife. Very probably anything but pleased! Just what had she gotten herself into, here? Heavens, she had only been looking for a romantic hero, and now what had she found? A new mountain of problems, including a man who could turn her inside out.

Suddenly, she felt herself grow angry, angry at the woman who had left her husband and her newborn behind in a hopeless situation.

They walked to the nearby café at the foot of the castle hill, which was the meeting place. Lou was glad of that, not wanting the attendant of the parking lot across the road to remember her and her parking fiasco. She barely dared look that way, fearing the man might recognize her. She should have taken Doc along. The dog always managed to calm her, and, besides, she could have sicced him on Alasdair's ex-wife if necessary.

Grace indicated a pink house that was almost indistinguishable from the other colorful houses along the street to the castle.

Oh my God, how do I look?, her thoughts screamed. She tried her best to get a good look at her reflection in one of the storefront windows. Sighing, she turned up the collar of her faded jeans jacket, under which her flowered dress showed. If she had had the slightest idea how this afternoon was going to turn out, she would have squeezed herself into her business costume and worn the Jimmy Choos, though those were pretty much ruined. Now it was too late, though. At least she would be able to flee quickly in her Chucks, should that prove necessary.

In front of the café, she took a deep breath and stood up straight, giving Grace an encouraging smile.

Once more into the breach!, she thought sarcastically.

The café revealed a comfortable but almost deserted

interior. At a table in a cozy corner, a woman jumped up, waving to them guardedly.

"Damn!" Lou exclaimed under her breath, seeing the slim brunette. This woman was a beauty, though her steely blue eyes couldn't compare to Alasdair's. These eyes were cold, calculating, and without the slightest friendliness. They made Lou think of glacier waters, and not only because of the colour.

No "Hello", no friendly "Good day", came from the perfectly made-up lips with the tattooed contours. A caustic: "I had really believed the girl was lying to me. But it seems she was telling the truth all along", immediately tried to put Lou in her place.

The answer "Whatever made you think my daughter would lie!" came from Lou's lips so casually and quickly that she was shocked by her own audacity.

I can play that game, too, she thought.

"Well, Alasdair has always had, shall we call it, eccentric tastes, Mrs...."

"Schulzinger, Louise Schulzinger. We're not married. Not yet!" *Heavens, how easily the lies slip from my lips!*

"And, concerning Alasdair's eccentric tastes, well, you're the best example", Lou riposted drily.

Without waiting for an invitation, she took a seat, pulling Grace onto her trembling knees like a shield. For just a moment, Felicitas Munro's perfect features distorted. But she had herself under control again immediately.

What did you expect, Lou? She's a professional actress. Just look at her. Miss Perfect, maybe even plays Broadway.

"Mrs. Leod is kind enough to act as a translator. You really mean to marry? A penniless Scottish farmer? Where did you say you come from, again?"

"Well, Mrs. Munro. Where I come from, and what

Alasdair and I do or don't do, is hardly the issue here", she rejoined. *I'm certainly not telling someone like you about my private life!*

"All right. Excuse me, please. Of course, that's none of my business. I just want to get to know my daughter better. Concerning an advertising campaign, where I help handicapped children…"

Lou interrupted the sentence by jumping up as if stung, pulling Grace up along with her. So, that was it. A smart move by Felicitas Munro. Unfortunately for her, there were two things in Lou's life she knew more about than anyone else: art and advertising.

"How dare you propose something like that! This isn't about Grace. You don't want to get to know the girl at all. Am I right? This is only about you, Felicitas Munro! All you want is to use Grace's deafness for your own publicity. Do you realize what that would do to the girl, *my* girl?"

With pleasure, she watched as Felicitas Munro's face turned the color of freshly fallen snow. Then, however, angry red spots appeared on the woman's cheeks. "Now, that's the limit! You dare… Grace is my flesh and blood. She's my daughter. I'm her mother… you dare, you nobody of a ….."

Counting to ten silently, Lou pulled Grace behind her back, keeping her composure with an effort.

"Slut. That's what you were going to say, isn't it, Mrs. Munro? Though I'm not sure you of all people should use that word!"

Turning to the translator: "Mrs. Leod, I'd be grateful if you didn't translate what's going on here for Grace. Would you be so kind and wait outside with my girl?" she asked the elderly woman, who seemed to want to hide under the table.

"She doesn't understand a word, anyway! Why should she go outside?", Felicitas Munro said dismissively, as the two left the café.

"Grace is neither handicapped nor stupid, Mrs. Munro. The girl notices tension and atmosphere more acutely than either you or me. If you had ever cared for your child, instead of only for publicity and your career, you would know that!", Lou growled, forcing herself to keep calm.

"I'm beginning to see why you two make a good match. You deserve someone like Alasdair. He can't pay his bills, is even about to lose his beloved Baby. Did you know that? I'd be careful who I give my heart to, if I were you. He'll take you down into bankruptcy with him, darling! I only want the best for my child, as any mother would!"

Each word hurt her more than anything had ever before. Still, she managed to answer with an icy voice, more calmly than she felt: " You have no right to use the word 'mother'! You've never in your life acted like a mother. You left Alasdair alone with a newborn baby. You left him to deal alone with all the problems a deaf child brings! You're no mother, Felicitas Munro! Leave my family alone! If you go near Grace again without permission, I'll bring my lawyers down on you, as well as your ex-husband!"

Trembling inside, she turned and left the café, followed by more imprecations and insults. She didn't turn around again. Holding Grace's hand tightly, she forced herself to walk slowly towards her car. She didn't feel like a victor, far from it. Was she really so much better than Felicitas? Wasn't she also leaving her own children in the lurch?

How much trouble was Alasdair in? She knew, of course, that his finances weren't in the best shape. He had told her so, after all. But she hadn't suspected that things were so terrible as this. And besides, who the hell was Baby?

Not enough that she no longer knew up from down with all these questions. No, she'd have to sit across from him soon, and had no idea how she should tell him about the meeting with his ex. Suddenly, she remembered the *Käsespätzle* she had promised to make him. Maybe she should pack her bags, in case he threw her out!

Grace looked longingly at a fish and chips takeaway. Decisively, she squared her shoulders, bought the girl a large portion, and then turned her back on the nightmare Inverness had been today.

Germany

Nice of you to check up on me, Constance, but I'm fine. You don't need to worry", Alexander tried to explain to his wife's friend. All his efforts were in vain, however, she wouldn't leave off. At last he capitulated sullenly, but helped her out of her mink coat like a gentleman and hung the expensive coat carefully on the coat rack. At least Constance was a woman who appreciated style. Louise would have made a scene if he had bought her a mink coat.

I feel sick just thinking about all the minks that are murdered for such an awful thing! Yes, he could remember every word of her comment.

"May I offer you a sherry or something else, my dear?", he turned to Constance, who gave him a charming smile.

"You're a real charmer, Alex. Thank you, I wouldn't say no to a Martini on the rocks."

Smiling, she took his offered arm. He gallantly held the door to his private room for her, or the smoking room, as Louise had always called it disapprovingly. Black varnished shelves and snow-white leather armchairs dominated this room. Louise had avoided it like the plague. He turned his back on the elegant woman to fix their drinks skillfully.

For just a second, he stopped, looking at the rough ice cube he had just taken from the bar's integrated freezer, then let it fall into the Martini glass. His life, with all its priviliges from money and the upper class, seemed to be reaching its limits.

Of course he was concerned about Louise. To be honest, though, he was mostly concerned about whether she was cheating on him. He was a man who moved in the highest circles. Bad press about a wife cuckolding the head of Schulzinger Consulting wouldn't be good, to say the least. There was already enough talk and wild speculation about his marriage, after the fiasco with the birthday party *sans* guest of honor.

To his annoyance, the detective agency he had hired hadn't been able to find Louise, either. And, well, despite Martin's connections to the upper echelons of the police, he had refused to get the GPS data for him. That was asking too much, he said. Argued that it could cost him his career. At least he had Louise's credit cards checked on. Nothing. It seemed his blonde babe wasn't born yesterday. She was cleverer than he would have believed.

Before serving the glasses, he loosened his tie, which seemed to be choking him.

"Everything okay, Alex?", Constance purred behind him. Next second, he felt her fingers massaging the knotted muscles at the back of his neck gently. He hadn't heard her get up.

No. Nothing is okay, nothing at all. My life is going down the drain!, he wanted to say. But he couldn't do it.

"You're all uptight, Alex. Let's have a Havanna, and help you let go for a change. Forget Louise! She doesn't deserve a man like you!"

Constance's words were flattering, salved his wounded ego. Since their wedding 22 years ago, he had feared this day. The day his young, beautiful wife left him for another man.

Was it really because of the difference in their ages, as his mother had always warned him? He and Louise were more than ten years apart, after all.

Several sherrys and a Havanna later, he allowed Constance's hands to reach under his shirt. It really didn't matter anymore, whether Louise was actually cheating on him or not!

Käsespätzle in Scotland

Scotland
A deluge of rain poured down from the sky, which was already quite dark for only 5 p.m. He had never been so glad that Grace had arrived home safely as today. Alasdair gave the rain no further thought, turned away with a shrug. It wasn't as if he wasn't used to this weather. Since Grace had come home from her meeting with Lou safely, and surprisingly cheerful, he supposed it would be the same with Lou. His German bonnie lass was tough, even if her appearance didn't suggest it.

He was anxious to hear what she could tell him about Grace's problems. He was also very much looking forward to having her cook for him. He had already changed his clothes three times. Though normally nothing could faze him, apart from Grace, his parents, and his ex-wife, now he was more than a little nervous. Even though this was hardly their first date. He hadn't shaved on purpose, because he knew Lou liked him a little rough.

What if she already had other plans for tomorrow? Maybe she didn't even like motorcycles. It might rain all day tomorrow, then even he wouldn't want to go on a long ride. Was he even ready for it himself? Could he show another woman all the beautiful places in Edinburgh that meant so much to him? He was once bitten, twice shy, after all. So much in the scenic old quarter woke memories of Felicitas, of happy times. That was why he had avoided the city like the plague for years.

Patrick had just about jumped for joy when he had asked him for a room for tomorrow night. His old school chum was so overjoyed, he had lent him his small, private two-room apartment, right on the Royal Mile.

Beyond price for a stranger. For free, for him.

He was in turmoil, emotions warring with reason, heart with mind. *Why are you doing all this for a woman who will leave you again anyway?*, his reason murmured, while his heart answered: *Who dares, wins! You must do everything you can to show her how much she means to you. Only then will she choose you!*

He was already dizzy from all the back and forth. Weren't men allowed to just dream sometimes, too? Shaking his head, he left the house, strolling over to his tractor, with which he meant to take Lou over to his most scenic pasture later.

The closer he got to his cottage and Lou, the uneasier he became. Hardly had he parked the tractor, when he noticed dark smoke clouds around the house. He belonged to the volunteer fire brigade of Kildermorie, after all.

Before his head had truly registered just what he was seeing, his legs were already in motion. He scooped up an old bucket filled with rainwater on the run. Alasdair took no notice of the water splashing on his trousers, nor did he care about the dirt he carried into the house, or that he almost ripped a door off its hinges with his shoulder. His only thought was of fire, and Louise in the middle of it. He skidded to a halt at the kitchen door, where he saw the strangest sight of his life. No inferno of flames, just one of dough and water. The whole stove was running with water, and stinking clumps of dough, burned black, were scattered everywhere. At least now he knew what had caused the smoke clouds that had alarmed him.

Lou was at the center of this chaos. He paused in the doorway for a long moment, laughing silently and memorizing the sight. She was wearing one of those corny tourist souvenirs, an apron depicting an otherwise naked man in a kilt. Pieces of dough, and an assortment of spots, decorated both the apron and her face. She was barefoot. The long slim legs vanished into an extremely short miniskirt, which accentuated her round posterior. A spotted red hairband kept her short brown hair in check, giving her the look of a little girl. She had just seen him. Her soft red lips formed a horrified 'O', which he would have liked to kiss from her lips immediately.

He leaned against the doorframe, his amusement obvious, and waited curiously what excuse she would come up with.

"I'm so sorry, Al. I tried, really I did, but…". Her voice was slightly hysterical, which caused him to put down the bucket immediately. Instead of scolding her, or grousing about the smoke, he simply took her into his arms, relieved she was safe. Her eyes searched his. He could see she was waiting for a tongue lashing. When he didn't say anything, she looked at him curiously.

"I'm sorry about your kitchen. I should have told you I can't cook…", she sobbed almost unintelligibly, and buried her face in his shirt in shame.

Snorting desperately, he tried to stifle his laughter in her hair, that smelled sweetly of apples, but it was no use.

"You aren't laughing at me, are you?", she asked suspiciously.

"Aye. Guilty as charged, lass", he whispered teasingly into her hair. "You could have just told me, Lou. We could have cooked together."

"But I wanted to do it alone, for you. I wanted to cook for you. Besides, we both know where that would have led!"

"Oh, we do, do we?", he acted innocent, while his hands came to rest lustfully on her bottom. "And just what is to keep me from just taking you right here on the kitchen floor?", he asked, more roughly than he had meant to.

"Phooey, Alasdair Munro! And I thought you'd wring my

neck for all this mess. Did anyone ever tell you you're quite an unscrupulous character?"

"Aye. The unscrupulous character also knows just how you could compensate him for this mess."

"Ha. Just as I feared. But if I'm to be any good for you, I need something to eat first."

As if in confirmation, her stomach growled at just that moment. He had no defence against her fluttering eyelashes, or the pout of her lips. Did women practice these looks in front of a mirror? Did they even know what these looks did to a man? For firearms, one needed a licence. For looks like this, they should be mandatory as well, in his opinion.

"All right, we'll take a rain check. Let's clean up a little, first. Then you can explain to me what went wrong here", he accepted, needing to cool off a little himself. It was really a miracle they hadn't found themselves on the floor, which was covered with flour and broken eggshells. They were both obviously more than ready.

The kitchen was relatively small, even for just one person. For two large people like them, it was tiny. That just made things more interesting, though. Again and again their bodies touched, skin brushed against skin. He had never realized kneading dough could be so erotic. Until today.

They prepared the dough together, before starting on "scraping" the *Spätzle*. Lou had managed to explain the principle to him, better than he would have expected after her mess. The Swabian Alb, Lou's home region, seemed to have some merits. Where his bonnie lass had failed, he succeeded, after just a bit of practice, probably because working with dough of any kind was second nature to him as a baker.

To have more room to work, but also so Lou couldn't do any damage, he picked her up decisively and sat her on the drying area next to the sink. From there, she watched him work with legs dangling, which reminded him of Grace, who had the same habit. This didn't keep her from distracting him again and again by stroking his rear end with her enchanting bare toes.

The resulting meal had really been delicious. Alasdair intended to cook the simple meal often in future. He would be sure to keep Lou from cooking, though. Who knew what she would burn down else!

After the meal, the sexual tension between them had grown so strong, he felt it necessary to provide a distraction for both of them. It had been easy to persuade Lou to an excursion with the big tractor. He had opened the windows of the drivers cabin to let in the breeze. They had left the dog in the cottage, where he had immediately started investigating the kitchen floor.

At this time of the late afternoon, there were hardly any cars on the road anymore. The bumpy farm tracks had Lou whooping with excitement, which tempted him into driving faster than actually allowed. Arriving at the upper pasture, he drove the tractor to one of his favorite spots, with a fantastic view of the Loch and the mountains.

"Priceless", she whispered from her seat and wrapped her arms around his neck.

"Aye. I had a suspicion you would like the view here!"

"I never had a better view", she confirmed, while nibbling teasingly on his shoulder.

Alasdair made no effort to stop her, as she pulled off his shirt. His body trembled under her gentle fingers, as they traced the eagle tattooed across his shoulderblades.

"I'm afraid I still have a debt to pay, my Scot", she declared with such a sexy voice he could hardly contain himself. He wanted to simply rip the clothes from her body. As he soon found, that was hardly necessary, as a lacy scarlet brassiere flew past his eyes. For a moment, he had to close his eyes, straining to keep his manhood under control, which was suddenly feeling very constricted in his tight jeans. Then he felt her tantalizing breasts with their rigid tips press against his naked back. Unable to control himself any longer, he pulled her in front of him, where, due to the narrow confines of the driver's cabin, she inevitably landed on his lap.

"You seem to know exactly how to make me burn, mo cridhe", he murmured hoarsely, before his lips found their way to the stiffly erect tips of her breasts. It wasn't easy to get rid of his clothes with so little room, but that circumstance, and the way they then had to contort themselves like acrobats to make love, only made the experience more memorable.

They made love passionately, with neither trying to restrain the other. Even later, when they were lying in the gras next to the tractor, laughing and still not fully clothed, they giggled like teenagers again and again. His fingertips stroked the contours of her face pensively.

"You were going to tell me about Grace's problems", he murmured tenderly.

Lou's reaction couldn't have been more violent if a Peeping Tom had suddenly jumped from the bushes. She flinched so badly that he involuntarily flinched with her. If his arm hadn't been around her, he wasn't sure if she might not even have run away.

"Lou?", he asked suspiciously.

He couldn't stop her from pulling away from him and putting some distance between them. What the hell was wrong? Fear spread through him.

"What the devil has she done, Lou?"

His bonnie lass cleared her throat loudly, while her teeth buried themselves pensively in her full lips. By now, her nervousness had spread to him.

"She….um…. Grace hasn't done anything…", she started explaining.

Suddenly he felt even colder.

"It's your ex-wife, who…well…she… she seems to want to get to know Grace better, so she lay in wait for her, together with a translator, and…"

His sudden jump to his feet, as well as the flood of Gaelic curses that burst from him, made Lou stop in mid-sentence. Like a tiger in its cage, he walked back and forth in the pasture, half naked as he was. That goddamn bitch. He and Felicitas had settled that at the divorce. Damn. His ex-wife had made no claim on Grace then. Why now? His eyes burned with rage. Alasdair could see how Lou quailed under his gaze.

"I'm so sorry, Al. Grace told her teacher and your ex-wife that I'm her new mother", she commented tentatively.

God in heaven. How much more embarrassing could it get?

"How could she do that? What was she thinking of, dammit!", he shouted at Lou, who flinched at his words.

"Al, I don't think you should be mad at Grace. She just so desperately wants a mother. She probably thought, since you and I…"

He realized that Lou was searching for words to calm him, words to make him think and reflect. But she was speaking to deaf ears. He was so filled with rage, it seemed he could no longer get a proper breath.

"Grace has no right to introduce you as her mother. Felicitas has no right to ruin my life once again…" he shouted and smashed his fist against the next tree, until his knuckles were split and bleeding. Before he could vent his rage against further trees, however, he felt her hands on his back.

Lou didn't say a word.

It was the way her fingers stroked his spine so familiarly, soothing, supporting, comforting. She opened his clenched fists, blew on the knuckles to take the pain away.

"Haven't you let her do enough to your life? Don't let her ruin you, Al", she murmured. "I won't let her destroy you, Alasdair. You hear me?"

He let Lou pull him into her embrace, buried his head between her breasts.

They spent half the night in the pasture, while he listened to Lou's story of the afternoon in Inverness, though they were freezing and the driver's cabin of the tractor couldn't stop the chill of autumn. He didn't tell his A' gearmailteach how proud he was of her reaction to Felicitas. After all, he knew Felicitas' dominating and intimidating ways far too well. It hadn't been easy for him to tell Lou the unvarnished truth of his finances. Now he was glad he had already told her most of it. It was nice to be able to trust someone so much, to be able to speak openly of one's troubles. He was also happy that Lou had accepted his invitation for a ride to Glen Coe and Edinburgh.

Though they didn't spend the rest of the night together, each going to his own bed to get some much-needed sleep, he somehow felt easier, almost euphoric.

Letting go

After far too little sleep, and far too gloomy thoughts, Lou could hardly get her eyes open next morning. Alasdair had been open about his finances. As she had feared, the Scot had his back to the wall. What she hadn't told him was her suspicion that his ex-wife was at least partly to blame for that. All the while she was walking Doc, she racked her brains for a way to help him. Finally, she had started out for the café to visit Marge, knowing Alasdair was out on one of the pastures with his father.

While partaking of a comforting pot of tea, and some delicious cookies, she had managed to persuade Marge to help her. While Lou photographed each room of the house, Marge searched out the builder's blueprints. It didn't take long to scan everything and send it to Debbie, with instructions to forward them to her husband, Christopher. Sometimes it was quite useful to be friendly with a lawyer, whose hobby also happened to be interior design.

Afterwards, she drove back to the cottage, where she put on her business costume and threw the mostly ruined Jimmy Choos on the passenger seat. Dressed for business, she set out again for Inverness and a visit to the Munro's house bank.

Mission: Save my Scot, commencing.

Her large handbag was stuffed with bills and receipts. For the first time in ages, she felt something like relief. This was a good way to start out anew!

Despite the immense distance from the parking lot to the bank, she balanced courageously on her high heels across the uneven cobblestones, undeterred. When she had finally managed to reach the bank, without any twisted ankles and without measuring her length on the cobbles, she said a silent prayer of thanks.

For the last time, she used her black American Express card, and remained unmoved as the bank clerk first looked at her uncertainly, then immediately started treating her like the Queen of England herself.

She was sure Alexander would now know her whereabouts, within two hours at the most. That was all right with her, wasn't it? No more lies, no more deception!

Back at the car, she took her smartphone and called Christopher personally.

"Hey Lou, everything arrived safely. Looks interesting. What exactly do you want me to do for you?" came so cheerfully from the smartphone that Lou could practically see her friend's slim, blond husband rocking his chair, as he usually did.

"Hello Chris, glad to hear that. I want you to find skilled craftsmen for me, from this region. Call for tenders for the work."

"You seem to be doing all right! Do you mean to open a Bed & Breakfast?"

Lou stifled a laugh. Christopher had always been very blunt.

"Something like that. Also, I want you to buy a motorcycle for me!" Concentrating, she gave him the exact details of the 74 Knucklehead that Alasdair was forced to sell.

"It has to be that exact machine. Nothing else!"

"You're starting to get weird on me, Lou. You don't even have a licence, do you?"

"Don't worry, Chris. I don't plan on learning to ride a motorcycle at this date. Chris, there's something else."

"More? It's starting to get expensive, darling!", her lawyer joked, amused.

"Chris, do you remember my divorce papers? I looked

through them with you a few years ago…"

"Of course I remember them. You begged off, wanted to think about it some more."

"Yeah, well, I've thought about it. If you haven't thrown those papers out, then I want you to ready the divorce documents!", she declared forcefully, as if to make sure the words got out. Her fingers tapped a nervous melody on the steering wheel.

"Seriously, Lou? Shit. I didn't think you'd ever find the courage to really do it! I've got all your data in the computer, so nothing has been lost."

"Will you do it?"

"Lou, I'm your friend, as well as your lawyer. Of course I'll do it. I don't think a divorce has ever made me so happy. You're absolutely sure?"

"Yes!", she declared, ignoring the tears that were smearing her carefully made-up eyes.

"And you still don't want to take more of Alex's money? You realize that you're entitled to half of all your common property?"

Yes. She knew that she could be set for the rest of her life. But at what price? Besides, Alexander had already, unknowingly, paid off Alasdair's complete debts with his American Express.

"Quid pro quo", she murmured, but answered:

"No, Chris. Leave it. I don't want Alex's money. Just prepare the papers quickly, please!"

Back in the cottage, she lit the fire in the hearth. What if Alasdair was just playing with her? Would he someday get tired of his older wife? Regardless of the doubts that gnawed deeply at her, she felt strangely liberated. As the dull scissors, to which her hair had already succumbed, cut into the plastic of her credit card, destroying it, she felt nothing but relief.

The strips of plastic burned in the flames, just as the photo from her purse did, the one where she and Alex, who had one arm around her, looked almost like a pair of gangsters. She let the fire burn while she packed her backpack for the ride to Edinburgh. When she was finished, she tipped a bucket of water over the stinking pile of wood and embers. Doc watched her skeptically.

"By the time I get back from Edinburgh, it will be dry again. I hope!", she defended her actions.

Alasdair wasn't enamored of this kind of fooling with fire. After all, he was a member of the Volunteer Fire Department. Now that she knew where the scar on his cheek came from – a roof beam had fallen on him, while he was saving some cattle from a barn that had been struck by lightning – she understood his concerns about fire and heat. He certainly would not be happy about melted plastic in his fireplace.

"What he doesn't know won't hurt him!" she murmured, while pulling the front door closed.

Lou had quickly gotten used to riding the motorcycle. Having started out leaning rather stiffly against his back, now she sat relaxed behind and snuggled against him. Her body followed each of his movements automatically.

Though the weather was somewhat nippy, and battalions of dark clouds marched across the sky, the rain they had feared didn't come. The recurring sunbeams that broke through the sinister clouds painted Glen Coe in an unearthly light. There were hardly any tourist busses on the road, apart from a couple of small ones of the local firm of Rabbies & Co.

Alasdair made the short dull part of the route through Ranoch Moor more interesting with some speed kicks, which had Lou squealing with excitement. Time and again, they had to stop so his bonnie lass could shoot photographs, intending to capture the moments so she could immortalize them on canvas later.

As Alasdair had feared, his old fringed leather jacket hung on her like a sack. But even that couldn't hide her natural beauty. Lou loved the fringes, which danced in the wind, at least as much as the mystical play of light. He would never have thought to find someone who knew the feeling and shared it with him. Though he didn't always understand why they were constantly stopping. When he looked through the seeker of her camera, however, heard her joyful voice explaining next to his ear, he managed to see with her eyes.

At first, he was actually a bit jealous of his baby, his machine. Lou's fingers stroked his ancestor's belt, and then the brooch on the tank, so intimately that he wished it was his body she was stroking.

They made a detour around the Visitor's Center. He drove to a seldom visited parking lot, below the Three Sisters of Glen Coe, instead. There they sat on a wooden bench and ate steakpie, with shortbread as a dessert, while Alasdair played the guide for Lou, which he usually only ever did on his bus tours. Unexpectedly, he rather enjoyed it. Lou already knew the sad story of Glen Coe, where the MacDonalds had been massacred by English soldiers posing as their guests, but she still hung on his lips. She had her own special way of discussing things with him. She didn't ask how something so terrible could have happened in the first place, but rather, how the survivors had managed to get out of the valley.

When they reached Edinburgh, it was already late in the evening. Instead of driving directly to the Old Town, where their apartment for the night was waiting, he drove up Princess Street, all the way to Calton Hill. That acutally wasn't allowed, but the advantage of having been a guide was that he knew all the byways. There was no better view of Edinburgh than that from Calton Hill, excepting Arthur's Seat, but that wasn't feasible, since it could only be reached on foot.

Edinburgh appeared as a sea of lights, reaching up to the castle, while the view in the other direction was of the ocean and the Firth of Forth. Even at this late hour, things weren't really quiet up here. Lovers held hands and gazed at the wonderful view. Small groups of young people climbed the unfinished copy of the Parthenon, meant as a National Monument for Scotland, but never finished. From somewhere, Alasdair could hear the sound of a guitar.

"Edinburgh never really sleeps, does it?", Lou whispered at his ear.

"No, not really. Come on, mo cridhe. Let's drive to the apartment and then go get something to eat, before you waste away", he joked.

Their apartment was situated right next to the Royal Mile, in one of the Closes. It was now shortly after 9 p.m., and the Old Town was still busy. Crossing the North Bridge, he followed the Royal Mile for a short piece, leaving it by Cockburn Street, driving through Market Street and St. Giles Street, and then returning to the Royal Mile, here also called High Street. From there, they turned off into Borthwick's Close, where Patrick's small two-room apartment was located on the fifth floor.

"This here is a so-called Close, because they could be closed off with gates or bars. The Wynds, on the other hand, couldn't be closed off", he explained to Lou, who was looking around the imposing courtyard, with her lips formed into a silent 'O' once again.

"Beautiful, in a way, but also oppressive",

she answered, head tilted back.

"Aye. Though the houses were formerly crammed together much closer than this. If we had had to live on the fifth floor in those days, lass, it would have been neither romantic, nor comfortable."

With Lou in tow, he rang for Patrick's neighbor lady, who had kept his key for him.

"Just imagine having to carry your groceries all the way up here…"

"Aye. Also imagine having only wood around us from at least the fourth floor upward, no stone steps or walls. Then you'll know why, in the 18th century, the majority of Edinburgh's inhabitants were killed by collapsing houses."

"You're joking!", Lou exclaimed, shocked.

"I'm afraid not. Edinburgh also had the byname Old Smelly, due to the bestial stink, which could be smelled for a long way around."

After rattling it a few times, he managed to open the door to Patrick's apartment, which had probably been warped a bit by the damp. The apartment wasn't very large, with just two rooms, a tiny bathroom, and a small kitchen. On the other hand, it was furnished cozily, and probably, with its many windows, full of light during the day. The anything but scenic view into the back courtyard was more than compensated by the splendid view of the Royal Mile on the other side.

Patrick had kept his word. The apartment seemed to meet with Lou's approval, judging by the look on her face. Alasdair had felt relieved when they had entered Patrick's realm and found neither empty pizza boxes, nor the garbage of weeks. His old friend probably had a new girl friend. Alasdair couldn't explain the change from Patrick's usual chaotic habits any other way. Even the refrigerator was filled to the brim. Hanging there, in an envelope with his name written on it, he found the receipt for the tour through the Southstreet Vaults, which he had booked on short notice at Mercat Tours, thanks to Patrick's connections there.

After refreshing themselves, they started out for Edinburgh's oldest pub, The World's End, at the end of the Royal Mile, where he had reserved two seats.

Though so much of Old Town reminded him of his former life at Felicitas' side, for the first time in ages, he felt neither anger nor sadness thinking of those faraway days. Instead of feeling uncomfortable, he felt as if he were burgeoning with every smile and every enthusiastic sound from the woman at his side. He felt as if he could move mountains!

There were still some street artists active, and they stopped now and then to watch. Again and again, he explained peculiarities of the Old Town, enchanted that his bonnie lass hung on his every word. He was even grateful for the cold wind blowing through Old Town, because it caused her to seek shelter in his arms.

Much too soon, they came in sight of the pub, and they plunged into the rustic atmosphere of live music, dark wood, whisky, and loud talk. The fish and chips lived up to their many awards and went well with the tasty house beer, and a whisky or two.

Afterwards, well fortified, they met up with the tour group at Market Cross near St. Giles Church, just in time for the horror tour.

"What a wonderful day that was," Lou whispered to Alasdair happily. He had both hands behind his head, and lay relaxed on his back in their common bed for the night. She almost thought she could see his smile in the near darkness of the room.

They had taken part in the horror tour through the South-street Vaults, where they had learned quite a bit about the Old Town of Edinburgh and its inhabitants. She could have done without the horror stories, though. Unfortunately, her English had gotten quite a bit better in the time she had been in Scotland, not least thanks to Alasdair. She had understood more than she really wanted to know. Of course, she hadn't missed how much her Scotsman had enjoyed playing her protector in the flickering candlelight of the Vaults. His plan had worked, for she had clung to him as if it was a matter of life and death. For one thing, she couldn't see well in the dark, and for another, the uneven ground they walked on had been full of chances to stumble.

Now, they were both lying, exhausted, in a very comfortable bed. Still, she couldn't fall asleep. Her thoughts were occupied with how she could explain the new man in her life to Alexander. Yes, she had decided. That didn't make the break that she had to make in her life any easier, though. How would her children react to a divorce?

Sighing, she laid her head, so heavy with thoughts, on Alasdair's arm.

"What's wrong, mo cridhe? Do you still have the creeps, or are you already bothering your pretty head about the decorations for the wedding cake we two have to master the day after tomorrow?", Alasdair murmured in her ear, sounding amused, then tenderly kissed her on the top of the head.

"Hmm", she evaded his question. "Exactly in that order."

A nightmare on the Royal Mile

The next morning began with the tantalizing aroma of bacon and eggs. After they had breakfasted with gusto, Alasdair showed Lou his Edinburgh.

There were still relatively few tourists around. They strolled hand in hand through the alleys of Old Town, and explored a number of quaint courtyards. They viewed the Castle from outside and examined the looms in the Tartan Weaving Mill, where they had one of the typical tourist fotos made, for which one was put into a Highland costume with Velcro fasteners.

This was where it happened for the first time. Lou was just examining a shoulder cloth in Munro Tartan more closely, meaning to buy it later, when she saw a young man from the corner of her eye, who seemed to be staring at her. She returned his look just long enough for both of them to recoil in shock.

Lou's pulse hammered in her ears. What was going on here? Alexander couldn't have found her this quickly! Still, that had definitely been the face of her younger son. Trembling, Lou leaned against one of the big cloth racks, while her Scot looked at her in concern.

"What's wrong, lass? You look as if you've seen a ghost!"

"I…um…no. Heavens, no! I just felt dizzy for a moment, that's all", she stumbled apologetically, while putting her arm around Alasdair's waist to pull him further quickly.

Maybe it hadn't really been Philip, she tried to persuade herself. On the other hand, she would have recognized Philip's brown hair, formed into spikes with hair gel, anywhere. She knew exactly what her own son looked like, after all. She was also certain that Philip had recognized her too, in spite of the new hair color and hairdo.

How did he come to be in Edinburgh? And, if he was here, where was Alexander? Damn. She wasn't ready to have the two men confront each other yet. Not now, and not here! Just thinking about it made her panicky. Alexander was choleric, and Alasdair was strong enough to knock out her future ex-husband with just one punch. They had to leave here, before they were discovered.

What a balls-up! She brought their tour to an end as quickly as she could without making Alasdair notice. Paying for her shoulder cloth, she had drops of sweat on her brow from fear. Twice more, she thought she could see her son's spiky hair, before they finally merged into the stream of tourists on the Royal Mile.

Near Gladstone Land, they barely escaped the notice of her sons, one of whom, at least, was looking searchingly along the street, but only thanks to her taking extreme measures.

Damn, Richard was also along!

"You could have just told me you wanted to view this old building, mo cridhe. Though I don't mind your ardent kisses, not even when you just push me in here with your sexy body. Even better would have been a dark alley, though", he murmured, one hand fondling her behind.

She gave him a sarcastic smile, then turned to the girl behind the counter to pay for their admittance.

"Our old man couldn't have had a more stupid idea! He has no idea where Mother is, or how boring this miserable Edinburgh is. I should't have listened to you. I could still be lying in my comfortable bed at the hotel!"

Philip ignored his brother's grousing. He had just lost sight of the woman with the tall, muscular man. It had been her. He was absolutely certain. The woman with the short hair,

hair the same color as his, had been his mother. He was certain, though he couldn't wrap his mind around her changed appearance, or the man she was obviously with. His mother was being unfaithful, just as his father and his brother had been saying. If he hadn't just seen her kiss this stranger with his own eyes, he still wouldn't believe it.

Of course, he knew of the problems in his parents' marriage. He was 17, after all, and knew what was what. None of his friends' parents had separate bedrooms.

He would confront his mother, demand an explanation. He had no problem with her finding another man, but having a lover in secret just wasn't like his mother. He couldn't do that, though, if either his father or his brother was along. The only thing he could do now was to limit the damage. He had to make sure they didn't meet Richard, of all people. So, instead of following them into Gladstone Land, he persuaded his brother to visit Holyroad Palace. After that, they would have lunch at the hotel. There, the chances of meeting them again would surely be lowest.

The day in Edinburgh went past much too quickly. They saw most of the sights from a Hop On Hop Off Bus, though they forewent the earplugs for the acoustic tour. Lou loved listening to the notably cheerful Alasdair, and his stories about the town he loved. Even though she had to stop him from relating some of the more horrific details. Luckily, they didn't meet any of her children again.

Late in the afternoon, they visited Patrick at the hotel where he worked, to thank him for the apartment. Alasdair's friend was a frenetic little guy, who could hardly stand still. He seemed to have Indian roots. Lou liked him immediately.

It happened on the way to the elevator, which would bring them from the Reception, on the second floor, back to the entrance. Just as they were getting on the elevator, Richard got off.

Her older son was so morose and grumpy, though, that he didn't spare a look for them. Lou had the presence of mind to take cover behind Alasdair's broad back, which, unfortunately, didn't help her much, as they ran right into Philip inside the mirrored elevator.

"Hi, Mom!", he greeted her with an impudent grin, which seemed to say: *Now I've caught you in flagranti!*

Alasdair's eyes went back and forth between them questioningly. The shrill ping of the elevator seemed to bring salvation from this embarrassing situation.

"I'll call you, Flip. Trust me!", she murmured, and pulled the bewildered Alasdair out of the hotel in double time.

"What was that? Or should I ask, who was that?"

Alasdair stopped right in front of the hotel, and looked at her for an explanation. Why did this have to happen to her? As if there weren't enough hotels in Edinburgh!

"Can I please explain it to you later? Not here, please", she brought out, as calmly as she could. Without waiting for her Scot, she was already walking in the direction they had come from.

"What's wrong with you all of a sudden, Lou? That young fellow looked a lot like you…"

Lou felt him watching her expectantly and keeping pace, though she hadn't been able to keep from walking with quick, long strides.

With a "Hey, lass!", he caught her arm and stopped her. "We're not running after a bus, or anything else. I think we need to talk, now!" He pulled her to a park bench beneath some trees.

They sat down and watched the many passers-by hurrying up the South Bridge for a moment.

"I'm listening", he said, and put a calming hand on her thigh.

"The boy was my younger son, Philip. Maybe you remember the slightly smaller, dark-haired young man, who looked so morose? He left the elevator before we entered. Well, that was my older son, Richard."

Alasdair said nothing, only gave her an expressionless look, which she couldn't interpret.

"You know that my husband is, well, let's say wealthy. I suppose he hired a detective to look for me. They probably found out which car rental firm I was using through the airline. It wasn't a secret that I was going to Scotland. I guess Alex sent my boys to Edinburgh so they could react quickly, if the detective found out where I was.

I haven't kept anything from you, Al, no secrets. I was just hoping Alexander would let me decide what I wanted to do by myself."

Alasdair rubbed his hands across his face, suddenly looked tired and doubtful in a way she didn't like.

"Aye, Louise. It's true. You kept nothing from me. I just wish I had had more time with you. Will you… I mean, will you…"

He couldn't say the word they both feared.

"Go?" she finished his sentence, almost inaudibly. Lou tried to smile bravely, patted his leg encouragingly.

"Aye, go. I suppose you have to." His melancholy voice almost made her cry.

"Of course I have to go. But that doesn't mean I won't come back!" This was her chance. Now she could tell him that her divorce was already in the works. But something stopped her.

"You could spend your next vacation here…", he started.

"My vacation? Alasdair, who do you think I am?" Why

should she spend her vacation here, when she wanted to spend her life with him? He looked like a whipped dog. Why were men so dense? Why couldn't he believe she would come back to him and nobody else?

"Let's talk about something more pleasant, please, Lou!" he changed the subject.

How could a grown man, with so much charisma and so much sex-appeal, have so little self-confidence? Frustrated, Lou closed her eyes for a few seconds and tried to think of a way to make him understand her feelings for him.

You, of all people, ask why? Aren't you yourself the woman with the self-confidence of a snail? Don't you hide all the time, to avoid being hurt or betrayed again? Don't you know exactly what it feels like, to know love and comfort only from books? While withering from lack of love in real life?

Alasdair squared his shoulders next to her, pulled her firmly to him. "Come on, Lou. I want to make good use of the little time we have left"

A wild wedding

After a wonderful ride back on Alasdair's motorcycle, through the fabulous scenery of the Highlands, and rather a short night, the morning began all too early. She had slept over at Alasdair's, to be close to him, but also, because she knew what a long, exhausting day was in store for them. Alasdair had vanished into the bakeroom long before her. She, however, had grabbed her smartphone and climbed onto the veranda terrace, to finally make the long delayed call to her youngest.

The air was filled with birdsong, the rustling of autumn leaves, and a loud, cheerful whistling, which she assumed came from her Scotsman. The sky was grey, promising rain soon.

The conversation with Philip was surprisingly calm and civilized, though it wasn't easy for her to explain to her son that she would be divorcing Alexander. At any rate, Philip promised to let her do the talking to Alexander and Richard, which was more than she had expected. For the moment, she felt some relief.

Alasdair was just stacking the different stories of the wedding cake, four in all, on top of each other. "You're just in time, lass", he received her with a broad smile, and threw her an apron with one hand, which she put on.

He had already kneaded the marzipan for her, and colored it as appropriate. All she had to do was form it, which proved harder than she had imagined. Her gaze drifted again and again to the man, whose unshaven cheeks were already streaked with flour again. Here in this bakeroom, at this counter on which she was trying to form marzipan flowers, everything had started with them. Judging by Alasdair's red ears and the looks he kept throwing her way, he was thinking of the same thing. The aroma of marzipan woke memories that made her own cheeks flush rosily. They were definitely both in the mood again, but there wasn't enough time. There was simply too much to do this morning.

Some hours later, Alasdair picked up Lou in front of his cottage, clad in his best kilt with all accessories. Thank God he had even managed to drive through the car wash with his jeep. His bonnie lass looked ethereal. Her red dress was complemented nicely by the shoulder cloth in the Munro tartan, which she had bought in Edinburgh. He had also given her a buttonhole flower of the same cloth, which decorated her enchanting décolleté.

The whole population of the town, as well as the invited wedding guests, had gathered before the little church. He wasn't the only one who couldn't take his eyes off Lou. It seemed his friends took more notice of the woman on his arm, than of the beaming bride herself.

The ceremony in the tiny church, followed by the handfasting under the big lime tree, had been charming. Again and again, he had glanced at Lou from the corner of his eye, pleased at the tears of emotion in her eyes. He asked himself silently what it would be like if, instead of Cormack and Emily, it was Lou and himself before the altar. If they were the ones who kissed each other so ardently as husband and wife, before all eyes. Since Edinburgh, he was in a panic that she might suddenly just be gone. For sure, nothing could stand between a good mother and her children, at least not if that mother were Lou. It was the same unconditional love he had for Grace. How could he blame her for that? Annoyed, he pushed the gloomy thoughts aside.

The wedding cake had turned out delightfully. With Lou's

help, he had managed to create a masterpiece. The compliments of the bridal pair and the guests were so fulsome as to be almost embarrassing.

Even the weather played along, providing sunbeams and a mild breeze, after only a short rain shower. Optimum conditions to party in the large tent, which he had erected together with his friends of the Volunteer Fire Brigade. It was decorated with a profusion of flowers, which the women of the village, under the direction of his mother Marge, and including Lou, had placed skillfully. By now, nothing about Lou could surprise him.

All right, so her cooking was a catastrophe, and she could be clumsy at times. On the other hand, she could use hammer and nails, as well as paint and a brush. Besides, she was the only woman he knew who, though wealthy, didn't care about money and appearances.

Late in the afternoon, after plying her with two glasses of champagne, he even managed to get her to dance. He didn't even mind her stepping on his toes every now and then.

"I warned you, Mr. Scot. I can't dance", she whispered in his ear, giggling, only to press against him even more closely.

"Aye. I remember, Mistress. I don't care, as long as you keep your heels under control!", he teased her. Gallantly, he whirled her out under his arm and pulled her back in. They were both so engrossed, they didn't notice the turmoil that suddenly broke loose.

Suddenly, he felt himself torn loose from Lou's embrace. A man, whose face somehow seemed familiar, glared at him angrily with reddened face. In bad English, the stranger shouted: "Take your dirty hands off my wife!"

Lou's face paled, her smile turned into a grimace.

Alasdair put up his hands in a calming gesture. Unfortunately, it didn't work. As if outside himself, he heard himself say: "Calm down, Mister. Let's act like adults, please!"

As if in slow motion, he saw the stranger's fist coming. It was aimed for him, but hit Lou instead, who had thrown herself between them.

The momentary silence was broken by the guests' screams. Lou was bleeding and crying.

Alasdair was torn away from her in the confusion, couldn't get back to her. Panic took him.

"Lou. Louise!" he shouted, flailing around. He was suddenly in the middle of a brawl. He could see Lou's sons, also in the middle of the brawl. God help him. He was ruining the wedding of his best friend, and had no idea how he was going to get out of this. He tried to evade the blows, and refrain from dealing ones of his own. He dodged Lou's sons several times, so he wouldn't be the one to knock them out. Unfortunately, it was impossible to avoid the brawl. Glass shattered, wood splintered. Chaos ruled.

After what seemed like an eternity, he managed to pull Lou's youngest son to safety along with him, out of the knot of struggling men.

"Did you see that, Barb? George Clooney fought Alasdair for his woman!", he heard from out of a circle of curious women, who were watching the brawl with interest.

"Really. I should tell George Clooney that he can take me with him any time, Cleo!"

"I'm sure George prefers women of eighty or so, Barb. You're experienced!"

There was loud laughter.

"Do we have you to thank for this, boyo?", he growled at Lou's younger son, while wiping the blood from his battered face with his sleeve.

The boy held up his hands placatingly.

"I didn't say a word, man! The detective agency checked

Mom's credit card bill … and found your name, Munro. My father came on a friend's private jet. It was none of my doing. Let go of me!"

He nodded reluctantly, took his hand off the boy's shirt collar.

"I'm really sorry, okay? I tried everything to keep my Dad and Richie away, honestly!"

"I believe you, boy. Come on, you have to help me!"

Taking the young man along, he managed to organize Cormack, his father, and some of the women, who helped him to bring the fire engine from the depot, unroll the hose, and connect it to the hydrant next to the church. The decorations around the dance floor, and the tables in the back, were ruined anyway, a bit more damage from water would make no difference.

A well-aimed jet of water separated the fighters in seconds.

"Man, I'm glad we already had the wedding pictures in the bag!", Cormack remarked, slapping him on the shoulder approvingly.

"As well as your wedding ceremony", Alasdair added, pointing at the preacher with his chin, who was just emerging from the heap of men, where he seemed to have done his share of fighting. Then Alasdair remembered.

"Lou. Louise?", he called into the room.

"Back here!", sounded from under one of the undestroyed tables. Heedlessly, he pushed his way through to her. He didn't breathe easily until he had pulled her from under the badly damaged remains of the table. Gently, he checked her for injuries.

"Do you need me?" Doc Carneby appeared next to them and looked inquiringly at Lou.

"Thank you, Doc. I'll pass this time! But, if you should have one of those monstrous needles along, maybe with a sedative? There's a man who looks like George Clooney. He could use one of those injections!", his bonnie lass growled sarcastically.

Carefully, he brushed his sleeve across her swollen lip, wiped the blood from her cheek. "Are you sure?"

"About the needle, or the vet?"

He swallowed the laughter that bubbled up in him, when he saw her face. So this was what Lou looked like, when she was really angry. Her younger son, beside him, flinched visibly.

"It's not your youngest's fault, lass", he heard himself defend the boy.

"Really, Mom! I didn't say a word about our telephone call!"

"All right, Flip. I believe you!" Turning to him: "I want you to save your friend's wedding, Al. I guess I have to clear up some things, here!"

She kissed him gently, turned to go. "Oh, and Al? Whatever happens now, I want you to think of the things I said to you!"

With all your colours, as you are!

Next day she had vanished. Gone, without saying good-bye. He could neither forget the way she had looked the day before, nor her words. Everything that had given him support, had completed and moved him, was gone. Erased in an instant. It seemed to him his life had lost all colour. He worked, drank, slept. Every damn day. He never went near the cottage. Once again, that house was only filled with bad memories.
After a week, the first postcard came from Germany. He ignored it. Was there anything worse than breaking off by postcard? He didn't feel up to it. What reason did he have to believe her excuses? Louise had left him. His bonnie lass had dropped him. It seemed to him, nothing was left of his heart but irreparable ruins.
After another week, with another postcard for him, and one for Grace, Marge lured him into the cottage by pretending the roof was leaking. There was no getting around his mother on things like this. With a heavy heart, and more than a little drunk, he opened the door. Damn, that had to be a hell of a hole in the roof! The wind had blown quite a few rose petals into the corridor. Strange. Come to think of it, the rose bushes growing around the house were long past blooming.
      Concerned, he followed the trail of blossoms into the living room, and froze. He rubbed his eyes in disbelief, couldn't understand what he was seeing.
The walls were papered with small Post-Its in different colours, on which were various sketches in charcoal and chalk. What brought tears to his eyes weren't the typically Scottish landscapes or sights, but seeing his own face looking back at him from every second sketch. There was also a thick ring

binder on the couch table, on top of which an envelope was leaning against a framed photo, a snapshot from the Loch, on which the two of them were smiling into the camera like teenagers in love.

Trembling like a leaf, he opened the envelope.

My dearest Al,

do you remember how we met? Do you remember how you asked me why I fell in love with you? I told you, because you are you, Alasdair. You see me. Not the rich wife. Not the artist or the mother. You see me. Without make-up, with all my scars, all my faults. You give me the feeling I am myself again. That's why I fell in love with you!

I don't want a vacation in Scotland, you fool.

I want YOU!

When I arrived in Scotland, I was a frustrated mother looking for a hero. I fell in love with your country, and with a man who is much better than all the Jamies, Mr. Darcys and Christian Greys in the world!

I know you won't like that I paid your debts without asking you for permission. And yes, I can already hear you shout: I won't be kept by my wife! Don't worry, I won't "keep" you. Not like that, anyway.

I'm afraid you'll have to work off every Pound for me. Just how you do that is up to you, though!

I've put in my divorce. I have to settle my affairs, and I have a vernissage coming up which I'm dreading.

Read the damn Post-Its and do your work!

Your loving Louise

The envelope fell from his hands, which suddenly wouldn't stop trembling. Something hit the ground with a soft ping. He picked up the platinum ring with the big diamond and smiled at it as if it were the greatest gift on Earth. Lou had taken it off. She had taken off her wedding ring, and left it with him in Scotland. The weight that simple fact took off his tortured mind was immense.

Beaming, he took a closer look at the Post-Its on the living room walls. There were comments like: "Because you snore just like me!" Questions that made him laugh: "Do I get your old leather jacket if I stay with you?" beside "I love you, because I'll never have to be hungry again. After all, you can cook!" Or: "I love you, because I float in your arms while dancing, even though I can't dance!"

But there were also notices like: "Important telephone numbers of craftsmen, for renovating the B&B rooms. Bargain hard!"

Another: "Important! Inverness, Culloden Road 17b, pick up your motorcycle!" had him sink to the armchair with his mouth wide open.

All of a sudden, there was colour in his life again.

Germany

"Stop looking like the sky is falling, Lou."

Debbie tried in vain to cheer her up. The vernissage was a big success. She was the celebrated star of the evening. Despite that, she felt terrible. Everyone wanted to shake her hand, congratulate her on her colourful, lively pictures. More than half of them had already been sold in advance.

On top of it all, Alexander had appeared with a beaming Constance on his arm, who smiled into the camera lights of the press.

She would endure it all, somehow. As always. With a smiling face and head held high, even though she would rather have thrown up. She hated crowds.

That Alasdair still hadn't gotten in touch brought her to the verge of despair. With tears in her eyes, she looked up at the only drawing that wasn't for sale. A life-sized Scot in a kilt, sitting on a 74 Knucklehead Harley-Davidson, looked down at her.

"If you ask me, that's a good likeness of your Scotsman!", Debbie commented on her gaze.

"How would you know, Deb? You've hardly even seen a photo of him", she answered sadly.

"Who needs a photo? He's standing right next to you..."

Before the champagne flute could fall from her hand, Alasdair took it from her. Without knowing it, he seconded Debbies statement.

"I like that picture of me, lass. A good likeness! Not as good as the original, though! And a picture can't do this to you!"

Before she knew it, she was lying in his strong arms. All doubts were forgotten. Even the applause of the guests, and the strobing flashes of the press, which now fell upon the two of them, no longer bothered her.

All that counted, were Alasdair and herself. Where he was, was her home. Suddenly, the world was full of opportunities and full of colour!

The End

MÓRAN TAING

Many thanks!

Dear readers, you're the ones who give my imagination wings! For that, I thank you with all my heart! If I've managed to entertain you with this book again, please recommend this book to others.

Of course, I would also be glad of a review on Amazon, or a message on Facebook, Twitter or by E-Mail! (info@piaguttenson.de)

You can find **news, dates for public readings, and things to know about Scotland** here: www.piaguttenson.de or at www.piaguttenson.blogspot.de my **Scotland Blog**.

Your Pia Guttenson

Tapadh leat!

I want to thank Basil Wolfrhine, for a wonderful cover, and all the precious time he invests in my works.

Simone, thank you for finding my mistakes, and often suggesting a better word.

Corinna, thank you for listening, for Gaelic, ideas and a great heart!

Ursula, thanks for your help with Gaelic.

Fritz, thank you for make my dream of a english translation come true.

And, of course, a HUGE thank you to my family, who always gets neglected a bit when I'm writing, but still stands behind me.

I LOVE You!

Glossary

Scots Gaelic / English

Dearg Amadain / Total idiot
A Dhia / Oh God
Cac / Shit
Daingead / Damn
A' gearmailteach / The German
Òinsich / Stupid cow
Pog mo thon! / Kiss my ass!
O mo chreach! / For God's sake!/ literally: Oh my ruin
Lass or Lassie / Girl
Lad or Laddie / Boy
Bonny / Beautiful
M'eudail / Darling
Mo cridhe / My heart
Athair / Father
Mac / Son
Mathair / Mother

www.schottenradio.de

Matching to the novel ...

... Celtic Music from A to Z!

CELTIC MUSIC on air
SCHOTTEN Radio.de
... geHÖRT zu mir!
www.schottenradio.de

THE STONE GATE

... and the adventure continues!

**The Stone Gate
Volume I - The Return**

**The Stone Gate
Volume II - Hope**

**The Stone Gate
Volume III - A new beginning**

Read now the new, revised and with numerous drawings illustrated version of this amazing fantasy novel.

All three volumes are available directly on the official website of the author and on Amazon!

Further information on: www.piaguttenson.de